IF
Your Wife
ONLY KNEW

Also by Cydney Rax

My Daughter's Boyfriend

My Husband's Girlfriend

Scandalous Betrayal

My Sister's Ex

Reckless (with Niobia Bryant and Grace Octavia)

Crush (with Michele Grant and Lutishia Lovely)

Published by Dafina Books

Last but not least, to the people who connect with me on social media: I value your love, support, and interest.

Okay good people! Buy the book, read it, and post your reviews.

Visit me online at www.cydneyrax.com.

May peace and blessings be multiplied unto all of you.

Acknowledgments

Writing *If Your Wife Only Knew* was an amazing process. I hope you enjoy the novel.

Thanks to my Heavenly Father whom I credit for stirring up the creative gift and for letting my dreams come true.

Thanks to Mercedes Fernandez, my editor, for the opportunity. And thanks to the Dafina family. And also to Claudia Menza (cheers to another one)! I am grateful for the support of my relatives both near and far (Houston, Arlington, Detroit, Chicago, Las Vegas, East Coast, and beyond).

I love my avid readers, especially Michelle Sloan, author promoters (Orsayor Simmons), and all the wonderful book clubs (R.E.A.D. Book Club and Bookin' It in Fort Bend County make me feel so welcome).

Thanks to anyone who allowed me to pick his or her brain about all kinds of topics (Wilt Tillman, Steven Burns, and several others). Shout out to my beloved author comrades (Margaret, Marissa, Cheryl, Chelsia, Pamela W., Lexi, Philana, and my literary twin Electa Rome Parks).

And thanks in advance to the media outlets and libraries around the world for your support regarding this book.

DAFINA BOOKS are published by

Kensington Publishing Corp.
119 West 40th Street
New York, NY 10018

All Kensington titles, imprints, and distributed lines are available at special quantity discounts for bulk purchases for sales promotion, premiums, fund-raising, and educational or institutional use.

Special book excerpts or customized printings can also be created to fit specific needs. For details, write or phone the office of the Kensington Sales Manager: Kensington Publishing Corp., 119 West 40th Street, New York, NY 10018. Attn. Sales Department. Phone: 1-800-221-2647.

Dafina and the Dafina logo Reg. U.S. Pat. & TM Off.

ISBN-13: 978-1-4967-0134-3
ISBN-10: 1-4967-0134-8
First Kensington Trade Paperback Printing: January 2016

eISBN-13: 978-1-4967-0135-0
eISBN-10: 1-4967-0135-6
First Kensington Electronic Edition: January 2016

10 9 8 7 6 5 4 3 2 1

Printed in the United States of America

IF Your Wife ONLY KNEW

A Love & Revenge Novel

CYDNEY RAX

Dafina
BOOKS

KENSINGTON PUBLISHING CORP.
www.kensingtonbooks.com

What I feared has come upon me; what I dreaded has happened to me.

—Job 3:25

Prologue

This time Kiara couldn't deny the facts—they were screaming at her. As she sat outside that night, crouching in the backseat of a rented car watching everything unfold, the details appeared fuzzy, but she knew her husband, Rashad. She saw him exit his white van. She saw the letters of his company, Eason & Son, displayed on the side. She saw him look both ways before he proceeded to walk up to a wood-framed house and ring the doorbell. Kiara raised her neck. She held her breath. This was the moment she'd been waiting for. Every woman who's ever been cheated on really wants one thing and one thing only: proof! And Kiara was about to get hers.

Kiara watched as a woman opened the door and stepped out onto the porch. Kiara popped the lock and got out of the car. She stood in the darkness of the shadows noticing how her husband lovingly wrapped his arms around the woman. They kissed. They closed their eyes. They embraced and rocked back and forth. Rashad reached around and playfully grabbed the woman's ass. She lifted up her skirt. They laughed, then Rashad followed the woman inside the house. Kiara crept closer until she herself was on the porch. In his rush to get inside, Rashad hadn't closed the front door all the way. He gave his wife the perfect view of his deceit.

Kiara made her move. She ran and grabbed the door handle. She stepped inside the hallway. They were too busy kissing and feeling on each other to notice her. Good! She walked up to Rashad and tapped him on his shoulder. He looked up at Kiara, his eyes filled with surprise—and then fear. And when she could take a good look at the female he'd just been embracing, Kiara shrieked.

"Who are you?" she asked. "Where'd that first woman go? The one with the big booty. She was petite, and had shorter hair."

Kiara didn't understand; because suddenly Rashad was standing next to an altogether different woman. An incredibly beautiful, slender woman whose long hair flowed down her back.

The woman smiled at Kiara and asked, "What took you so long? We've been waiting for you."

Kiara realized it didn't matter what the woman looked like. It didn't matter if the first chick disappeared.

"That's good to know," Kiara told her. "Because I've been waiting for you, too."

Kiara drew back her fist and popped the woman in the jaw. She grabbed her hair and yanked at it until the stitching came out. She pulled at her blouse and screamed at her.

"What type of bitch are you that you would sleep with a married man?"

But the woman couldn't answer. Her mouth was filled with blood.

When Kiara got done whipping her ass, she turned around and faced her stoic husband.

"Kiara, I'm sorry."

"Tell that to your Maker. Because there's about to be some wailing, screaming, and gnashing of teeth up in here."

She pushed an unresisting Rashad till he sprawled out on the floor. When he tried to crawl away she pounced on him, kicked him in his balls, and struck him with bloodied fists; she unleashed all of the anger for everything he'd done to her during their fraudulent marriage. And when she had beaten him into silence, Kiara stood up and looked around. This time she noticed another smiling woman whom she didn't know. Kiara took no chances. She raised her arm and smashed in that woman's face, too.

She hit the woman until she drew blood.

Then Kiara woke up screaming.

Chapter 1

Kiara Eason stood at the front of the decorated ballroom. Hundreds of helium-filled balloons bobbed against the high ceiling. A six-member band stood on a tiny stage loudly jamming seventies hits like "Dancing Machine" and "Benny and the Jets."

All the tables held party favors that bore the image of Max Julien in *The Mack*, in recognition of the first date between her grandparents, Flora and John.

"Mama Flora didn't leave out a single detail," Kiara said to herself as her eyes took in the festive gala. "I'm so impressed."

After a while, the band started playing "The Best Thing That Ever Happened to Me." A woman who looked like Gladys Knight but didn't sound like her grabbed the microphone.

"I've had my shares of ups and downs..." she began. Her singing voice crackled. She held the notes but sounded like a wolf howling at the moon.

Kiara let out a spirited laugh and grabbed the neck of her champagne glass. She strolled over to the female guest of honor and excitedly tapped her glass. Mama Flora dramatically swayed to the music then hugged Kiara after sipping the bubbly liquid.

"Forty freaking years with Grand Pop. I'm so happy for you. Y'all are such an inspiration to me and my hubby."

"Where is Rashad? Isn't he supposed to be here?" Flora asked.

"Of course, he should be here. And I don't know exactly why he's not. But I have a strong suspicion."

"You look like you're pissed, yet I sense you don't give a damn."

"Oh, I give a damn all right. It's just that I don't know how much more I can give to keep my marriage afloat. That's why I'm here tonight . . . with y'all. I need some inspiration, or maybe a swift kick in the butt."

Kiara walked a short distance over to the dessert table and grabbed two plates of anniversary cake.

"Want a piece?" she asked her grandmother.

"No, sweetie."

"Cool. That means there's more for me." Kiara laughed. She proceeded to devour one thick slice of cake. Then she wolfed down a second piece.

"You're worrying me, darling."

"Don't be worried, Mama Flora. I eat like this all the time."

"Has Rashad noticed that you're starting to overeat?"

"I doubt it. He's so busy with his contracting jobs. In fact, I'll bet he had to work late tonight. Yep, that's it. His favorite line is, 'A business owner always got shit to deal with.'"

"Do you believe him?"

Kiara shrugged.

She then unearthed her cell phone, which was inside her evening bag. She dialed Rashad's mobile number. No answer. She quickly called their house phone. It rang and rang.

Kiara decided to log into their cell phone account.

"What are you doing?" Mama Flora asked.

"I want to know the last time he made a phone call."

"You're checking up on him?"

"Damn right, I am. Because if he's been making calls, I probably have nothing to worry about. But if there are long gaps in between calls, that may mean something different. Something that will make me wonder."

"But didn't you just say that he's working tonight?"

Mama Flora studied her granddaughter, who gave her a distressed look.

"To be honest, Grandma, I don't plan to stay at this party all night. I just swung by to congratulate you and Grand Pop and to pick your brain."

Kiara and Rashad Eason had been married nearly ten years. And all Kiara ever wanted was to have a long-lasting, fulfilling marriage to the man whom she deeply loved. During the first four years, everything was perfect. They built their marital foundation together, striving to do everything they could to be each other's best friend. Then after their son, Myles, was born, things changed. Rashad felt pumped up about being a family man. And Kiara pressed him to do all he could for his precious heir. Rashad agreed. He was motivated by her job at the local college. Kiara was always a go-getter and he was proud to be her husband. The Easons wanted to achieve the American dream. Family, finances, and a badass crib. Kiara took charge of their household expenses, including balancing the checkbook, paying bills, and making investments. And they excelled. But for the past few years, Kiara noticed tiny details that made her feel restless. Their relationship felt too comfortable. And her husband's sex drive suddenly multiplied. But Kiara was exhausted from work, motherhood, social life, domestic duties. That's when she noticed her husband changing. He'd come home late and started petty fights. When she questioned him, he had a convenient answer. Rashad insisted that since the housing market was booming in Houston, he needed to jump on it and make extra money through his contracting business, Eason & Son. So that's why he was home less often, he said, and the pressure of work made him moody. Kiara didn't mind if Rashad was grinding for more money. But it did bother her if he was too tired to spend quality time with her. When he did find time, she felt happy and satisfied. Nevertheless, she desperately wanted to maintain the good parts of her marriage and make sure it lasted for the long haul. And who better to ask than the woman who raised her, Mama Flora, who took in Kiara after her birth mother died from breast cancer when the girl was only two.

Mama Flora raised Kiara to be cultured and educated. And she taught her granddaughter how to balance a checkbook, bake two-layer cakes, and properly clean a house.

"One day your future husband will appreciate a woman who is smart, multitalented, and beautiful. And that's what you are."

Kiara knew her grandmother had her back and she trusted any advice she could offer.

"So tell me, Mama Flora," Kiara asked as she took another sip of her champagne. "How exactly did y'all make it to this day? Don't leave out anything."

But her grandmother got interrupted and had to excuse herself before Kiara could get an answer.

As she waited, Kiara thought about Rashad.

"Where is my husband?" Kiara said to herself. "I swear to God he drives me crazy sometimes."

She skipped away from the pack of family and associates who were gathered in the country club. She crept down a darkened hallway. It was almost eight o'clock. The party had been going strong for one hour and Kiara felt anxious. She told her grandmother that her husband was working late. But what was the true reason why Rashad hadn't shown up?

She hid away inside the empty women's restroom and dialed his number for the fifth time that day.

Rashad finally answered and mumbled, "Hello?"

"Babe, where are you?"

"Mmmm," he groaned.

"Rashad, you sound strange. Are you asleep?"

"Naww."

She felt both relieved and foolish. "I mean, did I wake you? I've been texting and calling. Why aren't you here at Grand Pop's anniversary party?"

"Oh, damn."

"Please don't tell me you forgot, because I just reminded your ass last night. And I told you months ago to put this event on your calendar. *Rashad!*"

"Why are you copping an attitude?"

"You need to do better."

"Well, I'm so busy sometimes I forget."

"That's no excuse. You're way too old for this."

"Kiara, don't bitch at me. I'm not for all that."

She decided to use a different approach.

"Rashad, I know it's inconvenient, but get dressed real quick and come out here right now. Just to make an appearance. The fam has been asking about you and I know they'd love to see you."

"And it won't look good if I'm not there with you, right?"

The way he said it made her feel like she had committed a crime.

"I just don't like being at parties by myself. Plus, we *are* married, in case you forgot."

"I haven't forgotten. And I do apologize, babe. Forgive me. But hell, my sinuses were bothering me. I took some pills that knocked me out . . . so that's what happened."

"Okay, fine. I know you'll feel better soon. But it isn't every day that a married couple stays together for four decades. This party is not something we're going to see again. So please get dressed and come by, even if it's just for a few minutes, all right?"

"Kiara, chill. Tell everyone I'm sorry. But I'm not up to it. Please give my regards to your grandparents." He paused. "Forty years, huh? That's a longgggg time."

Kiara hated how he sounded when he said that, like he couldn't imagine being with the same woman for that many years.

Kiara knew her girlfriends envied her relationship. She could tell when she invited people to their home. Her guests stared at the spectacular house: the tasteful decorations and furnishings, brand-new appliances, and surround sound home theater system. They complimented its beauty—and rarely visited her again. These hating-ass "friends" compared their lives to Kiara's and couldn't stand that she was doing so well. In fact, Kiara's BFF, Adina Davis, was a woman that Rashad had forbidden her to hang out with any longer. He felt Adina was "messy" and a bad influence. It had been a couple years since the two women stopped speaking. And lately Kiara realized she missed her friend and she could use someone in her life who kept it real.

Nevertheless, although Kiara lost some friends, and other friends' marriages were now splitting up, she and Rashad were still hanging in there. And to celebrate their upcoming anniversary, Rashad booked a cruise to the Western Caribbean that would take place later in October. It would be good to get away from it all and try to restore the romance in their relationship.

"Yep, Rashad," Kiara continued. "Forty and fabulous is the theme of this expensive celebration. You should be here to see it. All that love. All that good food. It just might inspire you. It definitely has made me think. Anyway, I know even a room full of nasty strippers won't pull you out the bed. So whatever. See you when I see you."

She hung up. She knew she should have said her normal, "Bye, baby. Love you." But she felt mentally exhausted. She tried so hard to do the right thing in her relationship. When Kiara Eason committed to something, she gave one hundred and ten percent. This was true at her job. And it was especially true at home.

Kiara decided to forget about Rashad and his lame excuse. Instead she enjoyed getting her drink on, tearing up the dance floor, and chopping it up with family.

Not long afterward, Kiara cornered Flora again; the woman was resting her tired feet after she had tried to twerk to Michael Jackson's "Working Day and Night."

Kiara knelt on the floor next to Flora. "Grandma, please drop some knowledge. How do you stay married for decades?"

"It takes true commitment. You gotta love him even when it feels hard to do."

Kiara nodded and smirked.

"Don't fight over something that hasn't even happened yet. Never go to bed mad. And pick your battles 'cause every irritation ain't worth an all-out war. If you can do all those things, that's what it takes to get to this day." Mama Flora grinned and expelled a contented sigh.

"Hmm, that's all?"

"You sound disappointed."

"I'm thinking a lot of couples have done all this and more, yet they're no longer married."

"True. But I don't know about everybody else. I just know me and that man in there, we're besties. We love hard. We give each other space. And we listen to each other no matter what, even if we don't see eye to eye. And that's not hard to do these days when you wear bifocals."

Kiara laughed, yet she wasn't completely satisfied. That was why when Kiara bumped into Grand Pop minutes later, she wanted his side of the story.

Grand Pop was still handsome even though he walked a little slower since he turned seventy. But he trotted about like an old-school pimp.

"Grand Pop, have I ever told you how much I love you?" Kiara choked up and gave him a hug.

"Aw, sugah, I love you, too."

"And I want you to know that I'm praying that my husband will be just like you—strong, stable, smart, and dedicated to his wife." She shook her head. "It's unbelievable that you two have been blessed to see this day."

Grand Pop averted his eyes. He gazed at the ceiling and cleared his throat.

"Well, sugah, I hate to tell you this right now, but you would've found out about it anyway. I-I am filing for divorce before the end of the year. Sooner rather than later."

"W-w-hat did you just say?"

"You heard. We may have been together for forty, but I'm telling you now, ain't gone be no forty-first anniversary."

"Grand Pop! Nooo!"

"Sugah, you young but you ought to know by now that shigitty happens. That you can have it good for a long time, but good don't always stay good."

"I just can't believe I'm hearing this." Kiara stared into space and pondered the shocking revelation. "I mean, I've been to your house. I've seen all the beautiful photos that Mama Flora displays everywhere, in every room. She's smiling. You're smiling."

"They're photos, sugah. That's what you do. You smile . . . for the camera."

"Does that mean you weren't sincere? That your love for Grandma wasn't genuine?"

"It means I loved her the best way I could. In life, people try to stay happy, but things happen. Life gets changed around. Happiness turns upside down."

Kiara's heart sank inside of her. She reached out and hugged Grand Pop. She leaned her head against his chest.

"You two are my inspiration. Now what am I going to do? Does Mama Flora know? Why is she acting like everything is okay when it's not?"

"Baby girl, she's hurting. She just hides it. You may want to go find her. Talk to her. Give her your love. She'll always be your family."

She kissed Grand Pop's cheek as tears streamed from her eyes.

"I wish the best for you," she replied. "You will always be family, too. And thanks for letting me know what's going on."

She gave him one last squeeze and said good-bye.

The information was more than Kiara could bear. She decided to leave right away; she wasn't in the mood to party any longer.

Kiara finally made it home. She and Rashad lived on a quiet tree-lined street in Fresno, a suburb located south of Houston. Their corner lot residence had supreme curb appeal with its brick and stone elevation and opulent landscaping. It boasted a two-story living room, island kitchen, a game room, a spiral staircase, four bedrooms, and a custom-made deck built with Rashad's own hands.

Kiara drove into the garage and turned off the ignition. Once she got inside the house, she hurried to their first-floor master suite and got undressed. The hot water from the whirlpool jets massaged her as she cleaned herself inside their glass-enclosed Jacuzzi shower; then Kiara crawled into their king-size bed. Rashad was spread out and snoring. She kicked him. He didn't move. She kicked him harder. He sat up.

"What? Damn. What?"

"Sorry."

"You're not sorry. Why'd you kick me? What'd I do?"

"Oh, my God, everything isn't about you, Rashad."

"If you kicking me like a damned kangaroo, I've got to assume it's about me!"

"Babe, forgive me. I-I'm just so wired up." She waited for him to ask what happened. When he lay back down and turned away from her and snatched the comforter back on top of himself, Kiara continued. "Rashad, I know you're sleepy but you gotta hear this. My grandparents are heading to Splitsville."

"Is that a small town in Texas?"

"Rashad, stop playing. I think it's ridiculous for old-ass married folks to be breaking up. Grand Pop loves women. What's he supposed to do now? Register with OkCupid?"

"Hell, if he's a true G, he might."

"Oh, that would be so disgusting. At his age, where is he gonna find a woman that's better than Mama Flora? I think he's tripping. Whatever problems they had, surely they can work 'em out, don't you think?"

"Dunno. None of my biz."

"Rashad!"

"Why you sound so shocked? Couples crash and burn every day. Nick and Mariah. Wiz and Amber. And um, each time Kim Kardashian breaks up with a man it's almost like a national holiday."

"Humph! That's what you call hooking up with a famous penis. But we're talking about my family and people we actually know. This situation is serious."

"You're right. It is serious. And even though I'm acting like I'm not surprised, well, hell, I am surprised."

She sprung off the bed and started pacing alongside it.

"I didn't see this one coming. Women have so much to deal with already."

Rashad grinned as he watched Kiara vent. Even though they first met more than ten years earlier, he still admired his wife's beauty. Her oval-shaped face, flawless honey brown complexion, doe eyes, big boobs, and curvy shape made her a looker. She was his own little Ashanti, since she bore a strong resemblance to the attractive singer.

"Hello? Men have a lot on their plates, too."

"Rashad, there's no comparison. In fact, I think you ought to be glad and count the blessings you receive from being married to a woman like me. I bring something to the table because I work every day, and I mean seven-days-a-week every day. And I help to raise our awesome son. I cook for you, clean for you, spread my legs open for you, and do all kinds of things that you may not even deserve. You couldn't handle half the stuff that's on my plate!"

Rashad stopped grinning. "Calm down. You're going overboard."

"That's what I'm supposed to do. I must go overboard because when it's all said and done, I don't want anyone to be able to point a finger at me and say Kiara Mariah Eason screwed it up. Or that I was caught not handling my business. Mmm mmm. Nope. That's not going to happen."

"Okay, okay. I get it. You're dope."

"Don't be facetious, Rashad."

"But I'm not. I mean it. You *are* dope. You're Mrs. Rashad Quintell Eason. Now come get back in bed, shut off that overactive brain of yours, and take your pretty ass to sleep. I'm sorry to hear about what happened. But there's nothing we can do about them breaking up."

She raised one eyebrow and took a seat next to him on the bed.

"Rashad, go ahead and admit it. You really don't care because it's not your life! As long as you're not the one getting a divorce, you don't give a shit, am I right?"

"Huh? I'm saying that *their* issues have nothing to do with us."

"But actually they do." She gave her husband a pensive look. "I wanted us to be just like them and now I don't even know if we can make it to *twenty* years, let alone forty."

"Say what? Kiara, it is what it is, why can't you just let it go—?"

"Don't interrupt me. I feel we need to be on the same page as far as our relationship is concerned."

"But we are—"

"Let me finish. I've bent over backwards for us. And sometimes I feel you're not getting it. Or that what we've accomplished doesn't mean as much to you as it does to me."

"Of course it does, babe." He sat up and leaned over to kiss Kiara.

"Do not try and kiss me if it doesn't come from a place of love."

"Love," Rashad muttered, "is overrated." He blew her a kiss, turned over, buried his body into the comforter, and tried to go back to sleep.

"That's what I'm talking about," she wailed. "You're not taking me seriously. You're taking me for granted and I'm telling you right now, you don't want to do that."

He turned to face her. "Is that a threat?"

"Does it sound like one?"

"Do you really have to go there, Kiara? Damn, I turn in one unexcused absence for a party that I never had time to go to in the first place and now you're threatening me? As hard as I bust my ass every day, sweating like a pig, and sacrificing my safety on construction sites just to make sure you have every material good you want? Oh, so you're getting the big head and thinking you bring more than me to the table because you work, too? You're the HNIC at your nice air-conditioned job and you want the kudos here at our crib, too?" He threw back his head and laughed as Kiara's cheeks reddened. "Okay. I get it. Baby girl, you kick ass and you take names. You put in hella effort for us. And you're a bomb-ass mother. Hell, you're the shit at just about everything. And now that *that's* been acknowledged, it really makes me feel good that I'm about to go to sleep knowing my wife thinks I'm trash; and all because your grandparents are going to a place called Splitsville. Miss me with the drama, babe. Good night."

Kiara could not believe that Rashad went off on her like that. His crazy rant kind of turned her on, but right then she was pissed. Sometimes she let her husband's insults slide, but tonight wouldn't be one of those times. She let out a frustrated scream and snatched the covers until Rashad's body was completely exposed. He was lying on his side with his back facing her. She ripped down his boxers and spotted his butt cheeks. She jumped up on the bed, took her big toe and jammed it squarely into the center of his ass. She almost fell as she twisted her toe and she glared at Rashad as he squirmed.

He bucked his body and yelled, "What the fuck!"

"How's that for some drama? You better be glad that's all I did," she snapped. "I'm serious about everything I said, Rashad. I love you, but I will fuck you up. You've been forewarned. Good night."

After several minutes of pacing the room, Kiara calmed down and crawled back in bed next to her husband. Their highly emotional fights were common. Even though Rashad made her furious and she was inclined to check him here and there, she loved his dirty drawers. Even her former best friend, Adina, used to question her, "What do you see in this man? He's an arrogant asshole." Kiara would laugh and tell her, "I can't completely disagree, but I see things you don't see. He turns me on in spite of his ways. Love can't be explained. And it's not always logical."

In truth, Rashad made her feel deeply in love one minute, and she was ready to karate chop him the next minute. Ever since she first spotted him at a Houston nightclub, and noticed how well-dressed he was and his confident air, she knew she wanted to meet him. She spotted him standing around with some of his boys holding a drink in his hand and watching the action. His mouth was constantly running. But he saw her looking his way and he waved. Good! She got noticed just like she knew she would. Kiara confidently walked up to him and introduced herself. They snuck away to their own table. Rashad ordered their drinks. They made serious eye contact as they sat across from each other. At first their conversation was trivial bullshit as they complimented each other's outward appearance, and talked about the kinds of cars they drove, and where they liked to hang out. But as the night progressed, Kiara decided to lay it on him. She told him she wanted to be somebody, she wanted to live a good life, and she would work hard to achieve it. But the crème de la crème would be to have a successful man to share it with her. As they started talking about their lives, their hopes and dreams, Kiara knew Rashad was the one for her. She found out that he was a budding business owner; his goal was to make big moves as a minority firm in the city. He confessed he'd been buck-wild in the past, but now he was ready to settle down, if only he could find the right woman. The fact that he was deliciously hand-some also didn't hurt. Plus, he had other qualities she liked. After dating for a brief period they decided to get married.

And though they'd been a couple for one decade, Rashad still did it for her in the looks department. Her husband had short, wavy hair, a neat mustache, deep-set eyes that lit up when he laughed, an incredible body, and his big dick was a major bonus, especially since he knew how to work it.

Kiara lay next to Rashad and could hear his steady breathing. He'd already fallen asleep. She figured he must have been telling the truth about being sick and feeling exhausted. She felt a little guilty after that. She kissed his shoulder then wrapped one arm around his stomach. Rashad's warm, taut body felt good next to hers but she wished she had a better view than just his back. Instead of waking him up and asking him to hold her, Kiara felt thankful that her husband was there with her that night. Because as Kiara went to sleep thinking of the woman who raised her, she knew that once Grand Pop moved out, Mama Flora would morph into Macaulay

Culkin and his famous movie: she'd be all alone in her scary old house ... slapping her hands on the sides of her face ... and screaming.

At six a.m. the following morning, Kiara was on her way to work at Texas South West University, also known as TSWU. She served as a senior manager of communications in an academic department. Her job had been good to her, and Kiara was extremely satisfied to have stable employment and report daily to a place where she earned nearly six figures a year.

It was early May, a pleasant seventy-nine degrees. The glittering sun lit up the city as it buzzed with the sounds of life and activity. While she was waiting at a railroad track for a train to pass, she dialed the automatic account info number to their credit union. She enjoyed keeping on top of their finances. When she heard the balance of their joint checking account, she promptly hung up. She immediately made another call to Rashad.

"Hey babe, I'm almost at work but I needed to ask you something," she said

"What's that?"

"Did you make a big withdrawal yesterday?"

"Did I make a big withdrawal yesterday?"

"Yes, babe."

"How much?"

"What type of question is that?"

"A real one."

"Six hundred, babe."

"Uh no, I didn't," he said.

"No? You sure? Because according to the bank, a withdrawal was made."

"Look, a call is coming in that I've been waiting on."

"Well, whoever it is, they're gonna have to wait. This is important."

"Kiara, to you everything is important. Hold on a minute."

She grew more annoyed the longer she waited. And she knew that it wasn't good to argue with her husband before she went to work because the negative flow threw her off all day.

Rashad finally returned to the call. "Yeah, I just secured a major interior paint job I've been wanting at an industrial building on the southwest side."

"That's great, Rashad, but can we get back to my question. I was planning to pay off the new computers and printers this month and with that money missing—"

"Hey, tell you what. Since I'll be making a nice chunk of change, I will put the money back in the account."

"So you did take it?"

"Don't worry about it. I'll put the money back, the balance will be paid off, and we won't owe Dell, Inc., a dime. Problem solved."

"Problem isn't solved, Rashad. I have a feeling that you're holding something back from me and if that is the case then we need to talk. I want us to be open and honest."

"You want us to be open and honest? Really, Kiara?"

"Yes, now come on and tell me the truth."

"See, this is why I feel I should manage that particular account. That way, when I have to make certain moves, I won't have you all upset. Remember, I told you that a business owner got all kinds of shit he has to deal with."

"There you go. I just think I'm better at handling these kinds of things and I expect to be involved. You don't have time to work and oversee the funds. And as long as we have this joint business account, you definitely need to give your wife a heads-up when you do this kind of thing. Now I just pulled up in the parking lot. Do you know how hard it is for me to put a convincing smile on my face like I'm Super Woman before I come into the office?"

"That's the whole issue. Like I said, you do a kick-ass job, but you're not Super Woman."

"Rashad!" She felt her blood pressure rising. "I would never say something so shitty like that to you. Sometimes . . . I swear to God."

"Babe, I'm just telling the truth. You can't fly."

"Now you're acting silly."

He heard her sniffling. "Hey, I am sorry . . . but damn. Seems like lately . . . you've been over the top . . . with the emotions. You may need a reality check or something."

She sighed heavily and for the second day in a row didn't have the desire or energy to say her usual, "Bye, babe. Love you. Have a blessed day."

Instead she muttered, "Mr. Eason, I love you, but you're an ass."

She hung up.

Then she called the number to her credit union. She wanted to check the balance of a secret money market account that she had opened five years ago.

"Your balance on account number 753142 is twelve thousand four hundred dollars and eleven cents."

Then she checked on the balance of a CD that she secretly owned. It consisted of thousands of dollars, too.

Growing up, Kiara had heard far too many horror stories of her great aunts who had been born in an era in which the husbands made and controlled all the money. The wives took care of the kids and had to wait to be given an allowance. The men exercised total financial control. And a couple of Kiara's great aunts were stunned when their spouses went through mid-life crises that included running off with younger women and cleaning out the bank accounts. The wives were left penniless and struggled to find work even though they had no transferrable skills. Kiara never wanted to be in that position; she wanted to be prepared for whatever challenges married life could bring.

Kiara felt good inside when she heard the amount. She hung up and believed that one day her husband would realize that she really was Super Woman, but right then he was too blind and stupid to see her strength.

She may not have been able to literally fly, but Kiara Eason was determined to excel at life, and whether her husband was able to agree or understand would remain to be seen.

Chapter 2

Alexis McNeil expertly decorated the oblong conference table by covering it with a classy purple and gold table cloth. She arranged the breakfast service of doughnuts, bagels, and fresh fruit. Then she set up the containers of chilled fruit juices and pots of hot coffee. It was Hump Day. Although it was only eight-forty-five, the only thing she could think about was lunch. Lunch was her favorite part of Wednesdays. But first she had to get through this freaking staff meeting that her boss insisted on having.

Soon a dozen or so coworkers congregated in the meeting room. They all began filling their plastic white plates with breakfast items and exchanging morning pleasantries.

Alexis knew nobody cared about how she was doing so she made a concentrated effort to focus her eyes on the table. She quietly ignored the animated way her coworkers greeted one another as if they hadn't seen each other twenty-four hours earlier. She worked as the administrative assistant and one of her tasks was to make sure all the food was on par for their monthly meeting in the communications division of their academic department.

On that day Alexis wore a black jacket and matching pencil skirt with a gold silk blouse and massive ruffles that covered her neck. A double strand of white pearls rested on her blouse. And her twenty-two-inch Remi weave made her resemble a woman who could easily earn her money based on her looks.

Alexis had the type of beauty that alienated most women, yet her exotic features caused men of all races to admire her. She looked good from the front and the back.

Right then, Kiara Eason walked in and stood at the front of the room. She too wore a black dress suit and her hair was styled in a cute bob. An engaging smile, spirited personality, and commitment to excellence made Kiara a standout at TSWU.

She waited for her staff to finish drawing cups of coffee, or pouring ice water and juice. Gradually everyone quieted down and gathered in their seats around the table.

Alexis sat in a chair at the rear of the conference room and quietly observed Kiara as she commenced the meeting.

Womp, womp, womp.

Alexis immediately tuned out Kiara. She started daydreaming about other things she'd rather be doing. Then she picked up an ink pen and some paper and drew stick figures of people having sex on the beach. She laughed at her devious ways. She couldn't stand the sound of her boss's voice and she grew annoyed every time she was required to attend these dull staff meetings.

Twenty minutes later, Alexis heard the low chime of a mobile phone, a recognizable ring tone that caused her to smile. Every day she carried two cell phones: One was a BlackBerry that she used only for work. The other was an iPhone, the one her lover gave her three years ago when they first began seeing each other.

Alexis excused herself from the meeting. She scooped her tiny phone in her hand and rushed down the hallway to the women's room. There were a total of four stalls. Even though she knew all her female coworkers were in the conference room, she quickly checked first to make sure she had complete privacy.

"Hey there," she answered.

"What up, sexy? How is the meeting?"

"Same ole same ole. How is your day going? You gonna make it for lunch today?"

"You miss me, huh?"

She ignored him.

"Anyway, we still on. Can't wait."

Alexis returned to the meeting with a satisfied grin on her face. A couple hours later, she was on her way to her house to meet her lover for her weekly "nooner." She lived only ten minutes from the job.

Alexis pulled onto the gravel driveway and quickly let herself inside the house. She and her mother, Mona Hooker, resided in a cozy one-and-a-half-story bungalow that was built in the fifties. Although there was plenty of living space in the charming home, her mother was usually tucked away in her first-floor bedroom at the rear of the house. Alexis quickly checked on her mother. Mona was spread out in bed, covered by a quilt, and peacefully sleeping while her television was tuned to the TV Land channel.

When Rashad Eason knocked on the door minutes later, Alexis opened it and pulled him right inside the doorway by his shirt. He laughed and winked. They smiled at each other. She watched him; he moved with a confident, bouncy walk as he quickly slipped past her into the house. She kicked the door shut with her foot, and turned around to give him kisses on his mouth, his cheeks and forehead.

"Whoa, whoa. So you do miss me." He laughed as he kissed her back. "What up, Skillet?" That was the nickname Rashad gave Alexis. To him it meant she was "skilled at it," as in her bedroom skills.

"Come on, baby."

Alexis McNeil was every man's dream; she was lean and willowy. Her long legs looked fabulous in high heels. She had dark, penetrating eyes, thick eyebrows, a gorgeous smile, and a calm exterior. She resembled a younger Paula Patton and drew stares wherever she went.

She and Rashad's Hump Day scenario had been going on for two years. And no matter how many times they did it, she seldom got tired of seeing Rashad show up at her door. Alexis grabbed Rashad's hand and led him up the stairs which creaked with every step. Since she paid a decent share of the household expenses, Mona allowed her to occupy the entire second floor for extra privacy.

Alexis immediately locked her bedroom door and pulled Rashad's shirt over his head and dropped it to the floor. His ripped chest felt good when she brushed her fingers across his skin.

She peppered his neck with sweet kisses.

"Tastes salty," she joked. "Like nuts."

"Ohh, baby," he moaned. "That feels so good."

Alexis carefully unzipped his pants and chuckled when she saw the bulge in his briefs. They caressed each other while standing up. She got hotter and hotter. Rashad unzipped her skirt and slid it over her hips. He unbuttoned her blouse and she didn't care where he tossed it. She let him remove her panties and tried to keep from laughing when he attempted to twist her nipples between his fingers. Usually when he stopped by, he was dirty from having worked in dusty buildings. Alexis demanded that he be clean before they made love. So they took a quick shower and then sprawled out naked on a sheepskin rug.

When Rashad kissed Alexis on her thighs, toes, fingers, and lips, she quivered from the feeling he gave her. And all she could think about how she wished she could have this man . . . just like this . . . every day . . . except for the few times a week she got to see him. She wanted to cling to these moments, to her baby Rashad, and never let him go.

"You miss me?" he asked as he tenderly gazed down and inserted himself inside her.

His plump dick was erect and smoking hot. It felt good.

She squeezed his back and held him close, enjoying the warmth of his nakedness. "Why you keep asking me that?"

" 'Cause you never answer me."

"Jesus. Yes, Rashad. You already know. Stevie Wonder could see that I do."

"Okay, cool. What you miss?"

"Stop playing."

"How was work?"

"Boy, if you don't quit."

"Boy?" He threw back his head and chuckled again. "You're so cute when you're mad."

"I'm glad you think that. Now go down on me."

She closed her eyes and spread her legs. She raised her hips and thrust her pussy at him. He leaned down and started licking her, teasing her with his tongue. His tongue flicked across her clit. She gasped and squirmed and cupped her breasts. Rashad licked her toes, moved up her thigh, and sucked her nipples. She squirmed and moaned as he sucked. She enjoyed him in every way.

He hummed as he ate her. She thought she was going to die and loved every minute of him.

I'm much too in love with this man and that's a dangerous thing. How would I survive if we couldn't stay together?

Alexis McNeil knew she was a single woman dating a married man, but she felt she had the best of both worlds. She got to enjoy mind-blowing sex on a weekly basis. Her lover brought her nice gifts. And she never had to deal with the unpleasant stuff: washing his funky underwear, fussing at him for being a slob, dealing with his unbearable family members, or having to bury him if he passed away. That's what wives had to deal with. Rashad was her good-looking, well-endowed sexual healer, and that's what she preferred, or so she thought.

The minutes flew by. Alexis knew that their rendezvous would soon end. She held onto his neck, giving him tight hugs while he worked hard to get his orgasm. He thrust his penis inside her and she enjoyed how tight it felt. They created friction as they moved together. He stroked her with a nice rhythm. She gritted her teeth and cried out.

Rashad moaned then collapsed on top of her. She stroked the back of his head, believing that he loved her as much as she loved him.

Rashad handed Alexis a little cash, something he did once a month to help her out with any expenses she may have. Then he kissed her good-bye. He promised he'd be back and she knew he would. Alexis went to the bathroom, cleaned herself off with a hot wet cloth, and drove back to the office. She found a parking space in the staff lot and turned off the ignition. She ran her fingers through the long wavy strands of her sew-in and examined herself in the mirror before getting out of her car.

Once she was satisfied with her appearance, she headed inside her building and returned to her desk. Her workstation was centered in the hallway of the first floor so that she would be the first employee visitors saw once they entered the department.

Alexis was so busy having sex she didn't have time to eat her lunch at her house. So she sat at her desk and removed a deluxe turkey sandwich and a fruit cup from her lunch bag. She nibbled on her meal and resumed processing scholarship applications. She had only been sitting in her seat for ten minutes when she heard loud shouts coming from the hallway a few yards down.

"Where is that thot? If I see her, I'm going to beat her nasty whorish ass."

"What the hell?" Shyla Perry, the social network coordinator, came and stood by Alexis's desk where she could safely view the action. Shyla was a tall, short-haired, opinionated woman who loved to know what was going on with everyone in the office.

"Oh my God. Who is that crazy woman?" Shyla asked Alexis.

"Hell if I know."

The woman whooped and hollered at the top of her voice. "Show me that skank's office. Right now."

Beads of sweat formed on Shyla's forehead. She craned her neck to see.

Alexis busily tapped her fingers across her keyboard, but she couldn't help but hear the woman.

"I don't give a rat's ass that you think I should take this elsewhere. If a bitch got the nerve to fuck my husband, then I will come up to the job, beat *her* ass and shut this down. Shee-it. I don't play that." The woman kicked the wall with her heels and started going off again.

"Oh, my goodness," Shyla said. "This is nuts. I hope she don't have a gun. Call 911." Shyla frantically waved her hands at Alexis. But Alexis continued typing away with her eyes steadfastly on her computer monitor.

"Alexis, you hear me? Girl, what's wrong with you? Call the police."

"What's wrong with your fingers?"

"Have you lost your mind?"

"No. And why you losing yours? That's not your business. They grown."

"Do you hear how loud that lady is screaming? She's yelling at our graphic artist! This is a matter for security. Pick up that phone and call for help."

"Just because I'm the admin doesn't mean I have to do anything y'all tell me to do."

"Oh, my God. This isn't about you!"

"Then why put me in the middle of it?"

The wife yelled, "Heads are about to fucking roll around here like a bowling alley. Where is that shitty piece of ass?"

Shyla pleaded with Alexis. "See what I mean? She could be packing. Aren't you scared?"

"Why should I be? I'm not fucking *her* husband."

"Girl, something's wrong with you. The hell with it. I'll call the police from my office. You must be wearing a bulletproof vest or something."

Shyla ran down the hall yelling, "Fix it, Jesus."

Alexis rolled her eyes like she couldn't be bothered. She waited for the drama to fizzle to nothing. She and Shyla had never clicked. Shyla was one of those messy, annoying, know-it-all women that Alexis could not stand.

After a while, the irate wife finally stopped shouting

and calmed down when campus police showed up. Come to find out, the lady was in the wrong building. Neither her husband nor his lover worked in their facility.

"Woo, how much you wanna bet that wife feels like the town idiot?" Alexis was talking to the coworkers who had stood in front of her desk after the campus police escorted the woman outside. Shyla walked up and listened in on the conversation.

"Yeah, you see how crazy she looked? I felt sorry for her," remarked one lady.

"Her no-good husband probably driving her so crazy she doesn't know her left hand from her right foot. Poor thing," Shyla commented. "Some men will do that to you."

"And that's what side pieces do to you," replied the good-looking male custodian. "If the side didn't open her legs, he couldn't dip his stick in that big ole hole."

"Shut the hell up," Shyla snapped at the custodian. "That husband is a cheater. And that woman is one, too. I hope his wife finds the right building and beats the hell out of that woman."

"Even if he is cheating, the main chick handled it all wrong," Alexis replied. "If the man is messing around, why is she trying to run up on the other woman?"

"True that," said Tony Fu; he was the department videographer, who liked to lurk around and join in on the office happenings. He also was one of Kiara's favorite employees.

"He should have been the first person she was looking for."

"In my opinion," Alexis said, "a man that goes after the side is just pathetic."

"Alexis," Shyla responded, "are you actually saying that if you were married, and last time I checked you aren't and never have been, you wouldn't have any anger towards the side piece?"

"Like I said, he is the one who willingly shared his juices with someone else and did the wife dirty. The side never promised her a thing."

"You act like her husband's infidelity is all her fault."

"It could be, we don't know that, and we can't assume that the man is always to blame," Alexis responded. "But one thing I do know is that people cheat because there is a high interest in it or else so many men wouldn't be doing it."

Shyla heartily laughed. "Men do it 'cause some of them are damned fools that don't appreciate what they got. Or they can't keep that anaconda in its cage."

"Nope, wrong," Alexis said. "Think about it. Every market is determined by the law of supply and demand. When it comes to extramarital affairs, the demand for them drives the market. The demand comes from men. And the women handle the supply."

"Oh, wow, she's breaking it down like a math equation, huh?" Tony said.

"I'm just saying if men didn't want to step out, and if there weren't women that are willing to give these men what they want, there'd be no such thing as cheating. But that's what some people do." She shrugged. "And other times it's not that he's a no-good cheater. Sometimes he just fell in love. And that's something he can't help."

"You really believe that?" Shyla asked.

"Sure do."

"Girl, bye," Shyla said. "Some people." She walked away and glanced back at Alexis, giving her a curious stare.

That afternoon, Kiara passed through the hallway and stopped in front of Alexis's workstation. "Hey there. Can you please come to my office when you have a moment?"

"Sure."

Every time her boss asked her to come to her office, Alexis felt rolls of quivers in her belly.

Does she know about me and Rashad? Alexis would ask herself. The fact that she was sleeping with her boss's husband made Alexis feel some kind of way. And she still hadn't decided if she was ready to tell Kiara everything. Of course, Rashad begged her not to. And she was the type to play her position. But the way they ended up in an affair required both of them to be knowing participants.

The first time Alexis met Rashad was the day she arrived on the campus of Texas South West University. She was standing on a sidewalk peering down at a campus map kiosk.

"Hey, you look lost," Rashad told her. "Can I help you find something?"

He had just dropped off a check at Kiara's office, and had made a quick trip to the student union food court to grab some lunch when he noticed this pretty young thing. When a man meets a woman, he knows right away if he wants to smash; Rashad took one look at her body and wondered what she looked like naked. Up until that moment, he never seriously considered cheating on his wife.

"Oh, I think I know where this building is, but I'm not totally positive. But I'm sure it's down that way."

"What?" he said with a grin. Rashad doubted she knew what she was doing; her pretending ways captivated him.

"I said I know where I'm going."

"You don't look like it."

She twirled around and started walking east. But she only took a couple steps before she whirled back around. "Okay, sir. I'm sorry to bother you. Can you please help me? I've been lost ever since I parked my car and I hope I can find it when I leave. I've never been on this side of campus a day in my life."

Rashad burst out laughing. He was intrigued. She looked so sweet and vulnerable. She seemed like she needed protecting. He wanted to know her and not just have sex with her.

"I'd be glad to help. My line of work has me driving all over the city. So I know how it feels to be somewhere and not know where the hell I am. But don't worry, you're in good hands, young lady."

Alexis's cheeks flushed red.

"Don't be ashamed. We all need help sometimes."
He winked at her, which made her blush even more.

Even though Alexis assumed Rashad thought she felt foolish, in reality she was attracted to his good looks. His eyes were mesmerizing and filled with excitement. He had the most amazing teeth. He was super friendly and made her feel at ease. And he looked sexy in his clothes. Deep inside she felt she was being rescued. To her, all the buildings on the huge campus looked the same and she'd already wasted twenty minutes. No one else reached out to assist her. So Alexis told Rashad where she needed to go and he personally walked her to MacGregor Hall, the location of the HR department.

"You look like a college student. Smart and stylish."

She wore a belted coatdress and some black pumps. Rashad loved what he saw.

"Thanks for the compliment. I'm not a student. But my mama sure stays on me so I'll make something out of my life. If I didn't go to college, the next best thing is to get a job at a college." She gave him a reserved smile, which endeared her to him.

They arrived at MacGregor Hall and he walked her inside the lobby.

"Hey, I hope you get the job." He winked and reached out to shake her hand. Her skin felt smooth and warm. He wished he could hold her fingers a little longer; he resisted the crazy temptation to kiss them. But she eventually let go. He watched her board the elevator. Though he could have left right then, he decided to linger around on the first floor. He had to see her again. He stood and waited. And he was so happy when he watched Alexis get off the elevator after she was done with her appointment.

"Hey there," she said. Alexis was glad to see him, too. She thought about him all the while she was upstairs filling out paperwork. She wondered who he was.

"It's you again. I wanted to tell you thanks for helping me."

"My name is Rashad. What's yours?"

"I'm Alexis."

"I stuck around to make sure you're okay. And I just had to see if you can find the right parking lot."

They laughed together.

"Plus you're fine as hell and you also seem like a cool chick. Can we stay in touch?"

"You seem like a cool dude, and I don't mind staying in touch, but aren't you too old for me?"

"I'm thirty-one. That ain't old," he told her. "Watch this." In a moment of spontaneity, Rashad ran up toward the side of a nearby wall, jumped off of it, and did a handstand. He balanced his weight and with great agility walked around on his hands, yelling, "I'm the king of the world." Alexis was flabbergasted. This guy was something else. She giggled and shook her head.

"You sure are energetic . . . for an old man."

He got back on his feet and dusted off his hands. "Hey, baby, I would love to show you what an old man can do!"

Alexis felt breathless.

"I'd love to see that. Here's my number, cutie. Use it. Don't lose it."

Even though Alexis was nineteen, and she felt a little nervous about how she flirted back, she loved Rashad's energetic and confident air. She could already tell that he liked her, and that they shared great chemistry.

They talked on the phone every day. He made her laugh and gave her all kinds of compliments. She soon started working in an office on campus. They saw each other once a week and she snuck him into her mother's house to have sex. He continued to charm her and she loved the surprise gifts he brought to her. But a year later, when there was a reduction in force, Alexis got re-located to the communications division. That's when she found herself working for Kiara Eason. Right away, Alexis realized that her boss shared a last name with the man she'd been sleeping with. That's when she put two and two together. She asked Rashad if he was still married. He said yes, but "it isn't a happy marriage so please don't hold that against me." She got angry at him but he begged for her forgiveness. By then Alexis was sprung. She couldn't let him go.

Ever since then, working for Kiara kept Alexis on edge. She needed her job, but she loved and needed Rashad even more.

And now her boss wanted to meet with Alexis. She took her time and combed her hair, reapplied her hot pink lipstick, and curled her eyelashes. She grabbed her BlackBerry then walked into Mrs. Eason's spacious corner office, which was well lit by the sparkling afternoon sun.

"Yes."

"Close the door and have a seat."

Alexis wrestled with the fear within her belly, but she calmly sat down and crossed her legs.

"Um, while I was gone from the office, I heard about a disturbing event that took place. From what I was told, you were a witness, as well as Shyla and some of the other staff."

"Yes, that's true. But what does the alleged 'disturbing event' have to do with me?"

Kiara was taken aback by her tone.

"I wasn't finished yet."

"Sorry."

"Anyway, what it has to do with you, as well as the others, is that I think we should schedule a brief staff meeting to talk about it."

This heifer loves meetings.

"That sounds like a personal issue that the campus police department has already handled. The lady's husband didn't even work here. The only disturbing thing that happened is a woman made a big fool of herself. Couldn't be me."

"Well, Alexis, you definitely have a lot to say for someone who thinks the incident has nothing whatsoever to do with you."

"It's just my opinion."

"That's fine, but my concern is for everyone here to feel safe," Kiara continued. "In fact, it's my duty to create a secure environment. And while it is somewhat true that what people do on their own time is their own business—"

"At least we agree on that."

"Alexis, I beg your pardon. Is there something going on that you're not telling me? You've been snapping at me ever since you came in my office."

Alexis frowned and her eyes rested on an eight-by-ten

silver picture frame that was prominently displayed by Kiara's office telephone. She stared at the black-and-white photo of her lover, Rashad, snuggling cheek to cheek with Kiara. Their six-year-old son, Myles, was sitting on his mother's lap. Kiara was grinning and her eyes sparkled with joy. Rashad's lips curled into a proud grin. This must have been a new photo.

Alexis felt teary-eyed. The handsome boy greatly favored Rashad.

"This is some crap," Alexis said out loud and rose to her feet.

"What did you say? Why are you getting up? The meeting isn't done yet."

Alexis clapped her hands over her mouth.

"I think I have food poisoning. Excuse me."

Alexis stumbled out of Kiara's office and hurried to the restroom. She burst into an empty stall and fell to her knees. She flung up the toilet seat and placed her face over the white porcelain commode. It was cold and sterile. And the thought of her face being so close to where people emptied their bowels made her more nauseated.

"Oh, God," she said just before her stomach unloaded. Her mouth spread open wider and wider as she vomited. Her forehead beaded with sweat and she wished she could remove her jacket.

Once her stomach settled, she went back to her desk, opened a drawer with her key, and removed a clear plastic bag in which she stored toothpaste, a toothbrush, mouth rinse, and dental floss. She called it her "Freakum Bag" because she also kept two extra pairs of black thongs in it just in case.

Alexis returned to the restroom, thoroughly cleaned out her mouth, and got freshened up.

As much as she hated to do it, she walked back into Kiara's office and closed the door.

"Sorry about that. I feel better now that I've gotten rid of something that wasn't making me feel good."

"Where'd you go for lunch?"

"Where'd I go for lunch?"

"Yes, you said you experienced food poisoning. Maybe you should call that restaurant and let them know."

"Um, that won't be necessary."

Kiara gave Alexis a quizzical look. "Have you eaten there before?"

"Have I eaten there before? Look, don't worry about it. It's not even that serious."

"Just say the word and I'll call wherever you ate lunch today."

Alexis gulped. "Please. Don't."

"I won't. But if I were you, I would never go back to that place again. Now will you please send out an invite for a thirty-minute meeting? It can start at three."

"If you say so; I don't think this is needed. But you're the boss."

"I'm sure everyone is going to feel differently about this but, as a married woman, it's a topic that's close to the chest. It's never good when couples put their business out on the street. And from what I hear, this situation was completely out of control. I especially hate when married women lower themselves to the level of a—"

"You want to say 'whore'?"

"I did want to say it, and I will say it. The other woman is a ho!"

"You are entitled to your opinion, but why does that woman have to be called an ugly name only because she fell in love with the same man? Plus, you know nothing about the chick that the man is allegedly messing with."

"I don't have to know anything about her," Kiara

snapped. "If he's married, he's off limits point blank period. She should know that."

"What she 'should know' always isn't the case. Maybe he hasn't admitted he's married. You'd be surprised at how many men hide their status."

"Now, see, that's just something I don't understand. How can a man be living with his wife and going around acting like he's single and ready to mingle? I'd kill Rashad if he denied me. Then I'd kill the other woman, too."

Alexis tried to place her shaking hands in her lap. "I'm sure you don't have to worry about that with your man. You're one of the lucky ones." She forced herself to smile as she gazed at the family photo on Kiara's desk. "Your family looks sooo nice. And I can tell you've got a special one right there."

Kiara thought about it and nodded. "Overall, I probably am fortunate to have him. But he's the lucky one because he has me."

"Hmm. He's lucky, all right."

"Oops, so sorry. I'm not trying to brag or anything. And Alexis, don't give up hope. I'm sure in due time, the right man will come along for you, too."

"How do you know he hasn't already come along?"

"Oh, is that right? Well, I'd love to meet your man one day."

"Maybe you will."

"Do you have a photo of him in your phone?"

Alexis stood up. This was her opportunity to tell Kiara that she was sleeping with Rashad. Her BlackBerry was tucked inside its Union Jack curve case; she opened the case, then snapped it shut. "I do have a photo, but I will show it to you some other time. I need to get going on that meeting request."

Alexis was just fucking with her boss, for she knew

that she did not have a single photo of Rashad on her work cell phone.

That afternoon, once the entire staff gathered again in the conference room, Kiara stood before all twelve employees appearing resolute and stern.

"Normally, we do not meet about these types of topics, but considering what happened a couple of hours ago I felt it was necessary to bring everyone up to speed. I've met with the campus chief of police and one of the lieutenants. A woman whose spouse does work at TSWU came unannounced to our building today around one-thirty. She was screaming and causing a disturbance. Thankfully, she was unarmed. She wasn't arrested but was issued a warning. I'm not sure if she also entered any other buildings before she found herself over here, but the good news is no one was hurt."

"Why was she here? I missed the action," asked Ellie, the assistant manager of marketing.

"Her man ain't right, that's why she was here," Shyla said and gave a smug look. "Me and my man Wesley are getting married the first weekend in November, and I let him know from the jump that I do not play when it comes to cheating. In fact, if we're walking down the aisle towards the minister and if Wesley so much as looks at another woman, I will call off the wedding even before I say 'I do.' I will tell that minister, 'Before you get started, I *do not*. It's a *wrap*. And y'all don't have to go *home*, but you gots to get the hell up *outchea*.'"

Everyone except Alexis broke into laughter. She was trying to figure out how someone as disgusting as Shyla could get engaged when she knew for a fact she was a much better catch than that silly bird.

Long neck–having, goose-lipped, squawking-mouthed, chicken-legged fool.

"Well, since I wasn't here, I can't say why the woman ended up in our building, but you can only imagine," Kiara replied. "All I know is it sounded scary. People pop off over any and every thing these days. You know the state is debating if we all may carry concealed weapons on college campuses. So the tension is real, active shooters are in the headlines, and workplace violence is on the rise."

"We don't have to worry about anything like that happening here, though," said Tony. "Just about everyone who works in this department is happily married."

"True that," said Shyla. She sneered at Alexis and cackled.

"But, Tony, how would you know how happy they are?" Alexis spoke up. "You really know everything about everybody's relationship?"

Tony's face turned a deep red.

"Leave him alone," Kiara snapped.

"I'm sorry, Tony," Alexis apologized. "I'm just saying some people try to act like they're Beyoncé and Jay-Z. Outwardly that couple looks happy. But nobody knows what goes on behind closed elevators."

"Womp, womp," Tony said good-naturedly. "She's right about that one."

"Womp, womp. She's always good for ruining a fun moment," Shyla hissed in response. Alexis pretended like she didn't hear and she didn't care. But she definitely heard.

Later that evening, a couple hours after she'd gotten home from work, Alexis glanced at her watch for the twentieth time. The walls inside her house smelled like fresh pine. She toted around a bucket of hot water as she wiped kitchen counters that were already clean. When she was finished wiping, she got the broom and swept an immaculate floor. And several times she turned on the television in the living room just to turn it off every time a commercial came on that made a doorbell sound.

When she finally did hear a rapped knock on her door, Alexis took her time opening it. When she finally swung open the door, she stood and placed one hand on her hip.

Rashad beamed at her and opened his arms as he walked toward her, but she stopped him.

"I don't know what type of bitch you think I am, but you're about to find out."

"Huh?"

"You're late. Two hours late. Late Negroes get docked." She twirled around, walked back through her doorway, then slammed the door in Rashad's face.

Rashad buzzed her cell phone but she let it ring without answering. Alexis walked into the kitchen, opened the refrigerator, and grabbed a bottle of champagne and a container of orange juice. She calmly fixed herself a mimosa then fired up a cigarette.

She took her drink and went to open the patio door. She stretched out on the chaise longue, puffed on her cigarette, and waited.

She let the phone ring another ten times before she answered. "What?"

"Baby, I apologize. I'm wrong. I was late and I should have told you."

"You damn right you should have told me. I don't know what type of fool you take me for but you're messing with the wrong chick. I could be doing a whole lot more important things besides sucking your dick."

"Aww, sweetness, don't say that. I told you I'm sorry."

"Sorry won't fix this. Do you know how long I've been waiting for you?"

"Calm down, beautiful. It's gonna be all right because I'm here now."

"I needed you earlier, though."

"Why? What happened?"

"I had a rough day. I-I just thought you could help make it better." She caught herself. "But the fact that you didn't care about my feelings really has me fucked up."

"I wasn't late on purpose."

"It's not just the fact that you're late, Rashad. I really had a moment."

He paused.

"What type of moment?"

"I don't know how much longer I can take this. I sense Kiara knows something. She makes odd comments sometimes. And I'm not in this situation by myself. But when I need to talk to you about things, you aren't always available."

"I'm sorry I wasn't there for you when you needed me. What can I do to make it up to you?"

"I'll have to think about that one. And I'm not sure I can accept your apology."

"Damn, baby, why you being so hard on a brother? C'mon, let me come in. We can talk."

"We're not just gonna talk. I know you."

"We're gonna do two of my favorite things: talk and make love. How about that, baby?"

"You heard me, Rashad. I'm not in the mood to let you feel on my booty, my twat, or any other part of this good stuff."

"You playing, right?"

"The next time you see me will be Friday. You think you can remember to treat me right between now and then?"

He nursed his bruised ego with a silence that scared her. But then he said, "All right, sexy. I will see you in a few days."

Chapter 3

That Friday, Rashad rehearsed in his head what he needed to tell his wife. He arrived home from doing some subcontractor work around two o'clock, much earlier than usual. Kiara had been in the house all that day with Myles, who was battling a slight fever. She'd been busy tending to her son and doing lots of housework, plus she checked into the office via her tablet. After Kiara cooked and they enjoyed a late lunch, Rashad ran the water for her to take an afternoon bubble bath. She was standing in front of the vanity mirror tying a purple and gold headwrap around her bob.

"Thanks for the bath. You gonna be joining me?"

"Um, I meant to tell you, babe, I got some business to take care of tonight. I'll be leaving in a minute."

"It's almost four. You're working late again?"

"I gotta go when the money is calling. You know how this industry is."

"What type of job is it?"

"These old people finally paid off their mortgage and they need me to do three bathroom renovations and some other odds and ends at their house."

"Okay, well, just make sure and give me the check so I can deposit it."

"Um, all right."

"What's wrong? You don't sound right."

"It's just that I may do the deposit myself."

"Rashad! I told you I prefer to keep up with the money side of the business."

"Okay, all right. When the time comes to get the check, I will remember to hand it over to you."

"Good! You know, I miss you when you work at night. And Myles misses you, too."

"I'll make it up to the little man next Saturday. We'll go to the zoo or fly helicopters or something chill like that."

"Okay, babe. The zoo sounds fun but don't forget to actually take him because he's been asking me about it. He's fascinated by those homing pigeons."

She gave her husband a kiss on his lips. "I'm glad you do the type of work that you do. You have no idea."

"I'm glad, too. Glad I listened to my daddy and let him drag me around when I was a kid teaching me how to use my hands."

Before his father died, he left Rashad his firm, Eason & Son Contractors. He taught his son everything he knew about the business. And carrying on his dad's legacy was very important to Rashad.

"Bye, baby, love you."

Rashad went to the elderly couple's house. He did a walk-through and gave them a quote for the work they wanted him to do. But that task took no time. He soon left. He had somewhere else to be.

A half hour later, Rashad nervously stood in front of Alexis's front door. She waited a minute then opened it. She was dressed in jeans, a simple dark blue shirt, and some Chuck Taylors.

"You ready?" he asked.

She nodded. He got back in his van and started to drive off. Alexis followed behind him in her white Honda CR-Z.

They drove approximately forty minutes to an older neighborhood on the far north side of Harris County.

Alexis hopped out of her car and walked up to the door of a seventeen-hundred-square-foot one-story brick house. The home was surrounded by a white picket fence. Numerous toys were strewn around the front yard.

Soon a woman answered the door. She wore a kind smile on her face, but her eyes looked tired.

"Glad you made it out," she told Alexis. "This little monster is about to drive me crazy so you keep her as long as you want."

"Thanks, Glynis. I'll take her off your hands for a few hours."

Glynis and Alexis had the same father, but different mothers. Glynis was slightly older than Alexis and ran an in-home day care center along with Hazel, her co-operator. Alexis ventured in the main play area, which was an over-sized living room with green, yellow, and blue painted walls and tons of shelves filled with games and books. Several kids ignored her as they happily played in a corner. Then she spotted Hayley. Alexis's eighteen-month-old baby girl was wiggling in her car seat and tampering with the belt buckle. Her eyes were filled with tears but when she saw Alexis, a sweet smile lit up her entire face.

"Lessie," she said.

"Yes, your Lessie is here." Alexis reached down and nuzzled the girl's cheek with her nose. Lessie was Hayley's nickname for her mother. Glynis watched the baby throughout the week, and Alexis spent time with her daughter on the weekends. They had an informal agreement for Glynis to be Hayley's primary caretaker. No legal papers, no social workers; just Glynis's willingness to help out since she had the child care background.

"Mmm, I missed you, sweetie. Let's go get turnt up."

Glynis handed Alexis a tote bag filled with a stuffed animal, cleaning wipes, pacifiers, a sweater, and some GoGo SqueeZ pouches.

"Thanks. You know how much this means to me."

"I don't know why you tell me that all the time. It's not a problem. That's what sisters are for."

"But you're doing way more than what a sister should do."

"We're just doing what we have to do."

"I just hope Hayley understands this 'cause sometimes even I don't understand it."

Glynis hesitated, then nodded. The fact that she asked to help raise Hayley when Alexis got pregnant by an older, married man was something that had always caused a slight rift between them. Glynis couldn't have kids. Alexis dreaded the scandal her pregnancy would cause. Her half-sister stepping in seemed to be the perfect solution at the time.

Alexis told Glynis good-bye, then carried her daughter out to the curb. After Alexis carefully strapped Hayley in the backseat of her Honda, she took off down the street. Rashad followed. They ended up in a nearby park located next to a fire station.

Rashad removed his daughter from her car seat. He scooped her in his arms and gave her a dozen kisses. She laughed, screamed "Dada," and played with his cheeks. Alexis watched them and couldn't help but smile.

They walked over to the fire station and Rashad pointed out all the features of the big red trucks.

"She's getting so tall." Alexis was in awe as she stared at the child's eyes, hands, lips, and soft brown hair.

"Yes, she is. Just like her mama," Rashad said with pride.

Alexis hesitated. "I wish you'd come inside that house for once."

"I'm not exactly Glynis's favorite person."

"I know, but I don't know why we can't come up with a way to fix this situation."

"For now we're doing the right thing; we're doing the best thing."

"Best for whom? I think you're a coward. And you better be glad she's too young to know what's up. But what's going to happen when she gets older? What are you going to tell her?"

"I will cross that bridge when I get to it."

"I think that your foot is pretty much on the bridge already, Rashad."

"Look, I'm not ready for this to get out."

"You'll never be ready. So we may as well get it over with. I'm scared, too, but I want my daughter to have a bigger role in my life. And you ought to be able to have Hayley in your life the way she's supposed to be. People do it all the time."

"Alexis, please. I'm not trying to hear all that. Let's just enjoy right now, okay?"

Rashad focused on playing with Hayley and picking her up when she started whimpering. He gave her more hugs and kisses and she instantly quieted down.

"You definitely have an effect on her."

"You give Glynis some money?" he asked.

"Not yet."

"Well, you know how she is, so don't forget."

"Yeah! She acts like everything is cool, and she's been great. But sometimes I think she resents me. Like I'm one of those women who can get pregnant and she's pissed because she couldn't. I sympathize but that's not my fault."

After they finished spending time with Hayley at the park, they took her to a restaurant so she could eat chicken fingers loaded with ketchup and chewy carrot sticks, both her favorites.

They sat snugly together in a booth. They ate and played with Hayley and laughed at her antics. She loved to sing, wobble her head in a silly way, and talk incessantly about nothing. Alexis stared at her daughter, amazed by everything she did. Hayley made her brim with happiness; she wondered if Rashad was as happy as she was. Could he ever accept their daughter fully into his life or would he always try to keep it on the downlow? The few times that they got to spend together as a family felt wonderful. And she wished this scenario could be her life every day.

When they finished eating and playing, and when Rashad knew their time together was almost up, he picked up the girl and hugged her again.

"I love you. Don't you ever forget that," Rashad told Hayley, but he was looking right at Alexis when he said it. Alexis's heart skipped a beat when she met his eyes. In spite of their dilemma, she knew he was a great father. And she loved him more than she could ever admit.

When Alexis drove their daughter back to Glynis's house, the woman met them at the door before she could even knock.

"She's going to need more diapers and money for summer clothes and a couple more pairs of shoes, plus some other stuff."

"I already figured that." Alexis handed Glynis some cash that Rashad had previously given her and whispered, "Thanks." She didn't look Glynis in the eye.

"And um, I need to go back to the doctor soon for a

diabetes follow-up. That's another two hundred." Part of their agreement was for Rashad to finance Glynis's medical co-pays. That's one reason why he insisted on withdrawing cash out of his bank accounts. Cash left no trail.

Alexis paused and peeled off a few more. She really hated doing this type of thing and wanted so badly to make things better for her child.

"So how are things going? Y'all still playing house?"

"I really don't want to talk about it."

"I just want to be sure that you won't change your mind."

"I made a promise. I will stick to it. You can help nurture Hayley and I will continue to visit and provide the money you need for her care. That's how it's always been. And how it will always be."

Alexis told Glynis these things just to pacify her. But in her heart, she'd contemplated having her child full-time.

"All right. Just checking because you and your lover looked mighty comfy."

"How would you know that?"

"I followed you."

"Why? You think I'm going to kidnap my own daughter?"

"The way you live your life, there's no telling what you do."

"I wouldn't harm her. That's my daughter!"

"But I feel like she's mine! And if I want to follow you two and make sure the child is safe, that's what I will do. I love Hayley. And I don't want anything bad to happen to her."

"I don't want that, either."

"You probably don't. But sometimes I know you're way more concerned about that man than you are about that precious little baby. All she needs and deserves is love."

Every word Glynis said made Alexis's heart sag with indescribable pain.

"Please. Stop. I can't listen to your ugly words anymore."

"Alexis, you d-don't understand. Your life is not like mine." Fear made Glynis's voice shake as she talked.

"Hayley is my chance to feel like a real woman, my chance to be a mom, and I cherish it. These other kids that I care for, they're cool to be around, but their parents come and take them away from me every evening. At least this one stays the night. Anyway, my child needs me and I'm about to close this door and go tend to her. I'll be in touch."

"I know you will," said Alexis. She watched the door slam in her face and heard the little girl screaming and wailing.

Alexis slinked over to Rashad's van and stood next to it. He got out when he saw her staring at him through the window. Her face was pale and drawn.

"Come here," he told her. Rashad pulled Alexis into his arms and held her; he held on until her trembling body returned to normal.

They made it back to her house; Rashad followed Alexis upstairs. They sat on a cushy love seat in her second-floor den. He covered them with a duvet as they snuggled together underneath.

"What are you thinking about?"

"You don't want to know, Rashad."

"I don't? Oh, okay. Never mind, then."

"I don't know how much longer I can deal with this."

"Why you say that?"

"To be honest, Rashad, I feel like I'm living two lives

and not the life that I could be living. And knowing that fucks me up in the head."

"Babe, regardless, you're doing so well. You have a great job. You spend time with Hayley. She knows who you are. She loves you. I-I'm proud of you."

"I'm doing *well*? And you're *proud*? That's sounds crazy, Rashad. Is what I'm doing anything to be proud of?"

"I'm just saying I know things are tough, but they could be worse. A whole lot worse."

"Sometimes I wish—"

"Don't wish. I know this is hard on you. It's hard on me, too, but I'm trying to do the best I can. Why you think I hustle so hard? Why you think I had to lie today so we could go see her? Why you think Wednesdays and Sundays are so special? And today isn't even Sunday so that says a lot. Plus, my little man Myles has begged me to take him to fly his toy helicopter or go hang out with the animals at the zoo. Other things demand my time, too. So when I see you on the weekend, trust me, it's a big sacrifice."

"I never wanted to be a weekend wife."

"You're not a weekend wife."

"Then what am I?"

"You're mine. Even though it may not feel like it, you are mine. We're together now. Right?"

Alexis slowly nodded. In spite of how crazy her life was, and how much she wished it were different, she knew she cared for him. She loved that they had a child. And she was grateful that he spent time with Hayley.

"I'll be all right. Thanks for being here, Rashad."

Rashad's heart wanted to melt. He knew how Alexis felt about him and it touched him every time he thought about it. He gently kissed her long strands of hair.

"You may not want to hear this, but under the circumstances, I just need you to chill. Just keep doing what you doing. Hayley adores you. She feels her mother's love. I hope you know that."

Alexis gritted her teeth and rested her head on his shoulder.

That night, while Rashad was with Alexis and Hayley, Kiara made her own moves.

Once he left the house, Kiara kept prepping herself for what she was about to do. She was nervous. She poured herself a glass of wine, took a few swallows, then got up the nerve to make a quick call.

"Hello?"

"Hey now!" Kiara felt so excited yet tense. "Um, is this the homecoming queen from Elkins High School, class of '97?"

"Who is this?"

"Just someone from your past. Can you guess who it is?"

"Is this—is this Ki?"

"Oh, Adina," she screamed. "You remembered my voice. You remembered me!"

"Aw shit, I'm so shocked. What a way to start out my Friday night. Girl, wow. It's been a minute."

"It's been much too long. And um," Kiara said as she fought her emotions, "Adina, I know this is all of a sudden. And I know I should have called you before now. But you know how it goes. That's no excuse, but sometimes life kicks a sista in the butt. And when the time is right, she does what's right."

Adina grinned. Her eyes welled with tears. She'd always wondered if she'd ever hear from Kiara again.

"I-I just wanted to talk. I need to talk. Adina, I miss

you, girl. I love you. We should never have let a man keep us from being friends."

"I'm happy to hear from you, boo. I've missed you too. Um! You and Rashad? Y'all still kicking it?"

"Yes, we are!"

"Aw, fuck. I thought you'd be on a new upgrade by now."

Kiara heartily laughed. "Girl, you're a mess. And I have so much to tell you. Please don't think I'm crazy, but I was hoping if you're not busy, come on by. Like right now."

"Now?"

"Yes! Rashad is gone and we can have some privacy. Myles is here but he'll be busy in his room. So, please, Adina. I gotta release. And I really need to chop it up with you."

"I'm on my way."

Kiara ended the call. She went to freshen up. She poked around at her hair and stared at herself in the mirror a dozen times before Adina arrived. It was like she was getting ready for a first date, that's how nervous she was.

But all her anxiety left the second she laid eyes on Adina, the girl she met on the first day that they attended middle school and were seated next to each other in homeroom. The two little girls clung to each other and shared their lunchtime and recess together. They joined the volleyball and track teams together and both auditioned for the music club. Kiara had never enjoyed a better female friendship than with Adina and was ecstatic that she actually kept her word and came by.

Adina Davis stood on the porch, one hand on her hip, a bright, cheery smile on her face. One third of one side of her hair was braided and the rest was long, straight, and sleek. Her hair was always on point since she worked as a hairstylist in a popular salon. She had the biggest eyes in the world and for good reason; Kiara liked to tease her that she always noticed everything.

"Well, fuck, don't just stare at a sista; come give me a church hug or something. Shit!"

Kiara broke out laughing and pushed open the door to let her in.

"Girl, you are still crazy. And you look good. You haven't changed a bit."

After they embraced each other, Kiara invited her into the house. They sat in the living room. Kiara handed her guest a glass of red wine, Adina's favorite way to chill.

"Okay, boo!" Adina said, sipping on her drink. "What's popping?"

"First of all, let me apologize for not doing this sooner. I-I listened to Rashad and you know he felt that as a married woman, I shouldn't be spending so much time with a single woman."

"I was married too, in the process of a divorce. Damn. He's a trip. To not even let best friends be there for each other. What? He's scared you'd catch the divorce virus?"

"I guess. So let me get all that out the way."

"Water under the bridge. We're good. Go on."

Kiara gave Adina the edited version of what had happened in her life the past two years.

"Overall, believe it or not, I think Rashad is a decent husband. He's not afraid to get his hands dirty, and I can count on him to take care of us, but I dunno, Adina. Occasionally, I get these *feelings*. He can't always explain his whereabouts. I can tell when he's lying and he has no good reason to. And sometimes he starts an argument, leaves the house for hours, and when he gets back, of course, I'm sleepy as hell and in a bad mood. It just doesn't sit well with me."

"You think he's cheating!"

"I can't believe he is, but I guess it's possible. But why would a man that has an excellent wife step out on her and fuck around with other bitches? I can't prove it or anything, but if that explains his odd behavior, I'd be floored. I deserve better. I will have better."

"Ki, I'm not surprised by anything you're telling me. Sure, your man is a cutie and all that, but I always felt there was just something about Rashad. If it walks like a rat, what else could it be but a rat?"

"Why didn't you warn me?"

"Girl, please. Remember those times when I tried? You were not trying to hear a sista. You would've accused me of hating on your relationship like you claimed your other friends did. Humph," Adina said and rolled her eyes. "Plus, your man actually pulled me to the side one time when y'all first got real serious. He told me not to poison you against him because he was going to marry you whether I liked it or not."

"He did that?" Kiara asked.

"Rashad wanted your fine ass. You wanted him. Y'all were determined to be the next Nelly and Ashanti. I was a non-muthafucking factor."

"Um, well damn." Kiara nodded. "People always do stuff behind your back that you hear about later on. And again, I let him influence me in us not speaking anymore. He was my husband. But times have changed and I need some clarity on some things from your point of view."

"You got it. What's up?"

"I feel kinda shitty for what I'm about to say, but I do recall that you started to tell me something about him a couple years ago, but at the time—"

"Bitch, you practically cursed me out, called me all kinds of names."

"I know. I was tripping."

"It's cool. I understand."

"Tell me what you were going to tell me."

"Is this a setup?" Adina laughed and looked suspiciously around the room.

"It's not a setup. It's a step forward. So tell me."

"Like I tried to warn you, a few years ago, I saw Rashad pushing up on some broad. A tall chick. Cute girl."

"Hmm. What were they doing?"

"You sure you want to hear this? Because if I give you this info, Kiara, I do not want you hating me for revealing this shit."

"Tell me!"

"They were standing real close to each other and they kissed; slobbered each other down, girl, in broad daylight. I was shocked as hell. I wanted to roll up on him and ask him what the fuck was his problem. But I was caught in traffic as I was driving past. They were in the parking lot of a shopping center complex. And by the time I was able to turn up in that lot and get an even better look, I didn't see them anymore."

"Okay," Kiara said in a quiet tone but inside she was fuming. "That's all I wanted to know. If he did that back then in broad daylight, imagine what he could be doing when he's somewhere in a hotel room or wherever."

Adina paused. "But Kiara, I'm concerned too about why Rashad would do that when he has you. I mean, you're cute as hell but that never stopped a man from straying. So what's going on in the bedroom?"

"The sex is cool, but it was better, more passionate, and more frequent when we were dating . . . and the years before we had the baby. Now it takes a lot of effort to maintain the passion between the sheets. I accuse him of taking me for granted, but I might be guilty of the same thing. Our life has gotten way too comfortable."

"What you plan on doing?"

"I got a thing or two up my sleeve. And to be honest, you may hate Rashad, but I love him. I want to be married. I just need my husband to work with me, but if he doesn't, I gotta keep it moving."

Adina's feisty spirit grew quiet. She stood up and had a blank look on her face. "Girl, just be really careful about whatever you decide to do. You know I've been divorced for five years. And back then I couldn't wait to get away from Marlon. But truthfully, I miss him. It's hard out here. The dating scene is nothing like it used to be. We'll be forty in a few years. And it is scary as fuck to be divorced with a child, competing with all these other chicks, and you gotta deal with a body that isn't as fit as it was when you were in your twenties."

Kiara nodded and fear combined with anger rose within her. It seemed unfair that a married woman had to settle for garbage if she was unhappy in her relationship. But still, something had to give. She had to be happy for herself regardless of how her husband was acting.

"I will try to make good decisions, but I won't let Rashad hold me hostage in an unfulfilling relationship while there's a good chance he's running around with every Boo Boo Kitty in Houston. I'll figure out something."

"These men are something else, girl. And this is off topic, but one thing I've always thought you should do is stay on good terms with that man at your job. Eddison Osborne."

"That's way off topic," Kiara replied. "Why him?"

"I remember when you'd talk about him after I got divorced and he was recently widowed. And when you introduced us when I was up at the university, he seemed decent. Not so nice that a chick can run over him, but a man's man. Like he had his shit together. So you thought us two could hook up, but your friend Eddison wasn't interested."

"I wonder why not."

"Hello, because his fine ass was into you! I still thought he was cool. And I got some good vibes from him as a man who'd do right by a woman. I could be wrong—"

"No, you aren't wrong. Eddison is my boy," Kiara said with a smile. "A lot of ladies get in his face on that campus—because I've seen them do it and he is so cool about it all. But I consider him a friend—a great buddy."

"Some of the best relationships happen when men and women are tight like that, as friends, no ulterior motive." She sighed and shrugged. "I know you're still with knucklehead but you never forget a good guy. Hopefully the man is still feeling you."

"I wouldn't know, Adina."

"It's 'bout time you found out, though."

Kiara could only laugh. "Damn, have I told you how much I've missed your crazy ass? Now, I need you to go somewhere with me. You're going to love this."

She went and got Myles from his bedroom. And they piled in her car and sped along to Highway 6, right down the street from her subdivision.

Kiara then drove to her credit union's ATM and asked Adina to get out of the car.

"Check this out, Adina." She punched in her PIN for her bank account and waited for the receipt to print.

"See this? I just had to show you." Kiara gave Adina the receipt, which listed her total balance.

"Wow! That's a helluva lot of change."

"And it's about to get bigger," Kiara told her. "I always put a little money in the account every month. Because if I ever have to pull a Shaunie O'Neal, then I'm prepared to do so."

Shaq's former wife was said to be a pro at setting money aside while they were married.

"You rolling in scrilla. I ain't mat at ya." Adina laughed; the two women high-fived each other.

"A woman's gotta do what a woman's gotta do," Kiara said. "I love that man, and I want to remain married to him, but I can't let him make a fool of me *and* let him take away my happiness. Unless Rashad makes a change, then he's about to *see* some changes."

Chapter 4

It was May 12, the beginning of a new workweek. Kiara sat at her desk and tried to rub the sleepiness from her eyes. Tony Fu entered her office without knocking. He was holding his cell phone. His earbuds were plugged in his ears. He was bobbing his head and singing to himself.

"Tony!"

He started doing the Schmoney dance.

"I swear to God you are black."

"What you say?" He finally unplugged the earbuds and lowered the volume.

"I said you've got good taste in music and that's a fact."

"Sure, you did. Now, what do you need?"

"Oh, Tony, I've been having trouble with SharePoint all afternoon. Can you help me out while I sit at my little table over there and review some paperwork?"

"No problem. Anything for you, Mrs. Eason."

She grinned. "It's been a long time since anyone called me that."

"We haven't seen your hubby in a minute. When is he coming back up here?"

"Oh, shoot. I don't know. He's been very busy. Like

super busy. Like 'who are you' and 'what's your name again' busy."

"Uh oh."

"No, nothing like that. It's just that we both hustle our asses off. Like every Sunday, Rashad leaves in the dark and comes home in the dark. And I don't totally complain because, you know, a lot of times, after I'm done with doing laundry, doing a little gardening, and cleaning the house, both Myles and I are up here. My little boy runs up and down the hallways getting into stuff while I'm here at my desk slaving away. And I feel guilty because little Myles needs me. He needs both of us. And my husband works so hard, I feel he needs me too."

"What does he do to show you that he needs you?"

"What do you mean?"

She moved out of Tony's way so he could get to her computer.

"I was just wondering. Guys act pretty helpless when they want something."

"Well, if my man needed anything, I hope he'd tell me."

"So it sounds like he hasn't asked you for anything lately."

"Tony, don't play with me. What are you trying to say?"

"I'm not saying anything. I'm trying to fix your problem."

"My problem?"

"Your SharePoint problem."

"All right, Tony, I know you aren't thinking about SharePoint. I trust your judgment, so if there's something I ought to know, spill it."

A loud rapping noise interrupted them. Tony looked up. A man in a brown hat, brown shirt, and matching shorts stood at the door.

"Sorry. My schedule got way off today. No one else is around. Here's a delivery for Kiara Eason."

"I'll sign for it." Tony jumped up and scribbled his signature on the electronic device that the delivery man thrust at him.

"Thanks. Cool," Tony said. He set the massive bouquet of flowers on Kiara's round office table. The mixed arrangement sat in a tall vase and was made up of all Kiara's favorites: roses, daisies, mums, and spray roses in full bloom. The fragrance filled Kiara's nostrils as she pressed her nose against the exotic flowers and inhaled.

"These flowers are beautiful. That man is amazing."

"You gonna read the card?"

"What for? Rashad knows what I like."

"I just thought you'd want to know what he said. Maybe he's been a bad boy."

"Nah, he's just trying to be a better husband. I've been hounding him lately. That's what this is about." Kiara kicked off her heels. She leaped up and down and grabbed Tony by the hand. They did a little dance and Kiara couldn't stop laughing.

"Oh, he gone get some tonight."

"Hush, Tony. I just get very happy when Rashad listens to me. I told him that's what he needs to do. And these flowers prove all my hard work pays off—eventually."

"If you're *hạnh phúc, I'm hạnh phúc.*"

"Yes, Tony. I am happy." It was an expression Tony used all the time around the office and Kiara knew exactly what he meant.

That night when Kiara got home, she was in a good mood. Rashad may have slipped up in the past, but as long as he was doing everything he could to keep Kiara happy these days, she'd look past his minor indiscretions. So she made last-minute arrangements to drop Myles off at Mama Flora's, who said she welcomed the company.

She rushed home and got ready for her husband.

And when Rashad trudged into the house after parking his van in the driveway, she met him at the door.

Kiara grinned and stretched out her bare leg so it was the first thing he saw when he got near the front door.

"What's this?" He stared her up and down and smiled his approval. Rashad loved when Kiara wore sexy lingerie. She was dressed in all white. He could see her cleavage. Her feet were bare. Her bob looked messy and unkempt just the way he liked it.

"It's me. And I'm all yours, babe." She handed him a glass of red wine, then pointed to a tray of ice-cold beer.

"This is dope. What's up with all this?"

"I want to be as good to you as you are to me."

"What's that supposed to mean?"

"C'mon, babe. Stay with me. Please don't kill my vibe."

"You're cray cray, woman."

"That's not helping either, Rashad."

He lugged a heavy toolbox into the house and lowered it onto the floor in the hallway.

"Did I get any mail?"

"Babe, forget about work. Forget about mail. Forget about hammers and pliers and paint. Tonight is all about us."

"Where's little man?"

"That's what I'm telling you. I found a sitter. It's just me and you for the next twenty-four."

"Whoa, you're pulling out all the stops."

She beamed at him as she grabbed his hand and led

him into the media room. The entire room was lit up by fragrant candles. The aroma of roses and vanilla permeated the air.

Bump and grind music played in the background. The water from the aquarium bubbled. Everything felt homey and very sexy. If Kiara was honest, she knew that she hadn't been the most flirtatious with her husband as much as she claimed. She actually thought that if she sexually served it up to him, then whatever she did should last for weeks. But in reality, she knew that a strong marriage needed much more frequent romanticism.

Kiara threw herself into her husband's arms.

"I've missed you, and I've been thinking about the man that I first met when we fell in love. Just hold me."

He hugged her too and was impressed. Kiara could be hot and sensuous, and everything she was doing turned him on. He knew she'd cooked a great meal too because he could smell the aroma drifting through the house.

"You're amazing. So dope. You really know how to take care of a man." He picked her up and carried her like they were walking over a threshold for the first time after getting married.

He gently laid her on the sofa and after she scooted so that her head rested on the big throw pillows, he knelt beside her and gazed into her big brown eyes. She grinned with happiness and sighed.

"You do love me, huh?" he asked.

"You know that already."

"S-sometimes I don't feel the love."

"I know and I'm sorry about that. I stay on your ass because I do love you, in spite of everything."

"You're too good to me," he muttered.

"And you're good to me." She was thinking about her

flowers, which were wonderful. But she wanted more than just flowers.

"Hell, I'm not as good as I ought to be. I'm not perfect, but I'm trying."

"That's what's important. If we both keep trying, we're going to make it. I believe that."

Her voice caught in her throat and she started sniffling.

"Aw, damn. Here it comes." He grinned and kissed the tip of her nose.

"Can't help it. I may bitch from time to time but when I think about my life, I know I'm mostly blessed. I have a beautiful, bright son who is my world. I feel I don't even deserve him half the time. And I saw a little baby today after work when I went to pick up groceries, and it made me think."

"Think about what?" He sprung back.

"Rashad, I know we haven't talked about having another baby in years."

"Kiara, you know I got a lot going on already. It's not a good time."

"I know, but when is having a child ever a good time? Sometimes these things are not in our hands."

"If we keep a condom in our hands and always roll it on this dick, it is in our hands."

"You're so silly. But, well, if you don't think we're ready this year . . . to try again, I guess I will accept it."

"Look at you. I thought you were so busy trying to be Ms. Super Executive at the j-o-b."

"I am and I'm doing great. I guess I feel I'm at the point where if I took a short leave of absence to have a baby, it wouldn't hurt. But sometimes after a woman has a kid, she ends up quitting her job. Or the job forces her out because they think her priorities have shifted."

Kiara knew her proposal stunned Rashad. But he was a good father, and perhaps having another child would strengthen the weak parts of their marriage. But if it didn't work out, she couldn't totally lose. They made great babies, plus she knew she'd be guaranteed hefty child support for at least eighteen years.

"Whoa whoa whoa. All this talk about babies." Rashad looked like he had morning sickness and was about to vomit.

"Look, silly, I definitely don't have any of those scenarios in mind. I was just thinking of Myles. I've never wanted him to be an only child."

"Hmmm," was all Rashad could say.

Kiara reached up and pulled Rashad closer. He responded to her aggressiveness and gave her a long, sincere kiss.

"If that's what you want, we gotta talk about it and make that decision together, all right?" he asked.

"That's fine."

Kiara closed her eyes as Rashad kissed her. She thought that if he did everything she wanted, then the money she'd been saving up could be used for Myles. But if Rashad resorted to his old ways and messed over her, the cash could serve as her rainy-day divorce fund. In her head, it would be a retainer fee for a good-ass lawyer who could help her get everything she deserved for any marital hell she endured.

Kiara came up for air. "I just want my life with you to be good, Rashad. I mean it. That's all I've ever wanted."

"I want that, too."

She led him to the bathroom.

"Damn, you already got the bubble bath ready?"

She smiled and went over to stick her tongue deep in his mouth. Rashad loved to kiss.

He started to get aroused.

He unbuckled his belt and let her pull down his pants. He grabbed her boobs and held them like two coconuts. Then he bent over and began to suck her nipples. She tilted back her head and moaned. When he was done, she kissed him on his neck and sucked his earlobes. By the time he penetrated her, Rashad forgot all the baby talk. He was into his wife. He laid her on the floor.

"Hold on a sec," she said.

Kiara got up and ran to get a condom first and rolled it on him. Then she inserted his dick inside her. It had been a minute since they made love. This reconnect felt so good. Kiara hoped the intimate moment would remind Rashad of the blessing he had at home.

After a decent evening, Kiara returned to work the next day and politely greeted everyone on her way to her office.

When she sat down at her desk and powered up the computer, she barely had time to check emails before her extension rang. The ID said it was Eddison Osborne.

She picked up and placed the call on speaker. "Hey, my friend. How was your evening?"

"Probably not as good as yours."

"My night was wonderful. But how did you know?"

"So did you like the surprise?"

"What surprise?"

"The delivery you got yesterday."

"Um, yeah, but how did you know?"

"I checked the delivery status online . . . Oh wow. Awkward."

Kiara bolted from her chair and ran over to her small conference table. The card that she neglected to read when her bouquet arrived was still there.

She grabbed the note card. It read:

Thanks for a job well done. You are magnificent. E.O.

"Oh, no."

"What was that?"

"Eddison. I am so embarrassed. You did that."

"Mm hmmm."

"You did that." She couldn't help but laugh.

Then she giggled hysterically.

"Is everything okay, Kiara?"

"I wish you could see me right now."

"I wish I could, too."

"No, seriously, Eddison. You are a sweetheart. That's number one. And yes, I got the beautiful, wonderful flowers. That was so thoughtful of you."

"You deserved them. I appreciate how you came through for the kids recently when you presented at the Career Day Event."

"Oh, yeah, yeah, yeah. Well, it was nothing."

Career Day was last Thursday. Kiara was so accustomed to finishing her projects and moving on to the next thing, she had forgotten all about it.

Kiara slowly walked back over to her desk and plopped down on her seat. *I gave all that loving to one man, when it was really another man that made me feel special. And he called me "magnificent." Rashad has never called me that.*

"You still there?"

"Uh, yes, sorry. There's so much going on. In fact, let's meet up. How are you for lunch today?"

"I had something but it can be rescheduled. Anything for you, boss lady."

"I'm not your boss."

"Not yet!"

She gasped and lifted up the handset and spoke into the phone. "Eddison, what are you saying?"

"I'm just being respectful. You're a hard worker and you deserve the kudos. I'd love for you to be my boss."

Eddison's words made Kiara's heart completely fill with warmth. She always enjoyed speaking with her work colleague. He was an academic advisor within their division and sometimes acted as a mentor. When Kiara really thought about it, she appreciated how he was positive and encouraging no matter what. He reminded her of . . . herself.

Not to mention Eddison was also hot. He had the most beautiful redbone complexion—it reminded her of a café latte. He wore a neat mustache and beard, had the perfect size lips, and his hair—Eddison's brown hair was twisted in short dreadlocks. He was like the hip professor on campus that every staff person wanted to know and every female student fantasized about.

"I'll bet you're dressed very nice today."

"Oh, this old thing. I just reach in my closet and grab whatever is available."

"I don't believe that for a second. As a matter of fact, I know you're the type of woman who cares about her appearance, about all the details. That's you."

She swallowed deeply. She tried to think of Rashad. What was he doing right then? Was he thinking of her? Or was he knee-deep in work and she was the furthest thing from his mind?

"Eddison, I gotta go. And I will see you today. Say twelvish?"

"Not a minute too late."

Kiara and Eddison met at a popular Vietnamese restaurant. They were shown to a booth by the window. The sun's brilliance poured into the room and made the atmosphere feel happy.

Eddison pulled out Kiara's seat. She gave him a pleased

look and sat down. He was dressed in a nice gray suit with a polka dot tie. His black leather shoes were polished to perfection.

Eddison tried not to stare at Kiara while he reviewed his menu. He thought she looked pretty as usual, but this time there was something in her eyes that made him want to comfort her.

"First things first, Eddison. Thank you for the flowers. Again, you didn't have to do that."

"Did you like them?"

"They were pretty. They made me feel really good, too. You know just what I like."

They locked eyes.

An incredibly warm feeling flowed through her. His innocent flirts were something she always ignored. But right then, Kiara thought that maybe Adina was on to something. It wouldn't hurt to keep Eddison around.

"How're things going? Did you need anything?"

"Oh, no, we're good right now. But I did want to mention that I made an offer to Nicole Greene. Remember her from all the candidates we brought in for that job interview? I'm so glad you sat on the interviewing board for our department. Anyway, she will be starting this week."

"Right . . . I'm glad to hear that you filled your position."

"It's a shame that we can't pay a media coordinator more than sixteen dollars an hour. And it's sad because she's new to town and is starting over by herself with no family."

"And you know this how?"

"I got a chance to talk on a more personal level with her. She seems a bit introverted but it's okay. Nicole's very qualified. And the rest of the loud-talking staff will make up for her shyness."

"You've figured it all out, haven't you? You're so good at that."

"Ha! I wish my home life were as easy to manage as my work life."

"What's going on? How is Rashad? The man whom I always hear about but have never met in person."

"Eddison, I feel a little awkward telling you this, but hey, I definitely know your background. I can't believe you're still single years after your wife died."

"Why is that so hard to believe?"

"Well, look at you. You're—" She stopped herself as their waiter approached the table.

Service in the restaurant was a little behind since there was a huge lunch crowd. Kiara started to place her order. She could feel Eddison's intense stare, but she pretended not to notice. As soon as their waiter left, he probed. "You were saying? You said I'm so something, but then you stopped."

"Oh, Eddison, there're so many things I just don't understand."

Kiara could feel it coming. She looked him in the eyes and her voice grew quieter. "I lied to you. Kind of. Okay, I thought my husband sent me the flowers that you actually got for me. So I went home and I put it on him. I practically seduced him and it was cool, you know. It's been a minute and I know this is TMI, but, hey, it is what it is. Right now I need a male perspective."

He stared at her with concern in his eyes. "Go on, dear."

"I just don't understand what I'm doing wrong. Even though we had a great evening, I noticed that before I left the house this morning, he was acting a little cold and indifferent. When I tried to get him to open up, he shut me down. But then he warmed up a little later and it seemed like things were normal. But this hot-and-cold stuff . . . I try to pretend like whatever his problem is has nothing to do with me, but now I'm starting to wonder."

"It's normal to wonder. How do you feel about what he's doing? What do you want?"

"I want him to know I feel disrespected."

"Have you told him that?"

"He should know."

"No, he won't know. A man isn't a mind reader. Tell Rashad how you feel."

"I will. I have to. But I'd hate to think that I am driving my husband to not want to be around me for any reason. I'll try to make things right until I get sick of trying, if that makes sense."

All she wanted was to be comforted and understood.

Eddison discreetly placed his hand on top of hers. "Kiara. It's not you. You are the type who puts everything she has into a project to ensure its success. You are doing your very best and probably aren't getting the results you think you should. Am I right?"

"Yes. I have been like this since I was a kid. It's all I've ever known."

"Kiara, take it from me. Ambition is a good thing, but it can be a terrible master."

"What does that mean?"

"The things that we desperately want and are committed to getting sometimes take us down roads we shouldn't travel. We are driven to the point of getting ourselves in a jam."

"And I can't stand trouble. So what should I do?"

Eddison told her, "You can either have patience, keep doing what you're doing, and hope that eventually things will work out."

"Or?"

"Or you may have to figure out a different plan. If Plan A isn't working, go to Plan B."

"Dammit." Kiara was torn. "I'm actually already there. I hate when I'm right."

"I don't know everything that's going on with your relationship, but when I sit across from you, I see a young, beautiful, smart, sexy woman." He whispered the word "sexy" and the chills she felt caused her to tremble like she was cold. But Kiara was far from cold. Eddison's ability to notice her, to see her, and make her feel alive and valued, stirred something she hadn't felt in months.

"Me? Sexy?"

"You. Very very sexy. I don't know why you can't see it."

Eddison and Kiara's relationship was always sincere and friendly. She'd known his wife, Nina Osborne, who had been a strong woman who loved her husband. After Nina passed away, Kiara offered her support but he told her he wanted to grieve in private. But now it seemed like he was returning to himself. He became more open and transparent with her. He seemed happier, engaged, and trying to cherish each day. She felt he deserved all the happiness that life could offer him.

"Eddison, you're just being nice, and I appreciate your confidence in me, but—"

"But what? You don't agree with me?"

"It's not me that I'm concerned about."

"I see something that maybe he doesn't see. And if he can't see, then he's a fool."

"Eddison, I don't like how this conversation is going and—"

"You may not like it, but all of us have to come to the point in which we must face the truth. I had to face it when the military told me that Nina died. I did not believe it. I kept texting her. And she didn't text back. I never spoke to my wife again. I had to snap out of it. In truth, I just recently boxed up her clothes, her shoe col-

lection, her cosmetics that had been stored in an upstairs room. Took it all to the Salvation Army. I had to
let go of that life. Kiara, I hope you're hearing me. Let
me say it again. As hard as we may try . . . sometimes
we must face the truth."

Kiara heard him. And she felt scared. Right then,
things felt way too personal. But she blamed herself for
opening up. Eddison's implications were too much for
her to think about in that setting. She felt relieved when
her plate of hot food arrived. She quickly changed the
subject and was able to lighten the conversation.

Eddison continued eating and loved it when he could
make Kiara forget her troubles, loosen up and laugh.

"Hold on a sec, Eddison. I'm going to call Rashad."

"All right."

She retrieved her cell and dialed his number.

The call went straight into voice mail.

"Told ya. No answer."

"How you feel?"

"I'm over it. My happiness will not be based on
whether or not anyone answers their damned cell
phone. That's crazy."

"That's more like it," Eddison told her.

She picked up her fork and ate some shrimp and
chicken.

"Now this," she said, and laughed, "is living."

"That smile, though," he said, and stared at her plump
lips.

"Eddison, how does *your* food taste?"

"It's good. And yours?"

"It's great. I love it. And I love yours, too." She winked
as she scooped up some of the vegetables off his plate and
laughed as she ate them.

He picked up one of his egg rolls and held it high.
"Kiara, one day you're going to do something totally

different. Like dip my egg roll in your sweet and sour sauce . . . and lick it."

They both laughed.

Kiara figured Eddison was being flirty and she took it with a grain of salt. As they finished their meal, she decided no matter how peculiar her husband was behaving, she wanted to give their relationship her all.

Eddison could just be her handsome, minor distraction.

That night Kiara prepared dinner and helped Myles with his homework as she waited for Rashad to come home. But after waiting for an hour, she called Myles to the kitchen.

"It's about time. I'm starving. I'm so hungry I could eat a horse. And a pig. And a whale," Myles said.

"Sorry to disappoint you, but none of those animals are on the menu, son. Tonight we are eating spaghetti and meatballs, garlic bread, and corn on the cob."

"Is that all?"

"I did my best. I just want you to eat it and like it. Eating will make you big and strong."

"Strong like Daddy?"

"Yes, if you eat all your food, you'll be big and tall just like him."

"Where is Daddy?"

"Working."

"When will he be back from work? Will he wake me up and play in my room like he did last time? I want Daddy to help me put together my toy copter."

"I know, sweetie. I know." Kiara recalled how Rashad swore up and down he'd help Myles assemble the radio-controlled helicopter that he obsessed over ever since they bought it for him last month. Rashad promised they'd go out to the neighborhood park and fly it all day.

But weeks had passed with Rashad offering every excuse imaginable.

"Men work, Myles. And your daddy is a man."

"He's a good man."

"A good man . . . is an accessible man."

When Rashad finally stepped into the house around nine-thirty, Kiara met him at the door.

"Hey," she said in a crisp tone.

"Hi." He looked past her and saw his brown polyester upright luggage bag. It was opened and set on the floor. Kiara had purchased the complete set for him years ago. "Why is my favorite suitcase sitting in the middle of the hallway? Are you going somewhere?"

"I'm not, but you might be."

"Kiara, what's wrong now?"

"I've wanted to talk to you about something, but you're always gone. Or you don't have time. Or you're sleepy. You're sick. Always something."

"We were just together yesterday."

"That was then, this is now. How about tonight, Rashad?"

"I'm only one person. And after I get myself situated in a minute, I'd like to go play with my son."

"Do you know what time it is?"

"Myles won't care. Trust me. I'm going to be a good daddy no matter how much time I spend in the streets."

"I just want to know if you're doing anything else besides working."

He sighed and moved past her toward the kitchen. "Kiara, aren't you the one who said you don't mind me working like a slave?"

"That's true, Rashad, but you are doing more than slave work."

"Huh?"

"Hand over your cell phone. I need to make a phone call."

"Woman, you must be tripping. You got your own phone and then there's the house phone, too."

"Why can't I use your phone? Where is it?" She started toward him.

He began to back away. "You do not want to do that."

"You're right. I don't. I just want you to answer this. Are you fucking another chick?"

"Really, Kiara."

"I ain't joking. Answer me."

"You're so loud you're going to scare Myles."

Kiara stared at Rashad. He looked like he was ready for battle. She leaped at his pants but fell to the floor instead.

"You need to stop. This ain't a good look. You know my work ethic. You ought to trust me."

"Where's that going to get me?"

He reached down and pulled her up. He removed his cell phone from his back pocket. He handed her the phone.

"Who do you want to call?"

She paused but refused to take his phone. "One day you're going to find out."

He put his phone back in his pocket. "Kiara, just know that I-I don't want to hurt you. I want our family to be okay and I need you to be the good wife that you always are. You are dope, Kiara. And I-I'm sorry for neglecting you sometimes. But no, I don't have another woman."

Then he walked away from her.

"I didn't ask you if you had somebody, I asked you if you're *fucking* somebody," she yelled at him.

He ignored her and kept going till he reached their master bathroom. The walls and flooring boasted decorative diagonal beige tiling. His and hers vanity sinks were topped with granite. The room was dark but he saw that their Roman tub was filled with popping bubbles.

"Damn. Kiara still thinks about me even when I act like an ass."

Rashad quickly got undressed. He noticed the glass of red wine and the flickering candles on the side of the tub, which made him feel worse.

"I owe this woman."

Soon Kiara stood in the doorway watching him.

"Um, Rashad—"

"You gonna join me, babe?" he asked. He had already stepped into the tub, sat down, and was leaning back and relaxing.

"Nope. Looks like tonight this bath is just for you."

"I don't deserve you."

"I know. We don't always get what we deserve, boo." She smiled at him, folded her arms across her chest, and flicked on the overhead lights.

As soon as Rashad picked up his favorite white bar of soap, he knew something was wrong.

"Why does this soap look blue?"

She shrugged.

Rashad grabbed a wash rag and began wiping his body. He closed his eyes and moaned. The hot water felt good. Kiara burst out laughing. Rashad opened his eyes and looked down. Large dark blue streaks were all over his chest and arms.

"What the fuck?"

"I meant to tell you, sweetie, I accidentally put blue dye in the water instead of that aqua blue bubble bath. I kind of got it mixed up with Myles's Mr. Bubble container. Sorry! But I did find the real bubble bath and squirted as much of it in the tub as I could."

"How could you do this? Is this your way of paying me back? 'Cause it's not working."

"Then I guess I will keep trying until I find something that works."

The next night, Rashad came home promptly at six. A car that he didn't recognize sat in his driveway.

When he reached the living room, it was empty. So was the kitchen. Then he heard two voices. They were coming from his bedroom. He heard Kiara say, "Girl, he was the very definition of a man having blue balls."

Rashad heard shrieks of laughter. He headed for his bedroom and burst through the door.

The room smelled of Pine-Sol.

Kiara was leaning over the bathtub holding a soapy sponge in her hand.

Adina Davis looked up and smiled. She held a sponge, too.

"Well, if it ain't Rashad Fucking Eason. Long time no see."

"Kiara, what is she doing here?"

"She's helping me get back on your good side." Kiara began vigorously cleaning the blue blemishes from the tub.

"Did you put her up to this, Adina? Because that shit wasn't funny."

"Oh, wow, you blame me . . . and I've only been in your presence for less than two minutes. Rashad, you need to give your wife a little bit more credit. She can make decisions on her own."

"Shhh, Adina. Just help me please, girl."

"Y'all two crazy chicks won't be able to clean out that dye. I'll have to replace the entire tub. I hope you had a good time trying to get me back." He gave Kiara an angry look and walked out of the room.

A week later, in the middle of the workweek, Kiara was driving down a feeder road on her way back to the campus. She and Eddison had attended a Board of Regents meeting at one of the satellite campuses. He was tailing her in his dark titanium Chrysler 3000. He picked up his cell phone and voice-dialed Kiara.

"Yes."

"Hey, I want to talk to you about something important. Can you pull over in the next big parking lot? See that little park up ahead? It won't take a minute."

Kiara said okay and drove until she could make a right turn into a driveway of a moderate-size city park. She made the car come to a stop. Eddison parked next to her. He waved at her to come and sit in his passenger seat. She slid in the seat next to him and asked, "Hey, what's up?"

"I noticed you at the meeting."

"And?"

"You looked distracted, Kiara. I was a bit concerned. Is everything okay?"

"Everything is great, Eddison. Just . . . just great."

"Can you truthfully look me in the eye and tell me that you're happy?"

"Eddison." She placed her hand on the door handle.

"No, hear me out. Maybe I'm overstepping boundaries but, Kiara, I think you know . . . you know how I feel about you. I respect you and I'd never want to hurt you. But when I see you like this."

"Like what?"

"Like you're faking it and taking it. And you really don't have to take it."

She waited.

"Like, if you ever get to that point where you want something better, consider me."

Eddison grabbed her hand. He squeezed it.

"Every marriage doesn't work out. Not to say that yours won't, but if you've given it all you got, and you still aren't satisfied, weigh your options."

"Are you telling me you're a good option?"

"I'm telling you that I'm here for you. I'm not trying to break up your relationship, but I won't sit back and watch your spirit sink to nothing, either. You have way too much going for you."

Kiara told Eddison about the most recent events. About how she tried to get Rashad to open up to her but it backfired; and how she tried to get his attention with the blue balls joke and how her actions hadn't necessarily made things better between them since then.

"No woman can permanently change a man's ways. Basically, most men will do what they feel they want to do."

"I now realize that."

"Kiara, I'm just going to put it out there. Keep me in mind." He squeezed her hand then let go. "Think of me when you're feeling down."

Kiara could only smile and acknowledge the happiness he wanted to offer to her. "If I were to leave him, you'd be my option, Eddison. As crazy as it sounds, I've already thought about it."

"You have?" He looked pleasantly surprised.

"See, that's what I like about you. You do not take anything for granted."

Eddison lifted her chin and gently pulled her face near his mouth. When their lips meshed together, the warmth of his touch made Kiara instantly feel like she was being swallowed up by a warm, soothing blanket. He gently and lovingly pressed his lips against hers. Kiara didn't think about it. She automatically opened her mouth and let Eddison in. He extended his tongue and kept reaching till his touched hers. She widened her mouth and let even more of him in. Kiara wanted Eddison's kiss. Their tongues bathed each other's in urgent fashion. She felt like his tongue was making tender love to her entire body. She'd never been kissed that way before. The more she kissed him, the more her vagina got wet. And hot. And she felt she needed to stop. To slow things down. But she couldn't. Eddison felt too good and he smelled even better. She loved his scent and it turned her on so much that she let go of all logic.

Kiara noticed the second her hand wrapped itself around Eddison's neck as if it were a snake. She shut out warning thoughts and pulled him closer to her. She longed to feel him, to be as close to him as humanly possible. Little by little, she noticed her nipples grow rock hard. She wondered how it would feel if his hands rubbed her breasts. She couldn't believe she was sitting in a man's car in broad daylight with her tongue deep inside his mouth as if she didn't have a husband back home. That man may have been at home but what was he doing when he wasn't at home? That's what had been worrying Kiara lately. Her gut vexed her daily. She didn't know if she was losing this fight. All she knew was her marriage was in trouble.

When they finally let each other go, Kiara had tears in her eyes.

"Don't cry. I'd never want to hurt you, my love."

"Then what do you want?"

"I'd like an honest chance. If fate allows it, I want to be your man."

Kiara didn't say a word. She just opened his car door and let herself out. She drove back to work wondering how on earth she got into this position. And how on earth would she get herself out of it.

Chapter 5

"Hi, Mrs. Eason."

Kiara had been deeply immersed in her work. She looked up from her desk. Nicole Greene, the new hire for the media coordinator position, stood in the doorway clutching her tote bag close to her chest like it was a pillow.

"Good morning, Nicole. You're early."

"Traffic was light."

"No problem. I will show you around and introduce you to the staff."

It was twenty minutes before eight. And it was another Hump Day in the last week of May. Kiara had been so preoccupied reviewing the budget she'd forgotten that her new employee would check in today.

Nicole's purple optical frames slipped partially down her nose. Her shoulder-length hair was neatly tied in a ponytail and she wore a plain white blouse, brown pleated slacks, and a comfortable pair of flats.

"We'll go to your office. But first let's say hello to Alexis McNeil. Hey, Alexis. You remember Nicole, don't you?"

"Hi. How's it going?"

"As you know, this is Nicole Greene's first day. We want to make her feel welcome."

"Glad to have you. We have a really cool department with a lot of colorful characters." Alexis smiled. "I'm sure I'll see you again today. Sorry, but I have a deadline. You know how it is." Alexis said good-bye and resumed typing.

Kiara gave her attention back to Nicole. "We will fill out the key request forms and another one for a tablet. And you'll be going to new employee orientation later this morning."

They continued down the hall. "I trust everything went well with your relocation. I know you were in a temporary housing situation when you first moved from Alabama. But how are things now that you've gotten a permanent place?"

"Oh, that. It's going." Her eyes darted around nervously.

"Explain."

"It's just a fixer-upper that I found real quick. Rent isn't too bad compared to what I'd pay for a two-bedroom apartment."

"Obviously, there's something you like about the place."

"I love hardwood floors. It has a huge backyard and even some fruit trees. But the inside needs work. I'm grateful to have a place to stay."

"Definitely. What kind of work does your house need?"

"Painting. Drywall. Kitchen needs a backsplash. Completely new cabinets and flooring. Plus a few odds and ends. My landlord said if I get some work done on the place he will credit me on my rent. So I'm working on that now."

"Wow. As it happens, my husband is a contractor. He does it all. And his prices are reasonable."

"Okay. All right." Her voice was so quiet that Kiara barely heard her.

"Make yourself comfortable. You're part of our family now."

"Thanks, I appreciate that."

Once Kiara dropped Nicole off at orientation, she drove around campus and spotted Eddison walking alongside the law library. She pulled her car to a stop, tooted her horn, and rolled down the window.

"Hello there."

"Hi, Eddison."

He casually approached her vehicle. "May I sit next to you?"

"Only if you're on your best behavior."

"I promise to be good."

She unlocked the door. Eddison slid onto the passenger seat.

"Look," Kiara said, "we haven't talked since that day."

"I missed you."

"You always say words that make me feel better."

"Did you like the kiss? Did that make you feel good?"

"Yeah, I liked it. I enjoyed kissing you. Does that make me a bad person?"

"You needed it. And that makes you a normal person."

"Of course you'd say that."

Eddison grabbed Kiara's chin.

"Oh, God." She felt herself crumbling. Again.

She opened her mouth and let him kiss her. She couldn't believe what she was doing, but it made her feel desired.

He stroked her thigh. She got hotter and hotter. After a while they both came up for air.

"Wow." She laughed and blushed.

"Kiara, I need to know what you plan to do. Because you won't be giving me blue balls. That won't work for me."

Kiara tossed and turned in bed that night. Rashad was late. And she felt afraid. Her anxious mind imagined all sorts of scenarios. She tried to contact him earlier but he did not respond.

Just then Alexis texted her.

I have a personal emergency and will take a vacation day tomorrow.

Kiara wanted to text a response. But she accidentally waved her hand across the text, which caused her Android to automatically call Alexis. She tried to end the call, but couldn't.

"Damn. I hate this phone."

Alexis groggily answered. "Hello?"

"Um, sorry to bother you, but I'm responding to your message. Is everything okay?"

"Everything is great." Alexis's voice sounded muffled.

"Oh, okay. I thought you said you had an emergency."

"I do," she gasped. "I am dealing with it right . . . now." She sounded like she was gritting her teeth.

"Let me know if there's anything I can do to help."

She heard muffled voices. Alexis grunted, "Okay," and hung up.

Kiara knew the sounds of sex when she heard them. And she reasoned that Alexis must have been with that man she'd alluded to having a while ago. "Good, I'm glad she's getting some tonight. And it sounds like she'll be getting some more tomorrow."

Two hours later Rashad came home. Kiara was in

their bedroom with her tablet doing some work. He thrust a small vase of roses at her.

"Here you go, babe. Just because."

"Are you serious? Why'd you buy me these?"

"That's what you wanted, right?"

"I wanted you to answer my calls when I tried you earlier. Why didn't you call me back?"

"I did but your phone was busy. Or it went straight into voice mail."

"Oh."

"Yeah. So."

"But why the flowers?"

"You're my wife. That's why."

He planted a kiss on her forehead. Kiara felt conflicted. She compared Eddison's kiss to Rashad's. No fucking comparison. It seemed like life as she knew it was slipping through her fingers.

She had nightmares all night that Rashad caught her kissing Eddison. In fact, Kiara felt so troubled, she didn't seem like her normal self.

At work the next day, Kiara took a bathroom break. She was standing before the sink when Shyla entered the restroom. Shyla took care of her business and when she emerged from her stall, she noticed her boss staring at the mirror. Water steadily poured from the spigot. A glob of soft soap sat in the middle of Kiara's hand.

"Mrs. Eason? You all right?"

Kiara did not reply.

Shyla turned off the water.

"Mrs. Eason?"

"Huh, oh. Sorry. I-I've got a lot on my mind."

"It's okay, we all do."

"How are things going with you and—"

"Wesley? My fiancé and I are good. We are impatiently counting down the days."

"I can only imagine. I hope everything works out for you two. Hope that you are true soul mates and the life you want to share together will continue to grow and develop and that you receive every single freaking thing you want out of the relationship."

"Sounds like there's a story behind this little speech."

"Sorry for the overshare. But I'm already where you're trying to be. And let me tell you, marriage is very hard work. And sometimes we women get so caught up in the wedding that we completely ignore the relationship."

Shyla put on her concerned humanitarian face.

"Are you and Rashad truly okay? Like, y'all still good, right? I mean, it's not really any of my business. But I'm all about female empowerment. And if you ever need to talk—"

Kiara gave her an emotionless stare.

"I know you may not want to confide in me, but I am a perfect listener, if nothing else. And I know us women gotta stick together no matter what."

Kiara finally noticed Shyla's enlarged, hungry eyes. "Pretend this never happened. I was having a moment. I'm over it."

The next day around lunchtime, Kiara was in her office responding to emails. Rashad popped his head in her doorway. He tiptoed and tried not to make any noise. He placed his ice-cold fingers on her neck and she jumped in her seat.

"Oh, you scared me half to death."

Rashad smiled and placed several bags on her conference table.

She recognized the strong aroma.

"Asian?"

"Kim Son, baby."

"Oh, wow." She wondered if it was a coincidence.

That was the same restaurant where she and Eddison had had lunch the last time they ate together.

"All your favorites."

"Hmmm."

"That's all I get? A hmm? Where's a 'thanks,' a '*gracias*'? Even a '*Danke*' would help."

"Rashad, again, you've been catching me off guard. I didn't expect all this."

"I'm trying to make up for the times I've been an ass. You know that I ain't like that twenty-four-seven, baby."

"That remains to be seen. But thanks, I think." She glanced at her watch.

"What? You don't have time to eat lunch with me right now? I had a break and I thought I'd surprise you. Trying to be a good husband. This is what you said you wanted, right? Me showing more effort?"

She thought about Eddison and the fact that he wanted her to make a decision.

"You're outdoing yourself."

"That's what a good man does."

"A good man is an *accessible* man," she told him.

"An accessible man is a *broke* man."

Shyla suddenly stood in the doorway.

"Hey, y'all. I followed my nose. Something smells really delicious in here." She gave Rashad an admiring look. "You, sir, are one of the last good ones. I'm going to call my fiancé and tell him he'd better start bringing me lunch to work once we get married."

Kiara nodded and grinned. She would never want anyone like Shyla Perry to know her marital issues. "I'm telling you, you've gotta train these men early on before it's too late."

They all laughed.

"Well, I won't interrupt y'all." Shyla squealed. "That's so romantic. I *love* love."

Rashad's belly growled like a wild animal. Shyla apologized and dashed out the door. Kiara couldn't help but laugh. She knew her husband was ready to eat.

Right then, Nicole came shuffling into Kiara's office. She wore a turquoise short-sleeve blouse with a pair of tan slacks. Her shoes were ordinary, nothing like the shoe game of her female coworkers.

"Oops, I'm sorry I didn't know—" she mumbled.

"Speak up, what did you say?"

"I said I-I can come back later."

"No, it's okay. Actually, I'm glad you're here, Nicole. This is my husband, Rashad Eason. Remember, I told you he does renovations and carpentry work."

"Hey, what's up?" Rashad yelled at Nicole and gave her a casual glance. When she barely spoke, he proceeded to the conference table and made lots of noise opening bags and pulling out cartons of rice, chicken, shrimp, vegetables, egg rolls, and Mekong soup.

"Babe, you ready? I could eat."

"My husband is rude when he's hungry. Anyway, honey, I will give Nicole your card so she can get with you about doing some minor work for her. All right?"

He nodded and took a spoon and scooped his food onto a plate.

"Nice to meet you," Nicole mumbled, then she left them alone.

"Rashad, you weren't very nice to my new hire."

"You know how it is. My stomach is growling. I'm hot. And I stink. I don't need this woman knowing how funky I smell."

"You are so silly." Kiara's face brightened as she realized that her husband had surprised her with something she actually liked. She'd wanted things to turn around in her marriage for so long that she had just about given up. Maybe now was the time for her prayers to be answered.

But on her way home, she was thinking about Eddison, and that's when he called her.

"I was thinking about you and wanted to touch base."

"I was doing some thinking, too," she said.

"In a good way, I hope."

"Just keep being good to me."

She didn't want to tell him that her husband was acting like he had some sense. She knew Eddison was really feeling her. But she only had one heart. She just didn't know if it was big enough to handle her main man, plus the man that wanted to be her main man.

"Kiara, I-I'd like to stop by tomorrow."

"I don't know about that. I have a pretty tight schedule."

"Squeeze me in, please."

"It depends on what this is about."

"Jerome Fielder is giving a couple of freshmen a really hard time. They got into some trouble. I was hoping you can help them out."

"Geez, Rashad. I dunno—"

"Ouch."

"Oops, Eddison, I'm sorry. My bad. I-I didn't mean to seem like I'm blowing you off."

"I guess when I was preaching to you about the truth, I should have been thinking about myself . . . and if I can handle it."

"Don't even try it."

"Kiara, what can you tell me that will make me believe anything different than what you're showing me? You say you enjoyed that kiss, but now I'm not so sure."

"I did enjoy it . . . but it's complicated."

"You're having second thoughts?"

"I guess I ought to inform you that my husb—Mr. Eason is really trying right now."

Eddison grew quiet.

"Though it took him a while, I feel he is listening to me . . . he's taking baby steps. And this sudden turnaround is like a rescue tube has been thrown at us. I'm grabbing hold of it and hopefully saving my life."

Kiara cleared her throat. It was so quiet she glanced down at her cell to make sure she hadn't lost the call. But her screen still read, "Eddy O."

She thought about the kisses they shared: the most deliciously sensual kiss she'd ever had with a man. But she also decided it would have to be the last time she ever did that. If Rashad stayed on the right path, she felt it was only right to give their relationship a chance.

"I just want to clean up my side of the street and make sure things will stay good between us. As silly as it sounds, I don't want to lose your friendship."

He finally spoke. "I want you."

"Eddison."

"I said it, I meant it. It's not going to change."

"You're serious?"

"Just like you, Kiara, I can be positive too. And I believe if something is meant to happen, it will. Doesn't matter what, when, or how."

Kiara whispered good-bye and hung up. She thought about Eddison's words; it humbled her to realize that he actually did care about her. He was consistent and always proved himself to be in her corner.

She picked up Myles from school then drove straight home. He rattled on about his day, and how he had to handle Tommy Washington because the boy stole his toy helicopter.

"I told Tommy my dad finally put that copter together and he couldn't have it. And he said 'I dare you to take it back.' And when I tried to grab my toy, he shoved me. So, Mommy, I wacked him in his eye real hard. And he started crying like a kindergartener."

"That's nice, sweetie."

"So I'm not in trouble?"

"No, sweetie."

"Yes," he said and pumped his fist.

When Kiara parked her car in the driveway of the house next door, her son asked, "Mommy, why did you do that? We don't live here."

"Oh, right. I was just testing your alertness skills. Great job, son!"

She backed up out of her neighbor's driveway and this time parked at her house.

When she didn't see Rashad's van, her heart sank. When he arrived home a half hour late, she wanted to be happy but she wasn't.

Rashad lugged in bags of food.

"What's all this?"

"It's Friday night. I feel like barbecuing."

"I see."

"Aren't you happy? You love my brisket and ribs and sausages. You can make some of your potato salad, if you don't mind."

"Yeah, Rashad. Sure, I can do that. Whatever you want."

He stayed in the kitchen so he could sauté the meat and prepare his homemade barbecue sauce.

Kiara quietly went to their bedroom. That is where Rashad would pull off his clothes every time he got home from work. She locked the door behind her. And she went to the laundry basket and fished out his work pants.

She got her cell and called Adina. They'd spoken earlier by phone. Adina told her not to fall for his weak attempts at being nice. She said it was merely a cover-up for his dirty deeds and she needed to investigate to know what was really going on with him.

"Are you doing it?" Adina asked.

"Yes. Can you hear my heart beating? I haven't done this type of snooping in almost ten years of being with him."

"Baby girl, it's hard, but you gotta know what's up in your relationship. Aren't you sick of not knowing? Are you tired of feeling weird and shit?"

"Yes."

"So get to looking."

"All right." Kiara dug in Rashad's front pocket. She scooped up a handful of loose change. And she found a wrinkled business card from a lighting company, which she promptly stuffed back in his pocket.

"Nothing, girl."

"Check the back. Hurry."

"Okay." Kiara reached inside the back pocket and pulled out some crumpled papers.

"Nothing but some stupid receipts."

"Girl, you better look at those things. It's all about the receipts."

"Oh, wow. Here's one from a Greek restaurant. It's from two days ago. May twenty-eighth. Around twelve noon. Lunchtime. And it is for two Greek salads, and two pita sandwiches, and two Sprites."

"Hmm, he ain't that greedy. Who did the Negro buy lunch for?"

"Um," Kiara said as she stared at the receipt. "It says it was a carry-out. Paid for in cash. And the person who called in the order is Lessie."

"Whoop, now we're getting somewhere," Adina

yelped. "Some woman called in their order and your hubby paid for it. You know what you need to do, girl, so do it."

Kiara hung up and agreed that it was way past time to get to the bottom of her husband's suspicious behavior.

"Rashad, we need to talk." She returned to the kitchen with her cell phone in one hand, the receipt in the other.

"Ain't nothing to talk about."

"Yes, there is. And you didn't even know what I was going to say."

He was seasoning his meat. "Give me a second."

"That can wait. I want to know something. Who is Lessie?"

"Huh?"

"Do you know a woman that goes by the name Lessie?"

"Uh-uh, no, I don't. Why?" Rashad calmly placed the meat inside clear plastic bags.

"I found a receipt in your pocket."

He slammed the bag on the counter.

"No the fuck you did not."

"You want it? You wanna see?" She waved the paper in his face.

"Whoever you bought lunch for this week, I want you to call the bitch on the phone right now."

"You are crazy, Kiara." He shook his head furiously. The veins bulged out the side of his neck. "She is a client. I bought lunch for her. Satisfied now, crazy-ass woman?"

"She's a client?"

"Yes. Damn. Stay the fuck out my pockets."

"Rashad, sometimes I feel uneasy about our situation."

"That's because you're crazy as hell. You're doing exactly what insane bitches do. Sounds like something Adina put you up to. That's why I never wanted you to

hang around her. She couldn't hold onto her own husband and now she's trying to make you lose yours.
Black women can be so damned stupid."

"Your mother is a black woman."

"She can be stupid, too."

"That's true."

Kiara sniffed and gave herself a moment to think.

"So this Lessie woman is just your client?"

"I've done some work at her spot."

Kiara looked doubtful.

"Some work like what? Drilling? Laying pipe?"

He chuckled. "You're too much."

"Okay, then. If she is a client, call her. On speaker
phone. Just talk about anything."

"You must be out your fucking mind." Rashad went
to the refrigerator and found a space to store the barbecue for the next twenty-four hours.

"I am not about to embarrass myself calling this lady
out of the fucking blue all because your ass got gassed
up by Adina." He began yelling. "Is this where ten years
of being with the same woman takes you? Is this the
type of shit I gotta look forward to for the next thirty
years?"

"All right, okay, damn," Kiara said, backing down.
She'd read too many news stories about fights that got
out of hand. Petty grievances that led to a knife slashing,
gunshots, screaming, and 911 calls. She never wanted
that to be her life. But she did want answers.

"Maybe you don't know what to say or how to handle this type of thing in a professional way, but I do. I'll
be very nice. I'll act like I'm your secretary. What's her
last name?"

"What? Kiara, please stop it. You're not thinking ra-
tionally."

"And I have you to blame!"

Rashad couldn't take it anymore. He went to his room, put on a fresh change of clothes, ran to get in his vehicle, and practically burned rubber trying to get away from his wife.

Rashad stayed gone for two hours.

As soon he came home, he found Kiara in the bedroom. He told her, "For your info, I was at a sports bar. I had four drinks and some appetizers. I was alone. Is that all right with you?"

"Oh, so now you want to go out of your way to tell me where you were?"

"I sure do. Is that cool?"

"Whatever makes you happy."

Kiara already had on her nightgown. She decided to go sleep in the second-floor guest room.

"I'll be upstairs," she told him as she gathered a few of her things.

"Knock yourself out. I need to get some rest. Sleep tight, babe."

As she walked upstairs, Kiara wished that Rashad would come after her. She had told him she never slept well when he wasn't by her side. But she figured he was still upset with her for invading his privacy.

She heard him click the lock on their bedroom door.

Rashad's behavior frightened her to the point that she entertained morbid thoughts as she lay down and attempted to go to sleep. What would happen if nothing changed for the better? What if she was overly paranoid and he decided he wanted out of their marriage and she had to raise their son on her own? It was one thing to play around with the thought, but another thing to figure out how she'd handle an actual breakup.

She lay in the bed tossing, turning, thinking.

As drowsiness shepherded Kiara into a deep sleep,

she heard the bedroom door squeak open, then close. He slipped in the bed right next to her and held her from behind, cupping her breasts with his warm hands. He placed his face next to hers. His cheek felt like love. His prickly whiskers grazed her neck. He pressed his lips against hers, giving her slow, gentle kisses that made her shiver with desire. She turned, moaned, then squirmed until she faced him in the dark. She groped for his lips and hungrily kissed him back. She trembled with happiness as he told her over and over again how sexy she was and that he loved her. And when he removed her panties and tossed them on the floor, then pulled out his penis and entered her, she let him. They instantly came together as one. She was lost in him. She couldn't be upset anymore. She couldn't lie. She had to have him. The desire for him was too strong.

When Kiara woke up the next morning, she was alone.

Her panties weren't on the floor. They were still on her body.

Did we make love and then he put my panties back on me?

She got out of bed and headed downstairs to the master bedroom. Rashad wasn't there. She proceeded to shower and got dressed. When she entered the kitchen, the smell of turkey bacon, cheesy jalapeño eggs, and grits greeted her nostrils. Myles was already up and eating.

"Good morning, sexy." Rashad even wore her purple apron. "Have a seat."

He scooped some eggs onto a plate, selected a couple slices of meat, and dipped the spoon in the steaming hot grits which he poured in a small bowl.

"Um, really, Rashad? Grits?"

"Hahaha." He laughed. "Don't even try it."

Her voice was shaking. "Why are you doing this? What's all this for?"

"I don't want to fight. I hate it. I hate arguing. I know I've been fucking up in some ways and I need to step up my game. You're dope. I'm trying to show you that you are."

"I-I'm—"

"Speechless, right."

"Rashad—"

"You're welcome, Mrs. Eason."

"Thanks."

She sat her shaking legs down at the table and ate her breakfast. When she washed it all down with some orange juice, she said in a tiny voice, "Did you come in the room last night when I was asleep? Did you get in the bed with me?"

"Woman, I was knocked out all night long."

"So you didn't come?"

He laughed and made clattering noises as he set dishes and pots in the dishwasher.

Ten minutes later, Kiara headed out to take Myles to his early morning martial arts class.

All she could think about was the man in her dream. *Don't matter what, when, or how.*

Chapter 6

It was still Saturday and mid-morning in the city. Alexis sat alone at an outdoor café sipping on a mimosa and taking a drag from her cigarette. She felt like she was one of the last few smokers in modern society. Smoking was a habit she couldn't kick. An imperfect part of herself that she learned to accept.

As Alexis enjoyed the warm summer breeze, she thoughtfully observed a woman a few yards away. The woman was sitting across the table from a man. Alexis could tell the man was in his late thirties. They sat and ate their brunch. Alexis noticed how the woman gazed adoringly at the man. The man's cell phone rang. He glanced at it and answered. He gripped his phone against his ear. He ended the conversation and said a few words to his lunch companion. He rose to his feet and hurriedly left the café. The lady's face fell. Her sad expression vividly announced that her happiness had just walked away.

Alexis couldn't help herself. She stubbed her cigarette in an ashtray, rose gingerly from her table, and slowly walked toward the young girl, who looked to be around twenty.

"Hello. My name is Alexis and I couldn't help but notice what happened between you and that guy."

"Huh?"

"You know he's married, right?"

"You know him or something?"

"No, I don't know him. But I do know men and that one has a wife. Did you know that?"

"What? I-I—"

"Answer me this. Have you ever been to his house?"

"No. He lives with his great aunt. And his sister. And his niece. Their family is going through some stuff, so . . ."

"How long have you known him?"

"Almost two years."

"So in two years of being with him, he's never invited you to his house?"

"No."

"Has he introduced you to his family?" Alexis discreetly took a seat across from the chick. Her voice was calm and matter-of-fact.

"Well, no." The girl furrowed her brows. "No."

"Have you ever asked him if he's married?"

"Yes. Wait. No, not really. It never came up."

"So you're assuming he's single."

"He doesn't act married. We're always together."

"Always?"

"Well, he makes time for me when he's not working. And he works very hard. He drives semis. He's on the road a lot but he always comes to see me when he gets a break. We spend a couple weekends together out the month. We go out. We talk on the phone all the time. When he falls asleep, my voice is the last voice he hears." She grinned like she was proud of herself.

Alexis laughed. "When you do go out, does he hold your hand in public?"

The girl's face brightened. "Yes!"

"How sweet! What side of town do you live on?"

"West side."

"And on what side of town does he live with his great aunt . . . and the sister . . . and the niece?"

"Far north side."

"Figures."

Alexis quietly observed the girl, not desiring to hurt her but only wanting to educate her. She could identify with her and felt some compassion. At the same time, she hated the girl. Hated the situations that she and so many other women put themselves in. Yet Alexis chose to be in her own situation. And no matter how good it seemed, it was a hard life. The only life she knew.

"Have you met any of his close friends?"

"Oh yeah. There's Donnie Wade, T.L., and Bun."

"And when you met these friends, how did your man introduce you? Did he refer to you as his woman? His special lady?"

The girl thought. She frowned. "No, he just called me Regina. Like: This Regina."

Alexis nodded. "Hmmm. Why am I not surprised?"

She stood up and took a long, deep breath.

"Well, I gotta be going. Like I said, I noticed the interactions between you and your man and, um, don't say I didn't warn you, but he is locked down like a felon in the pen. Now if you want to continue being with this man, that's on you. But you gotta know what you're getting yourself into. Decide if that's how you wanna roll for the rest of your life."

Regina looked mortified. "The rest of my life? Assuming he is married, you actually think I want to be with a man like that for the rest of my life?"

"It wouldn't be the first time. Won't be the last."

Alexis waved good-bye and turned around.

Her long, graceful legs were like a giraffe's. Her hips swayed like the slow motion of a pendulum. She walked as if a hardcover book sat on her head and she was traipsing down a runway. She instinctively knew that the eye of every man was on her. And the eyes that weren't on her wanted to be.

Regina felt distraught the second Alexis left her alone at the table. Suddenly she bolted from her chair. She raced after Alexis, who by now had slid onto the plush leather seat of a two-seater black Mercedes. Her vanity plates spelled out "SPOILED." It was an old convertible but still turned heads when she drove with the top down.

The girl waved.

"Um, I'm sorry to bother you."

"You're not bothering me."

"Well, I wanted to say my name is Regina."

"You told me that already."

"Why do I keep meeting the same type of shitty-ass guys?"

Alexis reached out and squeezed Regina's hand with a gentleness that instantly soothed her. "Because there are way more shitty-ass guys out here to meet than non-shitty-ass guys," Alexis replied with a laugh. Then she said, "Seriously, Regina. I feel you. Because to be honest, I ask myself the same question."

"Can we talk? Something tells me I can learn a lot from you." Regina hesitated. "I-I already have."

Alexis emerged from her car and the two new friends returned to the café table, where they took a seat and ordered drinks.

Regina blurted, "You sleep with married men. Don't you?"

"Not men. One man."

"You act like it doesn't bother you."

"It is what it is. If I could control this situation, I would. I'd be like God. I'd have the power to make everything the way I want it to be."

"Really?"

"But he's not the first, obviously."

"You do this all the time?"

Alexis's eyes glinted with a sadness that couldn't be denied. "Do you mind?" She retrieved a new cigarette from her pouch and lit up.

"Nasty habit. I started doing this, started killing myself, ever since I was nine."

"That's too bad."

"I started smoking exactly one day after I found out the truth about my father." Alexis dreamily stared at nothing and was mentally transported to her childhood when it was her, and her mother, and her daddy.

"Tandy. That's my dad's name."

"Tandy. That's different."

"He was wonderful, too. We did fun stuff together. He took me shopping for clothes and cute little Barbie dolls that I loved to dress up. He'd buy us chocolate ice cream with waffle cones, and took me to the biggest parks in Houston so I could play and run around, even though my mother couldn't stand for me to get my clothes dirty. My dad treated me like his princess. That's how I felt whenever I was with him. I had such a good feeling of love, and acceptance, and belonging."

"But that changed?"

"Check this out. When I was nine, our class went on a field trip to the zoo. Daddy signed up to be a chaperone. The kids, we were all so excited and scared to see all the animals; the elephant display, lions, the squawking birds. But we had so much fun eating snow cones and stale yellow popcorn. And even though I was scared of the animals, I felt safe because Daddy was there with me. So I relaxed and kept enjoying myself. Just me and my daddy. And then this strange woman showed up at the zoo. I had never seen her before. I guess they arrived late. And a little girl was with her. The girl looked a year or two older than me. She wore clothes like she was going to church, not to the zoo. Her long ponytails were made up in pretty pink ribbons. She had on a neat little dress. Her mom was skinny and cute. The woman laughed a lot. And suddenly I noticed that my dad wasn't paying attention to me. He was talking to this lady and was all up in her face instead of in mine. He—" Her voice caught in her throat and it quivered when she continued. "My daddy took that little girl's hand and they all walked in front of me. I walked behind them. They were laughing, enjoying the animals, while I was forced to look at them. I didn't care about those animals anymore. And when I couldn't stand it any longer and went to yank his sleeve to get his attention, Daddy told me to hold hands with my classmate Vennie. I mean I liked Vennie. She was probably the closest thing to a female friend I've ever had. For some reason, me and other chicks don't always click. But Vennie and I held hands— but she was no substitute for my daddy."

"Well, what was that all about?"

"That day, after the woman and her kid left the zoo, and my daddy dropped me off at home, I was met at the door by my mother."

"Oh. He dropped you off? He didn't live with you?"

Alexis laughed. "That's how naïve I was. Hardly anybody's father lived with them. So I thought it was normal. He was still active in my life. But that's the day my mother revealed to me that Tandy had a wife, and that I had a sister named Glynis. Mama informed me we weren't his real family. All that time . . . I thought we were."

"Damn, that must have hurt."

"Daddy was the first man I trusted . . . and the first one that broke my heart."

Alexis waved a large circle with the thin cigarette

that made her want to choke. "That's when Capri Indigo and I became best friends. I began spending more time with Capri." She took a drag and blew smoke rings out her mouth, "Spent more time trying to smoke than I spent with my girl Vennie. Biggest mistake I ever made in my life. It was like a fork was in the road. And instead of going right, I went left. Story of my life. I should've stuck with Vennie."

Regina sensed that it was hard for Alexis to make friends. Maybe it was because she was so pretty that she intimidated insecure women.

"But weren't you scared to smoke? Are you scared now?"

Alexis read between the lines. "It's not like I'm a chain smoker or anything. Plus, we all gotta die of something one day. What difference will it make what the death certificate says? Death is death."

"Don't tell me you're not afraid of that, either?"

"I'm scared to death of it. My mother, she's been horribly sick lately. And I am petrified that I will walk into her bedroom one day, her room will be cold and dark, and she will be still and silent. And gone. And I won't ever hear my mother's voice again."

"Wow. Anything else?"

"I should be used to it by now but I'm very scared to be alone; I absolutely hate when I feel lonely. Men and women weren't meant to be that way. That's one Bible verse I remember." She laughed and continued. "Loneliness is like an endless, deep black pit. A big hole that can't be filled with anything except the ones you long to be with."

"With what's-his-face?"

Alexis nodded. "Being with what's-his-face feels like pleasure mixed with pain. Lots and lots of pleasure."

"And a whole lotta pain."

"You are correct, Regina. As weird as this may sound, sometimes I don't feel right with him, but other times I feel incomplete without him."

"So why do you do it? Why don't you stop? Do you like it? How often do you see your man?"

"I do it because . . . as bad as it may sound, it's what I want to do. Plus, the decent man shortage is very real in Houston. Many handsome, seemingly good men troll around like they're single until you find out they're not. By then it's too late. You're in love, or lust, and stuck on stupid."

"But you can still stop once you find out . . ."

"Are you going to stop, Regina? Can you tell me that you will never, ever see your own what's-his-face after today? Never have contact with him ever again as long as the sun keeps shining? Are you saying that the strong feelings you developed for the sonofabitch will completely dissolve ten minutes after you learned the truth about the man with whom you've shared many valuable years? After you've shared life-changing experiences? Sure, some chicks got that in them. Kick him to the curb or flick his ass off like he's a nasty booger and keep it moving. But the majority of us . . . we go back for more . . . more torture . . . more conflict . . . more struggling with desire for love and acceptance . . . more man sharing. It's a bitch."

"Well, Alexis, from listening to you, if he is married, I don't want to go back. I-I don't want to stay caught up year after year, if all he's going to do is keep going home to her."

"Regina, welcome to the Weekend Wives Club, because in essence that's what we are. Part-time wives. We get some of the privileges but not everything we deserve."

"If getting dick every now and then is what you call

'privileges' and he thinks that's all it takes to make me happy, then he must be fooling himself."

"You are learning, aren't you?"

"No, I'm processing. I'm pissed." Regina banged her fist on the table. "I am fucked up right now because this Negro had me wide open like the Grand-mother-freaking-Canyon. He made me feel like I was the only one. Like I was special and shit. Because if I do my research and find out he has a wife at home, I will feel very stupid. But now that I think of it, he did act shady and mysterious."

"All mysterious acting men do not work for the FBI. Side Chick 101, lesson number three."

Regina finally let out a jubilant laugh. "You are crazy, Alexis."

"I didn't used to be. But living this life makes you some type of way."

"Yet you like it. What? His dick all that?"

"Good dick is hard to find . . . until you are lucky enough to come across a better dick. But, sure, the sex is one factor, but it's not just that. We have stronger ties and it's so much more that I can't tell it all. But part of it is the fantasy. And my admitting this makes me sound so very pathetic, but when I'm with my man for the few hours he gives me, and the things we do together, and not just the sex, but the very important moments we get to share, I am able to live out my dream of us being meant to be. Him giving me undivided attention. Him buying me nice stuff not just to make up for his absence, but simply because he loves me."

"I see that nice whip you got. Your man got you that?"

"Hell, naw. Rashad ain't stacking that type of paper. He's doing pretty good, but he's not there just yet."

"Oh, that his name? Rashad?"

Alexis tried not to look as disturbed as she felt. "Do me a favor. Pretend you didn't hear that."

"Who would I tell? I don't even care. He ain't my husband." Regina thoughtfully studied Alexis, almost envying the woman. Alexis acted as if she didn't give a damn that she was cheating with a married man. And Regina couldn't understand it. She wondered why the woman couldn't do any better. Alexis was so darned pretty she was difficult to look at. Regina had never met anyone like her. From her sense of fashion to her the-hell-with-it attitude, she could still detect vulnerability underneath the charade. Even though Regina didn't know Rashad, she could guess why he would want Alexis in his life.

"Why do they do it?" Regina asked. "I mean, why wouldn't my boyfriend just tell me he was married?"

"Hello? His goal is to tippity tap tap tap that ass."

"Some niggas ain't shit."

"But women help men not be shit, don't we? We are cosigning. And whatever you sign up for is what you get. Yet if all us women stuck together and said fuck it, this shit is wack, it's over, and if we stop spreading our legs for men that are already taken, if we ignore their phone calls, delete their texts, stop listening to their charming asses, the world would be a much better place, wouldn't it, Regina?"

"Hell, yeah!"

"But . . . as good as it sounds . . . it'll never happen."

Alexis gave Regina her contact info and the two women went their separate ways. She hopped back in her Mercedes and decided to take a long spin to Fort Bend County. She decided to shop at a new signature Kroger store located on Highway 6, north of Fresno. It had high ceilings, was well lit and filled with fresh produce and meats. A lot of shoppers were crammed in the store on this particular day.

When she walked inside the front entrance, she began pushing a large, bulky basket.

"Hello, beautiful!" A well-dressed man smiled at her as soon as she entered the bakery department. She was distracted by all the bakery goods displayed on a big table.

"Hey," the man said again, this time with more attitude.

Alexis was preoccupied with viewing the pecan pies.

"I said 'hello,' lady; are you deaf?"

When she still failed to acknowledge him, he spat at her. "Stuck-up bitch."

"Hold up, what did you say?"

"So now you ready to talk? I gotta call you the bitch that you are before you act like you got good sense?"

"Excuse me, sir. You don't wanna go there. I didn't speak to you because . . ." She glanced at his left hand. "Because of your man tan."

He thrust his hand in his pocket and walked away.

"That wasn't very nice of him. Are you okay, miss?" A man with kind eyes stood near Alexis. He wore a simple pair of jeans and a maroon TAMU jacket. She glanced at his left hand. No man tan.

"I'm good. Thanks."

"Gotta be careful these days. Some men get real violent when a young lady doesn't holler back even though she owes him nothing."

"I-I know. That man rubbed me the wrong way. But—oh well."

"You get what you put out. And some guys don't realize that respecting a woman and approaching her correctly goes a long way."

"Story of my life, sir."

"You *can* write you own story, you know." His voice was firm but kind.

"I suppose."

"Anyway, as long as you're all right now and feel safe, I will let you continue with your shopping. Have a good rest of the day."

The man's presence and insight actually soothed her. He reminded her of her father. Alexis wished the stranger would notice her, really look at her, and discern that she could use a good friend. She wanted to hear his kind, slow-talking Southern drawl again, but he shyly smiled at Alexis, then walked away pushing his empty cart.

Alexis felt the familiar sting of rejection; it made her heart heavy with depression but she told herself she wouldn't be caught dead crying in a grocery store. She decided to suck it up and began to stroll through the produce and poultry sections. Alexis selected a few items and placed them in the basket. Next on her list was Raisin Bran. She decided to make a right down the cereal aisle.

As she guided her basket, Alexis felt herself growing calmer. But that feeling came to a grinding halt when she came upon a handsome older man leading a woman by her elbow. Alexis could tell they were married. He looked so protective of the lady. And the chick was no Halle Berry. She was more like Fred Berry on *What's Happening!!* She was squat and round. He was tall and chiseled. But at least she had him. And their toddler was sitting in a basket happily playing with his stuffed animal. In their place she imagined herself, with her baby girl, and Rashad next to her. An achy lump formed in her throat. When Alexis couldn't bear to watch them any longer, she turned her cart in the opposite direction and ended up in the frozen food section.

"Shrimp. I want some good breaded jumbo shrimp."
She searched until she found what she was looking for.
And when she grabbed two boxes of the seafood, she
twirled around. Her eyes rested on a man whose oval-
shaped head she knew like the back of her hand.

He wasn't facing her and didn't see her. He was far-
ther down the aisle closer to the frozen veggies. A little
boy stood next to him, lost in his own little world, making
helicopter noises and jabbering away like self-absorbed
kids do.

She watched her boss bark orders. And she witnessed
her lover quickly obeying. Alexis hadn't heard from
Rashad since the previous Thursday. He'd skipped last
Sunday's trip to Glynis's. So she went alone.

She felt breathless and hurt. Alexis decided to cut this
shopping trip short. Just when she was maneuvering her
basket to get away, Kiara walked up to Alexis.

"Hey, admin. I didn't know you lived on this side of
town."

"I-I don't."

"Rashad, look who we ran into today."

"Hello. Long time no see," he said with a nervous
look on his face.

"Oh, it hasn't been that long," Alexis said.

"Huh?" Rashad asked. He had a pleading look in his
eyes; like he was begging a woman with a loaded gun
not to pull the trigger.

"I see him all the time."

"Oh, really? Where do you see him?"

"She sees me driving around the city in my van. That's
what she's talking about," Rashad interjected.

"Men are a trip." Alexis smiled.

Myles began whining for popsicles. Kiara went over
to console her son.

"I don't think she heard me," Alexis said to Rashad

in a low voice. "Stop looking like you're about to shit on yourself."

He made a gesture like he'd call her.

She shrugged and turned around to look up into the kind face of the man she ran into earlier.

"Hey, it's you again. The nice guy. It's so rare to meet decent guys these days." She laughed and glanced back at Rashad, who was staring like he couldn't believe she knew any other man besides him. His arrogance is what annoyed her most about him, but it was also what drew her to him.

"Thanks for the compliment," the man told her.

"Do you live in this area?" she asked.

"No, I just like shopping in this Kroger. But if I'm blessed, one day I plan to own a home out here. It's so peaceful by the lakes. And there's some good fishing out this way."

"Oh, really?"

When the man took a couple minutes to talk to her, she could feel Rashad's eyes boring a hole on the side of her face.

"My name is Varnell Brown, by the way. Good to meet you."

"I'm Alexis McNeil. Good to meet you, too." She found herself blushing as she tried to concentrate on everything he was saying.

Alexis gave Varnell her number when he asked. She let him type his info in her iPhone. Rashad shot her a stony look but she didn't care.

All she cared about was making sure Rashad saw her. She hoped he was seeing her for the very first time.

After she got home from shopping it took no time to put away the few groceries she bought. She had nothing else to do so she went upstairs to her bedroom and turned on the television. She then went to stand in the doorway of her walk-in closet. Alexis owned one hundred fifty pairs of shoes and dozens of suits, dresses, slacks, and blouses. Most of the items she had purchased with money that a previous lover gave her.

Alexis dug out some of her favorite designer bags and spread them on the bed. She admired them for a few minutes, thinking about how good she looked whenever she wore them. Then she crawled in bed and lay down next to them. She wrapped her arms around a couple of her thousand-dollar satchels. A large lump formed in her throat. She began crying uncontrollably.

"God, please help me. Show me a sign that you care about me." When nothing noticeable happened, Alexis wept so violently her entire body pulsated. She gasped and whimpered until she eventually gave into sleep. She lay on her side with her purses pressed against her bosom.

An hour later, her doorbell rang. She went downstairs to open the door.

When she saw it was Rashad, she looked surprised.

"I'm spending the night tonight."

"Really?" her voice crackled.

"Yes."

"How'd you manage that?"

"I made up an excuse. And now I'm here."

She walked barefoot outside and saw his white van with the ladder rack parked in her driveway. Rashad held a backpack in his hand.

"You should have called first. You never know. I could have made other plans."

"I am your plans. And don't you forget it."

Once Alexis realized that Rashad was serious and he was hers for the night, she became a different person.

"You are a sonofabitch and you got a lot of nerve doing the shit you do."

"I love you, too."

She invited him in and offered to cook. But he said, "No. that's all right, sweetie. Let's order delivery." And they did. He bought forty dollars' worth of Asian grub. To Alexis, it felt like Christmas, even though she knew he was doing it for another reason.

"I know your birthday is this Saturday. But I'm booked solid."

"What else is new?"

"That's why I got you this."

He reached inside the backpack and pulled out a tiny black box.

Alexis offered him a delighted smile. "Hmm, what are you up to, Rashad?" She snapped open the box and pulled out a dainty sterling silver charm bracelet. It was outlined by sparkling diamonds.

"Babe, you gotta be joking! Didn't this cost a grip?"

"Don't worry about it."

"How were you able to buy this and get away with it?" He'd told her how he got busted with the lunch receipt and had to be more careful.

"I went to the library and ordered it off craigslist. I met the seller outside a Home Depot with a contractor of mine. Everything went smooth."

"I just feel so . . . how can I accept this when . . ."

"It's okay. You're my homie. I care about you. I don't think you know that."

"I don't like being called your homie, but it's good to know that you care."

Rashad slid the bracelet on her wrist, hugged her and kissed her. "Happy birthday with your old ass."

"I'm only turning twenty-three. That's not that old." She hesitated. "I hope this isn't a substitute for you. 'Cause I'd rather have time with you than the stuff you give me. It's nice but it's just stuff."

"Then give it back."

"You must be out your mind." She lovingly caressed her new jewelry. "I will treasure it always. You did good. I love you, babe."

"Enough of that. I'm starving. Can you go make me some lemonade?" Rashad asked her.

She complied and went downstairs to make a fresh gallon. She added ice cubes to his glass and brought it up to him.

"You're bae today," he told her.

Then together they opened each little carton of food and had a feast.

He was stuffing his mouth with a forkful of grub. "What good new movies do you have?"

She went to the oak cabinet, opened the door, and he pored over her collection of films. Alexis liked romance, adventure, and horror films.

"All this shit is old. Why don't we stream some movies? Let's watch the latest *Hunger Games* movie."

"That's what's up," she told him.

While he was still chewing on his food, he grabbed his glass of lemonade and started gulping it. Soon he began gasping.

"What's wrong?" she asked.

He tried to talk but couldn't. He motioned at his throat.

Alexis sprang into action. She made him stand up and she got behind him. She supported his chest with one hand and made him lean forward. She gave him a few abdominal thrusts. Soon he began to breathe normally.

"Thanks, babe. I hate when food feels like it's stuck in my throat. I keep forgetting that when I eat too fast I almost choke to death."

Alexis was grateful that he was okay, but she wondered what would ever happen if he had an emergency while he was at her house. Who would she call and how would she explain him being with her?

That night when they made love, Alexis was friskier than normal.

"Sit over there."

He immediately jumped up and took a seat on an armchair.

She removed her bra and panties and sat on top of Rashad, facing him.

They started kissing and he felt all over her ass, then sucked her tits.

He took off his boxers and she grabbed his dick and stuffed it in her pussy.

"You like this?" she asked. Alexis began singing Rihanna's "Birthday Cake." He stroked her real good while she hopped up and down on him. Rashad clutched her long hair in his hands while she arched her neck. She opened up her mouth and let out a long, roaring shriek. Her entire body shuddered. She kept repeating, "I love this. I love you." Alexis held Rashad's head between her hands and released all the sexual frustration she'd been having. She wanted Rashad so bad. He may still have belonged to Kiara, but as wrong as it was, Alexis felt no shame in having him with her all night.

They held each other tight as the light of the moon glistened through her window and cast ghostly shadows on her wall.

Rashad slipped out before the sun rose. Alexis stayed in bed as long as she could, relishing the memory of his presence and missing him already.

She later got out of bed, took a shower, and got dressed so she could prepare a Sunday brunch.

She brought in a plate stacked with hotcakes to her mother, who was sitting up in bed. She set the plate on a TV tray next to the bed.

"How you doing, Mama?"

Mona frowned at the plate of food.

"You must not be doing too well, but hopefully if you eat something you'll get to feeling better." Alexis patted her mother's messy looking red hair and kissed it. Alexis felt like she just kissed one of the wig-wearing creatures on the *Planet of the Apes*. She started roaring with laughter at her mom's crazy-looking hair.

Her mother shoved the plate of food onto the floor. Syrupy pancakes stuck to the carpet. Scrambled eggs lay scattered next to them.

"I'll feel a whole lot better once you stop disrespecting me."

"Mama, why'd you do that? What you talking about?"

"You heard me, Alexis. I didn't raise you to do what you're doing."

"So I'm not supposed to fix your meals?"

"I'm not talking about the stupid pancakes and the dumb eggs. I'm talking about all that noise you made all night. I had to cover my ears and I still heard you."

"Oh. Well. I-I don't know what to say."

"You may pay bills and help me out around here but you still gots to give me the respect I deserve."

"Okay, I will try not to be so loud next time."

"There won't be a next time."

"As long as I have needs, there will be a next time."

"Then you better go rent a hotel room 'cause I know that woman ain't gone let you sleep with her man in her own house."

"Rent a what? You must be losing your mind. Did you remember to take all your medicine?"

"Don't blame my common sense on some damned sickness. The sickness is that I failed at being a better mother. If you hadn't been so fast running around at four-teen doing things you had no business doing. Sneaking boys in the house while I was gone trying to make money."

"Mama, where is this all coming from? Like, last time we talked, you were fine. But I haven't actually spoken to you in days."

"Not my fault. I can barely get out the bed so if you haven't talked to me it's because you found better things to do than come check on me."

"No. I've been here. And I have checked on you. You were asleep."

"I don't know where you've been."

"Look, lady. If I wasn't at work or taking care of my business, I was here. I'm always here. That's the problem."

"Why be here? Did y'all two break up or something?"

"Huh? I don't know why you're asking me that. That's not something I feel comfortable—"

"Oh, so you don't feel comfortable talking about that married man that you always sneaking into my house like you're a teenager, but you have no problem yelling as loud as you can while you're slapping skins with him? You gone end up with two kids instead of just that one."

Alexis felt like the insides of her stomach rose up in her throat and blocked her ability to breathe. Her mama loved little Hayley to death and she enjoyed every moment when Alexis brought her granddaughter over to the house a couple times a month, but it had always bothered her that her daughter messed around with Rashad and got pregnant by him. She stuck by Alexis during her pregnancy, but when her daughter went into premature labor, she knew then that her young child wouldn't have the means or maturity to care for the baby. That's when Glynis volunteered to help care for Hayley.

"My ending up with his child wasn't totally my fault."

"That's what's wrong with you. You won't accept responsibility for anything. If you plant corn, you gone get corn. If you do dirt, you gone get dirt. You planting the wrong seed and that's why the wrong stuff keeps popping up in your life."

Alexis placed her hands over her ears. She watched her mother's mouth continue moving. She heard the muffled anger and squeezed her hands over her ears even tighter.

When her mother noticed Alexis's attempt to shut her out, she struggled until she could swing her feet to the side of the bed. Once Mona felt stronger, she rose to shaky feet.

She removed Alexis's hands from her ears and patted her on top of her head.

"I know you don't wanna hear it and that's fine. But I need to tell you the truth. We all make our own choices, and I told you a thousand times not to mess around with certain folk. It can get you in trouble that ain't worth its pain."

"It sounds like you're telling me you regret having me. Like I was a mistake."

"You're not a mistake 'cause God don't make mistakes, darling. And yes, it's been rough, but I don't regret having you. But falling in love with your father, that wasn't right. It brought so much heartache. And I never wanted you to know the same type of pain."

"I never wanted to have feelings for Rashad . . . or anyone else."

"You only had one man, a good man, and somehow you messed that one up."

"You know what, if I told you once, I told you twice that Patterson Currie, that good man that you think got away, he wasn't so good, Mama. He messed up my life."

Alexis had met Patterson Currie when she was seven-teen and working at her first job as a cashier at a smoothie shop. He told her she could make thousands of dollars as a model. Alexis decided to listen to him and go for it. She quit her job and got booked for shows at all the local malls. She made money and had fun. She was shocked and pleased when he gave her the two-seater Benz and other gifts. And sex with Patterson was amazing. But when she got pregnant, he sprung the news that he was married with four sons, and she'd better get an abortion because if she gained weight, her modeling days would be over. Alexis cried when she realized he didn't care about her. She was so ashamed she didn't dare tell a soul, so she took herself to get an abortion.

"As my daughter you never should sign up for any-thing just to be with a man. You deserve better. I de-served better."

"This ain't about you."

"As long as you're living here, it affects me, sweetie. And if that punk really cared, he wouldn't come by for a few hours and leave. If he loved you, he would never leave you, for any reason. For any woman. For any-thing."

"But—"

"Most married men won't leave their real family for a mistress."

Her words hurt Alexis so much. "S-sometimes it hap-pens."

Mona sadly told her, "It didn't happen to me so why would you believe he's going to do that for you?"

"Because I know Rashad loves me."

"That clown don't love you. He don't spend major holidays with you. He ain't there every time you need him. Quit wasting your time with a lying cheater, and get your do-nothing life together. Stop making a fool of yourself."

Mona's words made her tremble with anger. The truth tore at her guts and was good at making Alexis feel worthless.

As she fled her mother's presence, Alexis accidentally stepped on the pancakes. She picked up the food and put it back on the plate. Syrup stuck to her shoe and made squishy noises when she went down the steps. She ran to the kitchen and dumped the rest of the breakfast into the trash can. Then she sat down, laid her forehead on the table, and stroked the charm bracelet Rashad gave her and wept so loud she didn't care if Mona heard her.

Chapter 7

"You fell asleep where, doing what?" Kiara yawned as she questioned her husband. It was five in the morning. Her pupils were red. It felt like dirt was stuck to her eyelids. She got no sleep the night before. But when she heard the garage door open, she stopped Rashad before he could get in. He appeared exhausted.

"I fell asleep at one of the renovation houses I worked at. When I woke up, it was morning. And I came straight home. Is any coffee made?"

"That doesn't even sound right, Rashad."

"Well, regardless, that's what happened. I feel like crap, too; that floor was hard as concrete. Hell, it *was* concrete."

Rashad vigorously rubbed his back and a stupid grin formed on his face.

"Give me a massage?"

"Negro, please. You should have let whoever you were with last night massage your back."

"I told you what went down."

"I heard what you told me. But I doubt that it went down like that. You sleeping at a renovation house? What the fuck ever."

"You tripping. Don't act like this hasn't happened before."

Kiara thought about it. A couple of times in the past, he had slept at the job site . . . because he said he was too drained to make it home and he wasn't going to take chances driving. Back then she bundled up their child and drove to the job site to see if he was there. He was, because she noticed his work van. She went back home and never told Rashad she did a drive-by.

"Well, don't get comfy," she told him. She went and threw on some sweats, a t-shirt, and some flip-flops. She grabbed her keys and purse.

"Let's go."

"Go where?"

"You're about to show me where you were at. Come on."

"Kiara, I don't have time for this."

She stared at him. "Rashad, when we took our vows almost ten years ago, one of the things you promised was to make me feel secure. You remember that?"

"Yeah. And—"

"I know what you're about to say. But financial security isn't the only way in which a woman needs to feel secure."

"If you are saying you don't trust me, then why are you with me? Why would you be with a man you don't trust?"

"Prove to me that you can be trusted. And if you were where you say you were, you'd have no problem taking me to that spot. Right now. Let's go."

He gave a nonchalant shrug and went out to the garage to get in her car.

She got Myles, who was still completely knocked out, and struggled to carry him to the car. Kiara gently placed him on the backseat. She opened the garage door and they were on their way.

"Tell me where to go, Rashad."

He slumped in his seat and gave her directions.

They drove approximately forty minutes to the northern part of town.

"Turn down this street."

She did and he pointed at a one-story frame house on the left. It was surrounded by a white picket fence.

"You happy now? That's where I was."

She stared at the house, then frowned at him. She made a U-turn then drove back up the street until they were right in front of the house.

"What are you doing?"

She parked then put the car in neutral.

"Let's go."

"Okay. I'm putting my foot down on this, Kiara. We are not about to go up to this house. That's trespassing. You see those big dogs in the yard?"

"Wait. I thought you said it was this house?"

"No. That one. The one with those two Rottweilers. And you know you're scared of dogs."

Kiara nervously laughed. "This is insane. What am I doing here?"

"You need to slow it down, babe. This is not us. We don't do crazy shit like this."

"Then why am I doing this?"

Rashad reached over and tried to hug her. "You are stressed. You need a vacation. I could use some R and R, too."

She said not a word. She put the car in drive and kept traveling until they were back at their own house. They quietly went inside. Kiara made Rashad tuck Myles back in his bed. She lacked the energy and desire to do it herself.

When Rashad was done, he found Kiara in the kitchen, sitting at the breakfast table. He made her some hot green tea with lemon and handed a cup to her.

"Thanks," she told him. "I just want you to keep me posted about everything. Communicate." Her voice was hoarse. "I worry when you are gone all night, or for a long time."

He nodded. "That's understandable. But you should automatically know, when I ain't here, ninety percent of my time is spent trying to make money. The other ten percent is just little stuff I need to do. But I don't feel like I gotta check in with you first before I do anything that's just normal day-to-day stuff. Would you want to give me a full itinerary of everything you do before you do it?"

"Nope, not really."

"Good. I'm *your* husband. Ain't no other Mrs. Eason out there but you."

"I already know that. I'm just concerned about the wannabes."

He laughed.

"Rashad," Kiara said, standing up, "You know as well as I do that some chicks have no respect for another woman's relationship. Haven't you met chicks like that?"

"What? Not really."

"Oh, now I know you're lying." She came and stood directly in front of him.

"How you know that?"

"Someone told me they saw your ass kissing another chick. A tall, pretty woman. Does that sound familiar?"

"If that someone is Adina, be suspect. She's a hater. Plus she can't see worth a damn."

"Really, Rashad. Is that all you got?"

"It wasn't me, whatever she saw."

Kiara looked up in Rashad's eyes. "Well," she said, and shoved him backward into the kitchen counter, "I'm still waiting on you to prove that you're trustworthy, and until that happens you will see this very stressed Kiara Eason."

"Why you shove me?"

She smacked him across his face.

"This is just in case you've lied." She smacked him again. "And this is for taking me for granted." Her slaps annoyed Rashad, but he didn't flinch. He grabbed her around her waist and squeezed her into a hug. He felt guilty because he knew he'd done her wrong, but he wasn't ready to confess his sins.

"I don't mean to take you for granted, babe. And, forgive me for stressing you out. But you're not with just any man. I am considered a business pillar of this community, at least that's what I want to be. So I have big goals. To reach them, I must be on my grind. Yes, I work around pretty women. I do lunch with them. I treat them. But they're my clients. And don't forget, one reason I work so hard is for you. I'm trying to pay for our cruise trip that's coming up this fall. Another deposit is due."

Kiara decided to back down. She knew Rashad was trying to stay on her good side.

"How could I forget the cruise?"

"Babe, we both work so hard," he said in a tender voice. "Besides that, what else do we do? Don't you want to get out of Houston? Go get our sexy back?"

"Well, yes. I do, but—" Her throat clogged with hurt. Her spirit couldn't completely rest, no matter what he told her, but Kiara was weary of arguing. And as much as she asked her husband for the truth, it was a fact that many women who had issues with their men simply couldn't handle the truth even if they got it.

Truth demands decisions. Truth forces changes. Was Kiara ready for major changes, things that would totally affect her family life, if she had the truth?

Later that afternoon, Kiara told Rashad she had some business to take care of.

"No problem. Me and Myles gonna hang out. He wants me to help him plant seeds in the yard. Something he learned from his Cub Scout meeting."

"That's the type of thing I like to hear from my husband," she told him.

Kiara hopped in her car and drove until she reached a Chili's Grill & Bar that was closer to Adina's neighborhood.

They greeted each other and slid in a corner booth across from each other.

"What's up, my friend?" Adina asked.

"Girl, I did what you told me. I confronted him. He denied everything."

"Of course he would. Why would a cheater admit to something if you have no evidence? Or even when you do have evidence, it gets twisted into another convincing lie."

"So now my ass is back at square one."

"Not really," Adina said. She gave Kiara a pensive look. "I really hate that things had to come to this, but what the hell."

Adina retrieved a Kindle Fire.

"Damn." Kiara laughed. "Why did you bring that?"

"Because I knew one day it would come in handy." Adina powered it up and swiped the photos icon.

"I kind of held back some info from you, because I really wanted to protect your little heart. But since your husband is on some bullshit, shots are about to be fired," Adina told her. She held up the tablet in front of Kiara.

"Here. Look. Tell me what you see."

"That's Rashad. And he is kissing a woman." Kiara strained to get a better look.

"Girl, help me out."

Adina came and sat next to Kiara so she could take a closer look. "That's the fucking shirt I bought him for Father's Day a few years ago." She laughed. "That bastard lied his ass off. I'm glad I smacked his face." She looked closer. "Oh, shit. I know this woman. And she is not my husband's client." Kiara took a photo of the photo. "That's it. I deserve better. And I'm about to fucking get it."

Kiara drove home wiping tears from her eyes. But she dried them right before she pulled into the garage.

When she walked inside the house, she heard the sound of the television. Rashad and Myles were playing a video game.

"Hey, baby boy," she cooed, "why don't you go up to your room? I need to talk to your daddy. I won't take long."

"Awww, Mommy."

She gave Myles the look. He threw down the game controller and shot up the stairs.

Kiara calmly went to the master bedroom. She walked inside the custom closet. Rashad had installed the shelving when they first moved in.

"Too bad all that talent is such a waste," she said. Kiara reached up and yanked a few shirts from the rack on Rashad's side of the closet.

She stormed from the closet, went to the living room, stood in front of Rashad and held up his clothes.

"Watch this."

She walked to the hallway, and looked down at Rashad's suitcase. It was still sitting on the floor from when she first placed it there. She felt Rashad come up behind her. She bent down and dropped the shirts inside one by one.

Kiara went back to the closet.

Rashad was following right behind her.

"What are you doing?"

"Making myself happy."

"You are nuts."

"You better hope I don't kick you in your nuts."

She spotted a few pairs of his retro Air Jordans, gathered them in her arms, and went to toss them in the suitcase.

He just stared at her.

"I found out you lied about kissing that woman." She opened her cell phone and showed him her new screen saver: the photo of Rashad in a lip lock with Alexis.

"Every time you do something foul, I will throw your shit in this bag. The day it fills up is the day we're through."

Rashad began yelling at her and trying to get his stuff out of the luggage. She shoved him away and went to get a can of pest control spray. She squirted it all throughout the hallway.

Rashad started coughing and immediately left the room. Kiara knew he suffered allergic reactions to roach spray.

When Kiara went to work the next day, the first person she saw standing outside her office was Eddison. As usual, his dress style was impeccable. He wore a light brown suit. He held a large tan mug in his hands. She noticed steam rising from the cup and she detected the rich aroma of a cortado.

"Hello there."

"Eddison, really?"

After a tough night, his presence soothed her.

"As you can see, I am here to make sure your day starts out well. I wanted to pop in and say hello, make sure you're good."

"I'll be just fine."

She led him into her office and offered him a seat. He handed her the mug and she took a sip. It tasted delicious.

"Is everything okay? Can I do anything to help?"

"Eddison, you are like my knight. God knows I need that. But I gotta figure out a thing or two."

"Kiara, just say the word. I will help you in whatever way you need."

"I know you will. You're an amazing man."

"And I'm also trying to get you to reconsider helping my students."

"Look, thanks for the drink. You're such a sweetheart, but as far as these kids, I can't help you. I'd like to. But I can't."

"Can't or won't?"

She sighed and felt frustrated.

"Kiara, please reconsider. These are good kids. We don't want their future to be thrown away over this. If we help them, we can change the direction of their lives."

She chuckled and set down her drink.

"I knew you'd do it." He reached out and squeezed her hand. "Thanks, I owe you."

"You owe me nothing."

"I do owe you. I will pay you back . . . with dividends." He stood up.

"I'll be in touch, Eddison, plus I think we need to have a conversation."

"Let me know when you're ready."

She waved bye to him and watched him swagger down the hallway.

"Lord have mercy, that could be mine one day."

She knew Eddison had her back and it was likely she was going to need him very soon.

But now she had to focus on the business at hand. She had an important mission that day. But it wouldn't take place for another hour or so, when Alexis was scheduled to arrive at work.

Her cell phone began ringing. It was Rashad. She put his call into voice mail. He was the last person she felt like dealing with right then.

Kiara yearned to be comforted. She was afraid that her marriage was over. And she had to explore other options. She closed her eyes and thought about that dream that she recently had. It seemed so real. She imagined herself in Eddison's arms again. He made her feel so safe. He was all about the details. And his bringing a coffee seemed so little, but it meant so much.

Alexis texted her and told her she'd be in at nine-thirty. Kiara did not respond. But when her administrative assistant showed up at work, Kiara was waiting for her at her desk.

"Put your things away and come see me."

"Yes, ma'am."

Kiara went to her office. Confronting Alexis would be the most difficult conversation she'd ever had with a woman.

Alexis was there in minutes and immediately shut the door. Her eyes were filled with tears. She couldn't believe how much of her tears lately had been caused by other females. Something had to give.

"Oh, Mrs. Eason. I think I know why you want to see me."

Kiara's cell phone was face-up on her desk, her screen saver clearly visible. Alexis saw the photo of her and Rashad kissing. She started trembling.

"I feel terrible," she said. "That picture is old. I was young and stupid. Have you ever done something you regretted?"

"Before you get started, don't. This isn't about you. He could have slept with any whore. If it ain't one, it's another."

"Excuse me? Okay. I-I—"

"I only called you in here just to let you know that I know. I do not approve. Both of you ought to have known better; especially Rashad."

"I'm so sorry."

"That changes nothing. I want to kill you, but what good will it do?"

"It'll never happen again, I swear."

"I hope you mean that." Kiara stared at her. "And now I'm going to sit back . . . and watch how you'll be dealing with this situation. That's it. You can go now."

"I still have a job?"

"Alexis, please get out of my face and close the door when you leave."

Kiara trembled with anger after Alexis fled her office. She was angry and felt so stupid. She wondered how many times Alexis laughed at her behind her back. She wanted to fire the girl, but she knew she had to walk a very thin line as far as the legal implications of her situation.

Alexis's hands were shaking as she left Kiara's office. The event that had just happened really messed with her mind. In fact, she went back to her desk, expecting to get an email or a phone call from Kiara or HR, but none of her worst fears were realized. It was difficult to concentrate on her work the rest of the morning.

Right before lunch, she couldn't take it anymore. She trekked down that long hallway and stepped inside Kiara's office. Her back was turned. She was on the phone talking in a loud whisper.

Alexis stood and listened.

"You need to be getting you some business, Rashad, because I'm sure enough about to get some."

A pause.

"Blame yourself. You got the rest of the day to think long and hard about what you've done."

Kiara slammed down the phone.

Alexis started to turn around and discreetly leave, but Kiara saw her before she could flee.

"I really need to remember to close my door. Did you need something, Alexis?"

"May I have a word with you?" Alexis closed the door and took a deep breath. "You may not believe me, you may hate my guts, but I've wanted to tell you, but he said not to tell."

"And of course, you do whatever he says."

"No. I don't."

"Your actions suggest otherwise, because you never went out of your way to let me know you were fucking him."

"But I wanted to. I just didn't know how. I had never done it before. I didn't know when to bring it up—"

"How could you do it?"

"To be honest, when I met him I had no idea he was married. He never wore a wedding ring."

That part was true. Due to the nature of his work, Rashad almost severed his ring finger when his hand got jammed up in some construction machinery. After a couple close calls, he decided to stop wearing his band and Kiara agreed.

"Oh, that only tells me that if a man doesn't wear a wedding ring, then he definitely won't wear a condom."

Alexis gasped. She hoped she didn't know about the baby. "I, um—"

"Where'd you do it with him? No, don't answer. What does it matter at this point?" Kiara stared curiously at the young, stupid woman, the pretty princess who always looked like she was in control.

"What he did was his choice. But, Alexis, make no mistake. He didn't rape you. It takes two consenting adults to do what you did."

"You're right. He didn't twist my arm." Alexis stood awkwardly in front of her boss. "But I promise you, it wasn't intentional. Not deviously done."

"How long did you sneak around with him?"

"Um . . . too long."

"What did he tell you about me? He said I was a wife that didn't meet his needs? That I was terrible in bed? That I didn't understand him like you did?"

"He wouldn't really talk that much about you—"

Kiara rolled her eyes. "Please. I don't believe that. And I don't want to hear it. Why torture myself any further? The damage is done." She sniffed and couldn't believe she was having this conversation. "Life goes on. And in case you're wondering, you still have a job."

"I do? Oh, thank you, thank you, Mrs. Eason."

"Don't thank me yet, Alexis. Now, is there anything else you need to say?"

Alexis wondered if Rashad had told Kiara about Hayley, but knowing him, the answer was a big "hell no."

"No, ma'am. I have nothing more to say."

* * *

Alexis drove around during her lunch hour. Eating was the last thing on her mind. All she could do was ponder what had just happened. God knows she didn't know what she'd do if she were in Kiara's shoes. If she was a wife would she stay? Would she go? Never in a million years did Alexis think she'd end up living the life she had. If she could turn back the hands of time, what would have happened if she hadn't met Rashad, fallen in love with him, a love so deep that it turned her into a woman that she didn't want to face in the mirror?

On the day she found out she was having a baby, Alexis wondered if she could pin the pregnancy on another man. But it wasn't in her heart to do such a thing. She was twenty. Had never married. Yet she was in love with a man who went home to another woman every night.

When she decided to inform him, Alexis sat on top of Rashad, facing him with her legs clamped around his waist as she grinded on him. Skin touching skin. Moans. Pleasure mixed with pain. He was holding her by her luscious hips lost in the world of forbidden love that took place behind locked doors.

"Damn, baby, I love how you give it to me," he said.

She moaned and tilted her neck back, wanting that good feeling to last forever.

"I love it too. I-I love you, Rashad."

"I love you, too."

"And I'm having a baby."

He opened one eye and cocked an eyebrow.

"You're having a what?"

"I'm pregnant."

"You sure?"

"I wouldn't tell you this if I weren't."

His face looked transfixed, like he was trying to understand.

"Hey now, that's dope."

"You sure?"

"Yeah, baby, I'm sure. But you can't tell anybody."

And from that day on, Rashad Eason quietly bought everything Hayley needed. He was all for Glynis watching the child during the week. He committed his weekends to seeing the child. He was worried that her premature birth was his fault. But when Hayley eventually rallied and got stronger and bigger and healthier, he was relieved and on top of the world. He fell more in love with Hayley and he knew her existence would kill Kiara. But Rashad's heart couldn't give up his child, not after he'd already held her and bonded with the precious being. His love had to protect her. She was his everything. So he would do all he could financially to care for Hayley, but no, Kiara would never have to know about her. And he trusted Alexis enough to know she wouldn't tell, either. He encouraged her to find employment elsewhere, and she applied for other positions, but nothing ever came through. So she remained in Kiara's department and tried to play it cool. She continued to fuck her boss's husband and tried not to let it all bother her. But in the back of Alexis's mind, she always wondered what would happen if Kiara ever found out.

During the lunch hour, Alexis tried to gather her strength. Although she previously thought she wanted her boss to know about the affair, now that it was out in the open, Alexis didn't feel any better. But she decided to try to act like everything was okay. She didn't want to make a bigger mess of things by constantly harping on the affair.

Later on, Alexis knocked on Kiara's door and carried in two big boxes.

"These came earlier for you. I'm just now remembering to bring them."

Kiara stared at Alexis. Although she wanted to claw out her eyeballs, Kiara had a reputation to think about. She was a well-known woman at the university and she couldn't jeopardize everything she'd established by unleashing violence on her subordinate.

She had to play things out smarter.

Kiara opened up one box. It was from Nordstrom. She removed its contents and stared at the two stunning strapless maxi dresses she'd ordered online.

"Wow, aren't these pretty?"

"T-they are gorgeous," Alexis said.

"They're supposed to be for our anniversary cruise. Happy fucking anniversary to me," Kiara sang as she held up one dress to inspect it.

Alexis didn't say a word. She quietly slipped away from the office. But Kiara didn't notice.

A pair of brown leather sandals were also in the package. Pricey and chic. She tried them on and they fit perfectly.

"This sure brightens up my day," she said and glanced around, only to realize she was talking to herself.

Embarrassed, she put down the shoes and ripped open the other Nordstrom delivery. This box looked exactly like the other one. When she tore back the shipping bubble wrap, she noticed that the same two maxi dresses and pair of shoes were inside the box. The dresses were exactly like the ones she ordered, but the shoes were white leather.

"What the hell? Why did they send me two sets? They better not have charged me for this expensive stuff."

When Kiara reviewed the order slip, she realized that someone had made a mistake. She got two shipments for the price of one.

"Hallelujah. What a blessing."

When her conscience whispered it would be deceitful to keep the extra items, she shrugged it off.

"God is good all the time. Even when someone else fucks up."

A few days later, Rashad stopped by TSWU to see his wife. Kiara had been giving him the cold shoulder at home ever since she let him know that she'd had a conversation with Alexis. He tried to assure her that it was a one-time thing. She shot back, "It better be." Now he wanted to smooth things over with Kiara by showing her that he could be a good husband.

And he knew he'd have to be more careful. When he passed by Alexis's desk, they discreetly acknowledged each other. Alexis knew the deal. Previously, when he came by the office, she pretended like she didn't know him. But she really had to play her position now.

Kiara was in her office in the middle of a conversation with Nicole when Rashad interrupted them.

"Hi, babe," she sweetly replied to her husband, not wanting Nicole to know her personal business.

"I was in the area. What's going on? You ate already?"

"Yep. I'm good."

As he stood there making small talk, Kiara knew he was trying to gauge her attitude. Of course, he wanted her to be forgiving. And Kiara was so happy that Rashad couldn't read her mind.

He is a sonofabitch that was willing to jeopardize our marriage over pussy. Kiara felt robbed. Why should he have all the fun while she just stood around and accepted it?

She didn't want Rashad to make a fool out of her. She wanted to make a fool out of him. And she could do it a number of ways.

Kiara decided she had no reason to feel guilty about Eddison anymore. She was ready to let him make a move on her any way he pleased. But first she had to handle Rashad. He must pay for his betrayal.

She glanced at her husband, then stared at Nicole.

"Rashad, can you do me a big favor and set up an appointment to go see Nicole's place this weekend? She really needs some help and I told her how you're talented and efficient and wouldn't mind helping her."

Her question caught him off guard. "Are you serious? Um, these days I'm really swamped."

"But you'd be more than happy to squeeze in your wife's colleague who'd really appreciate your help, right?"

Nicole grimaced as if she didn't enjoy being the topic of their conversation.

"I-I um—"

"You were saying?" Kiara asked. "Nicole, look for Rashad to contact you soon so he may assess the work needed and give you an estimate."

In the back of Kiara's mind, she wondered if Rashad would make any moves on Nicole. Kiara sized up her employee and figured right away that Nicole wasn't on her level. She couldn't imagine him being attracted to a woman like her. But even if he flirted, it would prove that cheating was in him and that Alexis wasn't just a one-time fling.

At the end of the week, Kiara met with Eddison in his office. She decided she'd hear him out and be as professional as possible.

"Thanks for taking time out of your schedule for this important cause."

Eddison placed a packet of papers in her hand. "Meet Collette and Gherman. They're sophomores. English majors. They're both from inner city families. First-generation college students."

He proceeded to tell her how the students got themselves in trouble that included an alleged sex tape, a video uploading that went viral, and accusations of the invasion of some college roommate's privacy.

Kiara felt instantly concerned.

"Some kids are immature and don't think before they do certain things," Kiara remarked. "And these pranks they pull just amaze me. It never should have gotten this far."

"I agree. Collette and Gherman received a dozen death threats. Of course, they're both black, which has a lot of the black student body really riled up. They feel Collette and Gherman are not being treated fairly, so racial tensions are high. Anywhere, here's where you come in."

Eddison leaned in and outlined to Kiara a course of action the kids could take so that they'd be reinstated, a pending lawsuit could be dropped, and the negative publicity the school received could be alleviated.

"Now that those two are out of the way, what are we going to do about us two?" Eddison asked.

They were totally alone. He had a corner office on the fourth floor of his building. They could look out of the window and see a cluster of oak trees and people walking across the campus.

Eddison stood up and went to close the door. Then he whispered, "Come here."

He looked so good. His locs were freshly moisturized and he smelled like sandalwood.

She got up and followed. He walked into a lavatory

that was only accessible through his office. It was a private bathroom. There were no windows. Once Kiara was inside, he shut the door. It was now completely dark. The room only had a toilet and a tiny sink and a small counter. Their noses were practically touching as they stood face-to-face. She could hear him breathing.

"This feels naughty," Kiara whispered.

"Not as naughty as this." His arms clasped about her. He pulled Kiara into his arms. They instantly started kissing.

"Oh, Eddison." She trembled. She hugged him back, then rubbed her fingers through his hair. It felt like Eddison was hers and she loved that feeling. Being close to him and sensing his body heat only made Kiara hotter. He felt around for her blouse. Soon his fingers were struggling to undo the buttons.

She helped him. His lips were on her breasts. She lifted them up so he could suck them.

She felt herself getting wet. She could imagine all the people walking past the building they were in, going to and from class, while she was hidden away with a man that she liked, getting her freak on.

Before she could think about it, Kiara unzipped Eddison's pants. He didn't stop her. She grabbed his penis. It was rock hard. She knelt on her knees and took him in her mouth.

"Oh, my fucking God."

She got him off, and hearing him moan turned her on. She grabbed his hand and pushed it toward her panties.

"Pull them to the side for me."

Then she heard a light knock on the door.

"Mr. Osborne?"

Kiara started to yelp, but Eddison's hands covered her mouth.

The knock grew louder. "Are you in there?"

He quietly reached back and locked the door of the lavatory.

"I'm using the restroom. Can you come back later?" It was the department office assistant. She was a clueless young lady who wasn't bothered by closed doors.

"Okay, I just needed a signature for an invoice that needs to be paid. And I brought you your mail, too."

"I'll sign it. Leave it there. Thanks."

Once it was completely quiet, Kiara could breathe evenly again. It was so dark she was glad Eddison couldn't see her face. But even if he could, he'd know for sure that Kiara was happy that she was with him. And she couldn't wait until they did it again.

Chapter 8

Nicole Greene couldn't believe it. She took a long look around her house and wanted to pinch herself.

I did it. I escaped Alabama. I'm in Texas. Life begins again.

It was the first Saturday in June and Nicole woke up early. She hummed as she unloaded the last of the boxes that she'd packed up when she relocated. A do rag was tied around her head. She wore no makeup and her feet were bare. She placed water glasses, casserole dishes, and pots and pans in the cheap wooden cupboards.

When her cell phone rang suddenly, her heart beat wildly. She picked up the phone and didn't recognize the number.

She saw that the caller left a voice mail, but when she listened to it, she just heard breathing, normal breathing, but no words.

Somewhat alarmed, Nicole decided to block the number from ever calling her again. She couldn't take any chances.

All in all, things were looking up. She had a job at a good school and she was eager to start her life over. And that day she patiently waited for Rashad Eason to show up. Her house didn't look or feel like a home just yet and she was praying that with his help, she'd one day feel totally safe and satisfied with her brand-new surroundings.

Hours later, Rashad and Nicole were seated at her spindly wooden dinette set which she had bought at a flea market.

"Sorry about the wobbly legs."

"No need to apologize. I know the struggle."

She grabbed a notepad and a pen.

"I want this, this, and this done. I can only pay with installments. Is that all right?"

"Don't even sweat it. I've done my assessment and I can do the job in four months or maybe a little longer. It just depends how fast I can get in the supplies."

"That'll work. I'm so excited. I signed a two-year lease and I want to see a place of beauty while I live here."

"I'm the right person for the job. Now what time do you get off every day?"

"At five."

"You should ask my wife if you can report to work at seven, take a half-hour lunch, and leave at three-thirty a few days a week. That way I can meet you at your spot at four and do a few hours' worth of work in the evening."

"You think she'll be okay with that?"

"I think so. She's the one who suggested I work with you."

"She must really trust you."

"What you mean by that?"

Nicole didn't respond. She pushed her glasses up her nose, and offered him bottled water.

Her refrigerator door was covered with colorful magnets from all over the country: Florida, Denver, St. Louis, Chicago, Los Angeles, and New Orleans.

Rashad asked Nicole, "You like to travel?"

"M-my ex used to travel a lot. He brought these back to me."

"Where is he now?"

"I-I have no idea. I-I—"

"Hey, my bad. Just making conversation."

"Well, make the conversation. Don't let the conversation make you."

The sassy tone of her voice stirred him. From then on, Rashad observed Nicole through different eyes. She wasn't much to look at, but her spunky presence intrigued him.

The more time he spent in her house, the more relaxed he felt. He started working there right away. As they agreed, when it was time for Rashad to start the project, he'd give her a day's notice and she'd make sure to leave work at three-thirty the next day. Sometimes she cooked while Rashad worked. Nicole felt very comfortable tossing and dicing vegetables in a Crock-Pot while she watched Rashad do his thing. And she could tell that Rashad was a hard worker. His crew consisted of two other men who'd help out. Other times he came alone.

"You're a genius," Nicole told Rashad. Temperatures were sizzling outside. She wore a halter top that showed off her bare upper arms and shoulders, both of which were lined with henna body art. She hung around in the kitchen and admired the way he was doing prep work to refinish the cupboards. "Men who work with their hands are like so smart and talented to me. You have a gift. And Ms. Kiara wasn't exaggerating. You are good at what you do."

Rashad blushed. "Oh, it's nothing."

"And you're modest."

He'd been called a lot of things, but "modest" wasn't one of them.

When Nicole would cook, she was too bashful to ask
Rashad if he wanted something to eat. But as she became more comfortable with him, she felt adventurous.
She stirred the food in the pot and asked Rashad if he
wanted a taste.

He nodded. She dipped the spoon and filled it. He
opened his mouth and she gently pushed the food inside
until it disappeared.

"Mmm, it's good." He smacked his lips. "What the
hell is it?"

"Just a little something I threw together. I created my
own special seasonings but it's a secret. You like it? It
tastes good?"

"Some things look better than they taste, and some
things taste better than they look."

They locked eyes. Nicole changed the conversation.

"Have you ever seen John Legend in concert?"

"He's dope. He puts on a good show."

"I wish I could do fun stuff like going to concerts."

"Why don't you?"

"I-I just haven't."

"You that shy? Nahhh, you not shy. If you feel cool
around somebody, you open up."

She smiled and nodded and began pouring out her
heart to Rashad, telling him about all her dreams and
wishes for her life.

"I've had it hard in the past. Every day was filled
with uncertainty. I worked my ass off to get my degree
and I held down a job at the same time. Studying was
tough and I didn't know if I was ever going to make it.
And the situation with my ex didn't help. He was on the
wrong side of the law, if you know what I mean. But
since I've been in Texas, I have a feeling things are about
to change for the better." She smiled at Rashad. And he
smiled back.

* * *

The next day when he came over, Nicole tried a new recipe.

She beat the chocolate batter with an electric mixer till it was light and fluffy. She scraped the bowl with her spoon. It was batter for a berries and cookies cake.

"Here," she said. "Lick this and tell me if it tastes good." He looked at her and immediately opened his mouth. He hungrily licked the spoon.

"You like that?" she asked.

"Nope."

"What?"

"Just kidding. I love it. It's sweet. And tasty. You're good with your hands, too, Nicky."

That's what he started calling her soon after he started working at her home. Kiara knew he'd accepted the job to do some remodeling at Nicole's. So far she couldn't tell if anything had jumped off between them. Rashad became more diligent about acting like he was on the up-and-up, and actually, compared to times past, he was on his best behavior. He kept decent working hours, except occasionally he'd be gone for long stretches on Sunday. But his seemingly changed ways didn't fool Kiara. She knew her husband, and knew he could revert to his old ways. So she kept his luggage front and center in their hallway, ready to deposit more of his belongings in it if necessary.

Meanwhile, throughout the month of June, the more time Rashad spent at Nicole's, the comfier they became with each other. She let him bring his iPod and he hooked it up to her speakers so he could listen to his favorites: August Alsina, Kendrick Lamar, J. Cole, and Childish Gambino.

"Oh, you kickin' it with my favs," she said and started swerving to the music as if she was at a concert.

"I like just about everybody out here . . . except that punk-ass Trey Songz. He's suspect."

"I hate him with his goat-sounding ass. Oh na na na." Rashad started making howling noises and pretended like he was baying at the moon. "America, you know I have to pop that corn."

"Pop that corn? You're so silly, Rashad."

They fell out laughing and Nicole couldn't remember the last time she had such a fun, relaxing day. The good time she was having helped to erase the memories of what she had suffered in Alabama.

Rashad worked while Nicole kept him company, asking him questions. She was starting to become attracted to him. Of course, in her head, the good ones were always taken. But she wanted to get inside his head and see what type of man he was.

"How long you been married?"

"Where'd that question come from?"

"I don't know. Just asking."

He told her, "A decade."

"Cool. I've always wanted to get married," she said in a dreamy voice. "I heard that a woman is supposed to let the man find her, but in this Gabrielle Union era, in which a woman falls in love with a man who's legally married; well, she waited on him till *he* officially became hers. She showed me that a woman must take charge to get who she wants."

"Is that right?" He grinned. "Okay then, Gabby," he teased.

"Here's another one for you. What was it about Kiara that made you want to wife her? Like, were you attracted to her personality? Was she an excellent cook? Or was it all about her big booty? I've always wanted to know what characteristics a chick must have to get a decent husband."

He could only laugh at her curiosity. "No two men and women are just alike. Different people have different needs and wants."

As a habit, Rashad seldom liked talking about his and his wife's relationship, especially with a chick that he wanted to smash. And at that point, he'd seriously wondered what it would be like to make love to Nicole.

"So you're not going to answer my specific question about Kiara?"

"Some stuff you don't need to know."

"How come?"

Rashad wasn't ready to tell Nicole that she possessed several characteristics that made him want to have sex with her. He loved the way she talked, he admired her sexy shape, and he appreciated the way she made him feel. At times, Nicole would stare at him while he worked and that let him know she was impressed with him.

"Hello? I'm talking to youuuuuuu!"

He decided to act like he was busy concentrating. She stared at him, then changed the subject to a lighter topic.

"What are your favorite cartoons? And don't try to deny it 'cause you look just like a nigga that watches cartoons."

"Yeah, right."

He wanted to laugh because when he had time he did like watching the *Teenage Mutant Ninja Turtles* and *Sonic Boom* with Myles.

The more they chatted, the deeper they bonded. Rashad could see himself with her.

And after working awhile, he told her, "Hey, you busy? Nah, you not. Come with me."

Nicole asked no questions. She grabbed her purse, cell phone, and keys and locked her front door. He opened the passenger door of his van and waited for her to hop inside.

"Excuse the mess."

"No need. I know you an important business man."

She sat next to him on the passenger side. She liked that he was in the driver's seat. He drove respectfully, unlike a lot of fools out on the streets who wanted to show off. To Nicole, Rashad was a real man. He was so different from her ex, who was several years younger than she was.

"So you just gone get in the car with a strange man and not even question where he's taking you?"

"You're not strange. And I trust you."

When was the last time my wife said she trusted me, he asked himself.

Rashad drove till they ended up at Harbor Freight Tools.

"You ever been here?"

"Nope."

"Good. You'll love it."

They walked in side by side. For the second time in her life, Nicole felt like she was a wife. She noticed other people looking at them and she enjoyed the attention she got from being with Rashad. Her ex used to make her feel that way in the beginning, but they never made it down the aisle.

As soon as she and Rashad stepped inside the door-way of the store, Nicole frowned. This place had the look and feel of a large dollar store, but it smelled of sawdust . . . steel . . . plastic . . . and men.

"All I see are tools and equipment and a bunch of guys acting like they're in a sex toys shop."

Rashad laughed.

"Harbor Freights is to men what the Michael Kors Outlet is to women."

"Whatever, dude."

She walked with him, never leaving his side, while he

searched for packages of nuts and bolts, a drill holster, and a cordless jigsaw.

"What's all this for?"

"Stuff I need so I can do the best job for my favorite VIP."

She didn't hide the smile that his words put on her face.

When they got back to Nicole's, Rashad took the purchased items out of the shopping bag. He tossed some nuts and bolts in his tool belt. He placed his hands on his hips and glanced down at his slacks.

"It's amazing how something so small . . . so light-weight, and so pointy has so much *power*."

Nicole stared at the front of his pants then burst out laughing.

"I'm talking about this here nail." He grinned and held out his hand. "I see what type of mind you got, miss lady."

For the first time since Alexis and Rashad started hooking up, he became noticeably less available. Although she feared it might have to do with Kiara finding out about the affair, he only told her he "needed to take care of home." But Alexis had a lot of pride. She felt something in her bones. And even though she promised herself not to stay involved with Rashad unless it had to do with Hayley, her jealous nature told her to check his ass and find out what was happening.

Playing her position was starting to get old.

Rashad was painting in Nicole's bedroom when Alexis called. Normally he wouldn't answer, but he did this time.

"Yo, wassup?"

"You. I was just calling to see what you're doing."

"You know me. Always working."

"I figured that," she responded, lying her butt off. "What job are you doing now? That same one you've been working on?"

Usually Rashad offered Alexis all the details on the projects he had. But he never specifically told her he was helping Nicole.

"Yep. That's where I am, doing that little fixer-upper."

"The baby needs some new things. Maybe I can come to where you are and hang out," she told him, just to see what he'd say.

"If you need money, I will find time to drop it off. But you coming here, uh, no, that's not dope."

"Why not? You've let me do it before."

"This client is always here. That would be unprofessional."

"Oh, okay." She sounded disappointed. "We miss you. Haven't seen you in a minute."

"You can thank Kiara for that. She tries to keep her foot on my neck. Why'd you have to admit that we did it? Don't you know how to lie?"

"What? I know that you aren't blaming all this on me."

He heard the anger in her voice. "Look, no. I don't blame you, babe." He thought about Alexis. Up until recently, she really had been a discreet lover.

"You've been really cool throughout about everything. I will make it up to you. I can come see you but we gotta be real careful, now more than ever. Kiara acts like she is one step away from kicking me out the house. And I won't put up with that. I put too much money in our house to be thrown out. So let me figure out something for us. Stay strong."

The next day, when Rashad was working at Nicole's, he took a quick look around her bedroom. She only had a twin-size bed. He noticed how the small mattress dipped in the middle.

"That can't be fun to sleep on," he said, pointing to her bed.

"Yeah, it feels like a damned hammock."

"We gotta fix that."

"How?"

"I know people."

The next day, he had a friend help him move a queen-size bed, frame, and mattress into her house.

"It's been a long time since anyone did something this nice for me." She choked up. "I'm so grateful. And I owe you."

"No need. We straight," he said, playing it off.

She ran and bounced on the bed and squealed at how tight and sturdy the mattress felt. She settled on her back and felt happier than she'd been in a long time.

"Yep." She nodded. "We are straight. For real."

She closed her eyes and before she knew it, she nodded off on her new bed. Rashad silently stared at Nicole. Her chest rose and fell as she slept. He walked over to the bed and admired the peaceful look on her face. He took a chance and opened up her dresser drawers. He found a blue blanket and spread it over her.

"Bye, Nicky," he said, and closed the door. He knew he had more work to do but he needed to drive over to Lowe's. He knew where Nicole kept her spare house key. He quietly slipped it in his pants pocket and left, locking the door behind him.

Chapter 9

It was the last weekend in June, only four weeks since Nicole had begun working in the communications department. She was getting acclimated to the city and was feeling like she made the right choice by moving to Houston and especially in accepting the new job. She enjoyed her work and had fun interviewing students and filming feature stories about their college lives.

That Saturday, Kiara had to work on a project that required some of her staff to film a very professional and costly video for Texas South West University's fall orientation. Rashad decided, since his wife would be gone all day, he might as well stop by at Nicole's.

"Hey, you," he said when he walked in her house.

"How'd you get in here?"

"I used my key."

"You used your key? Since when did I give you a key?"

"Since you accidentally let me know you leave an extra one under the welcome rug. That's dangerous, by the way. You don't want just any man coming in your house, do you?"

"No, Rashad. I don't want just any man coming in my house."

They locked eyes. He felt she could see straight into his heart. He wasn't sure if he liked that or not. He broke the stare and started removing paintbrushes.

"I thought I'd get started on the bathroom. Is that cool?"

"Anything you wanna do is fine with me."

"Is that right?"

"That's very right."

"So why you don't have a man?"

"Excuse me? What you talking about, Rashad?"

"I kind of noticed that no man is ever over here. Anything that needs a man's touch, you always have me doing it. So don't be offended if it seems like I'm judging. But am I right?"

"You're right. Since I've moved here I haven't really met anyone. Haven't had time. But I know it won't always be that way."

"What kind of man you looking for?"

"You want to know the truth?"

"Give me the truth. I can handle it."

She giggled. "I like a jack-of-all trades. A man who is responsible and can get things done. Someone who is smart and athletic. A man's man, though, you know what I mean? He should only bat for one team."

"I hear you. Anything else?"

"Love mustaches. I love thick lips." She canvassed Rashad's entire face while she talked. "I am crazy about beautiful, dreamy eyes and nice hair. And he should be on the right side of the law. That's a must-have."

"Sounds like you describing me."

She simply grinned.

"You like me, Nicky?" His voice was husky. "Be honest."

"I-I um . . ."

"It's okay. You don't have to be scared of hurting my feelings. Maybe I don't even compare to that dude you left behind in Alabama."

"No, there is no comparison. He was hot, but I'll admit you are much, much hotter than him."

Rashad suddenly grabbed Nicole's chin between his hands. "You shitting me?"

"No, I mean it. You are exactly the type of man I've been praying for."

"Hmmm, word?"

Nicole stared lustfully at Rashad's lips. The corners of his mouth turned into dimples when he smiled. She could tell by the way he carried himself that he had mad bedroom skills. She'd already dreamt about him being on top of her, making love to her, and holding her in his arms. Maybe she was wrong for fantasizing about her boss's husband, but what woman in her right mind would knowingly send her good-looking, talented man into a single chick's house?

Nicole wondered why Kiara never came over to her house unannounced like a normal wife would. That alone let her know Kiara wasn't normal. She trusted Rashad too much.

That's her problem . . . and it will be the cause of her heartbreak.

The next day was Sunday. Kiara had an important project to finish and made a decision to go straight into work. Work gave her peace when home didn't feel right. Kiara got dressed and caught Rashad eating in the kitchen that morning. She knew he was about to leave the house himself so he could do some contracting work.

"Hey, Rashad," she greeted him. "I don't wanna take Myles to the office with me today. So you gotta take him with you."

"Huh? Nope, that ain't happening. I got a lot to do and he'd just be in the way."

"He will be quiet and will leave you alone. Just make sure and bring plenty of snacks, some LEGO toys, and his books."

"Even if I did all that, I'd still feel like I was baby-sitting."

"I don't care what you feel like. He's yours too and today you're going to *babysit.*" Kiara grabbed her purse and keys and ran to the garage. Rashad yelled after her but she ignored him. The next thing he knew, his wife was gone. She had never just up and left Myles with him on a Sunday. He loved his son, but he didn't like the trick Kiara pulled on him.

"This is some bull. She's just trying to keep tabs on me."

Rashad finished eating his cereal. His mind raced in a thousand directions. He actually wasn't working anywhere that day. This particular Sunday was dedicated to Hayley. Alexis was waiting on him. And he promised her that he'd come through to take them to a water park the minute it opened.

Just as he was thinking about how he was going to break his promise, Alexis texted him. He had recently purchased a smart watch that he could use to communicate with her. It resembled a regular watch and he hoped it would be safer than using his regular cell phone.

U up? I'm excited.

He texted back.

We got a little prob.

What?

He went out to the garage to make sure Kiara was really gone. Then he decided to call Alexis.

"Myles is with me today."

"Are you serious? What are we going to do? We can't cancel."

"Hayley won't even know if we cancelled."

"But I would. We'll just have to bring your son with us."

"No fucking way. I don't want to do that."

"She's his sister."

"I know that, but this isn't a good way to announce all that. He didn't ask for this."

She was stonily quiet and he knew he'd hurt her. It was something he didn't want to do and he hated when it happened anyway.

"I think I know how to handle this. Get ready. We're about to come over to your place right now."

He woke up Myles and fixed him a quick bowl of cereal. Then they were on their way. But instead of going up to Alexis's door and knocking, he stayed in the car as it idled a few houses away from hers. When she was ready to leave in her own ride, he discreetly started driving to the far north side. He made a phone call as Alexis drove behind him.

When Rashad arrived at Glynis's house, he took Myles with him and rang her doorbell. Rashad was so nervous. He knew how Glynis felt about him, but he needed a huge favor.

"Hello there, Glynis. I know this is short notice, but can you please watch my child today? Just for half a day."

She observed Myles and smiled. "He's a cutie. Go on in, son."

"Thank you. You are so cool to do this—"

She rolled her eyes and snapped. "It's gonna cost you extra."

"Name your price."

He went into the house to find Myles and explained that the nice stranger would be his sitter for the day. He could barely look the boy in his eyes. He felt like crap but didn't have time to figure out a better plan. When Rashad got his son preoccupied with Glynis in a back room filled with toys, he quietly picked up his baby girl, gathered her things, and hurried out the house.

He was going to tuck Hayley into his car but decided against it. He let Alexis do the usual securing of their daughter. Then they were on their way.

All while he was driving, he kept thinking of Myles. He decided to use his main cell phone to make another quick call.

"Hello? Are my eyes deceiving me?" she said.

"Very funny."

"You never call me on Sunday morning like this. What's up? Have you decided what to do with Myles?"

"Um, yeah. That's what I wanted to talk to you about." He hesitated. "Kiara, I really am gonna be tied up today. So I found a sitter for him."

"A sitter? Who?"

"It's this lady I know."

"You left my child with a strange woman? What the hell, Rashad? Are you out your mind?"

"Uh, naw."

"Who is she? Do I know her?"

"No, but she watches kids. She has an in-house day care." Already he felt like he had told his wife too much. He instantly regretted telling her.

"But don't worry. He's in good hands. And it's just for this one time."

"Rashad, I swear to God I don't know what the hell is going on with you but I smell something foul. I know one thing, you better not be fucking this woman, whoever she is."

Kiara felt that even if they both had to work on Sunday, Rashad could do his part in taking care of Myles occasionally if she had to work too. She was trying to trust him, but she never would've guessed he'd leave their child with a 'sitter' that she didn't know.

"I swear to God I'm not doing anything with her," he explained. "It's nothing like that."

"Then I want to meet her. I want to know who the hell you got—"

He hung up. He texted her.

Sorry, I'm in a dead zone.

Kiara texted back.

U gone be dead all right

An hour or so later, Kiara was busy at work when her phone rang again. She looked at the caller ID. It was Rashad.

"Hello?"

She didn't hear him say anything. All she heard was a loud sloshing noise.

She kept listening and saying hello. She quickly realized his cell phone had accidentally dialed her. From the noise it was making, it sounded like his phone was in his pocket.

"At least I know I'm the last person he talked to since he butt-dialed me." Kiara started to disconnect the call, but she kept holding on. She worked and listened. After a while, she heard voices.

A little kid squealing and chirping.

"What the hell?"

Her stomach hollowed out as if she were riding a roller coaster. "What the hell is he doing? Whose kid is that?"

The more she listened, the more she felt like she couldn't breathe. She listened until she heard him speaking into his phone.

"Hello? Hello?"

"Where are you, Rashad?"

"Did you call me?"

"No, fool. Your phone called me." She paused. "I heard everything."

"So?"

"Rashad, I'm going to ask you one more time. Where are you?"

"You heard kids' voices?"

"Yes, and it wasn't Myles."

"I told you the babysitter owns a day care."

She fell silent, wondering if he was telling the truth and questioning if he wasn't, what was the truth?

"I hope you aren't lying to me."

"I'm not. For real. She does own a day care." He paused. "How much did you hear?"

"Rashad, something isn't right. Why don't I know about this lady? What's her name?"

"That ain't important."

"Why do you continually hide things from me?" She felt like a hypocrite when she said those words, but her fear made her not care. "Rashad, there you go again; leaving out everything about you that I need to know."

"Look, woman. The only person that should know everything about me . . . is God."

And he hung up. If Kiara had no proof about his actions, she shouldn't be so pissed off.

That's why Rashad made sure to give himself a little bit of physical distance between himself and Alexis while they were at the park.

Alexis stood nearby listening to the entire conversation. She could tell Hayley was having fun because of her screams of laughter whenever she played with her in the water.

She was glad for her daughter. But she noticed that Rashad seemed so distracted. His body was there, his mind was elsewhere.

"So you had to lie and make up something to Kiara about what you're doing, Rashad?"

"You know how it goes. We've been doing it this way all along."

Alexis nodded. She could hear a voice telling her, *Be careful what you sign up for.* Mona Hooker constantly reminded her to know her worth as a woman. She begged Alexis to understand that she never had to settle for less than what she could be having with a better man, a gentleman. The seeds her mother had planted inside her were starting to develop.

"I know it looks like you're ashamed of your flesh and blood. You barely played with Hayley while you're here, and you dumped your son off so you could hide him from his sister. And you keep walking two steps ahead of me at this fucking water park." She stared at the man whom she felt she loved. "In this arrangement, none of us are getting the respect we deserve."

"Oh, okay, how about this?" Rashad pointedly grabbed her hand. He let little Hayley walk in the middle of her parents. He grabbed her hand, too. They all started walking down the gravel sidewalk, enjoying the breeze of the palm trees.

"Better now? You like this?"

She gave him a weak smile. "Better now. I like that."

But Alexis spoke words she did not feel. She began imagining a life with a man who acted proud to be seen with her. One who didn't have to hide her and one who openly celebrated her and Hayley.

Soon Rashad was ready to go. He and Alexis had driven in separate cars, so he left her with Hayley at the water park while he went to pick up Myles. Afterward, he drove his son to the toy store and bought him everything he wanted as long as he didn't spend more than two hundred dollars.

"You my little man, you know that, right?"

"I know, Daddy."

"And I have been the best father I can be and I plan to be even better."

"Okay, Daddy," Myles answered Rashad, but he was more interested in observing his new toys, especially the radio-controlled quadcopter which looked as much fun as the helicopter he already owned.

When they arrived home, Kiara was quietly sitting in the darkness of the family room. The air was stiff with tension. Once Myles ran upstairs to his room, Rashad came and sat beside Kiara.

"I apologize for how the day went. I'm not good with handling last-minute surprises, Kiara. I had to make do."

"You don't 'make do' with your flesh and blood, Rashad."

"I know that. But I did the second best thing."

"Who is that woman?"

"All I can say is she is a registered day care operator that I came to meet when I did some work in that area."

"What's her name?"

"Do we really need to go there?"

"Unless you're fucking this babysitter, I don't see why I can't know her name."

"She's not a babysitter. We-we call her Glynn."

"We? Who is we?"

"Me, Kiara. Me."

She gave him the side-eye. "Rashad, what is happening to us?" Although her husband told her Alexis was a fling, her gut told her what her husband wouldn't and it scared her. But her love for him and her family compelled her to give the union another try.

"Babe, it's called rough patches. But the rough can turn smooth. If you chill out and just keep being a good mother, a great wife, everything will work itself out."

"One more question, why did I hear kids' voices in the background?"

Rashad could have had a 'these are my confessions' moment, but the truth would've killed his wife. He didn't want her to feel that pain.

"She runs a twenty-four-hour day care."

"Really? How fucking convenient for your ass."

"Another thing, Kiara, you heard what you heard because you were snooping when my phone accidentally called you. You should've just hung up."

"Are you serious? That's bull."

"When you look for trouble you will find it. Stop looking for it, Kiara. Stop making things worse than what they ought to be."

He left his wife alone in the silence of her thoughts, and in the uncertainty of their marriage.

That night, when Rashad went to sleep, he knew that he was in deep trouble. His heart was now attached to three different women, four if his little girl was included. And even though there was no way he could give quality time to all of them, he knew he lacked the ability and desire to give up any of them.

Chapter 10

The next Tuesday afternoon when Kiara wasn't expected to be in the office for hours, Shyla and Nicole strolled back into the workplace after enjoying a two-hour lunch. They took their sweet time parading past Alexis like they didn't have a care in the world.

The gorgeous beauty sat solemnly at her desk dreamily staring into space. And she had no idea her coworkers had drunk a little alcohol during their lunch break and were in some type of mood.

The two ladies stood directly in front of Alexis, making sure she could see them. Nicole dramatically boosted up her smart phone and aimed it. Shyla and Nicole stood cheek-to-cheek and poked out their lips in a sexy Marilyn Monroe pout.

Alexis heard the camera click several times.

"This one is going on my IG," Nicole said. "Give the haters something to hate about."

"Yeah, girl," Shyla was saying. "I know what you mean. Like when I posted my engagement photos on social media, haters came out the woodwork. These birds can't stand to see another chick happy. But hey, I can't help but spread my joy. My baby takes real good care of me. That is why I know I have met my soul mate. He courted me the right way. The way you start out is the way you'll end up."

Shyla admired her engagement ring. "And he paid three months' worth of salary for this bad boy. That's a lotta paper. My man hustles hard for me. Sometimes I feel so unworthy." She cackled until Alexis couldn't stand it anymore.

"You know I've been thinking the same thing," she replied. "Sometimes when I find out that certain women get engaged, I immediately question how the hell did that happen? She ain't even worth all that. These days basic bitches on the come-up while real bosses gotta wait. Somehow, that shit don't add up."

Nicole said, "Ooh, I didn't know she talked ratchet. She always tries to act like she is so sophisticated and we're soooo beneath her."

"Oh, this one can go from thinking she white to acting black real quick. I told you, you gotta watch the fake ones," Shyla remarked.

"There's nothing fake about me," Alexis responded.

" 'There's nothing fake about me' claims the chick with twenty-two inches of horse strands glued to her scalp."

"Nicole, you're one to talk. I see you started wearing colored contacts. That's about as phony as you can get."

"But no one would ever know I wear contacts unless I tell them. Your head of bone-straight Indian hair is screaming, 'Faaaaaaaaaaaaake.' "

"That's dumb," Alexis responded. "I knew you wore contacts and you never told me."

"Excuse me? Did we become best friends and no one ever told me?"

Shyla almost fell over laughing. "I *love* this new you, girl."

Alexis was stunned. Nicole didn't seem like the same

chick that she met less than two months ago. She'd become much feistier, like she was feeling herself.

"And you're hating on me because you think you can size up folks," Nicole continued, "but you got it wrong when it comes to me. I may seem quiet, but don't try me. Because if I have my way, they'll be calling you Sexless Alexis."

Alexis couldn't believe it. There was nothing worse than getting dissed by a basic bitch in front of a basic bitch.

"Nicole, at least I look fierce, which is more than I can say about you with your irrelevant Dogzilla-looking ass."

"I am a lot of things, but ugly ain't one of them."

"You have a nasty attitude and yes, you are one uglyass bitch. Plus you have no personality. You are about as charming as Ebola spit."

"At least somebody likes this spit."

"Tell her, girl." Shyla laughed.

Dislike oozed from Nicole's face. Alexis didn't understand where the hate was coming from. She barely knew her. But she rationalized that Nicole was intimidated because Alexis was so stunningly pretty. Alexis McNeil had been treated rudely a thousand times by insecure chicks ever since middle school. But just because she was used to it didn't mean she liked it or would stand for it.

"I don't give two shits about your pretend boyfriend, Nicole. You are really a joke."

At this point, Shyla was shrieking and wiping tears from her eyes.

"Shyla, if I can recall, you used to boohoo to me about how you couldn't get a man to save your life. And now that you have one, you're always trying to give other women advice. You better hope y'all even make it down the aisle."

"Oh, don't you worry about that. I am secure in my relationship. And don't hate on me because Wesley put a ring on it. If a man wants you, there is no stringing a woman along for years. Won't be no 'Twelve Years an Old Maid.'" Shyla placed her hand on her back. She started walking bent over like she was ninety-nine years old. "A real man'll snatch a real woman's ass up and wife her in no time, just like bae did me," Shyla said. "And I do not apologize for that."

"I may not be wifed up today, but my time will come. I have no worries."

Before they could go in on her again, Alexis turned around and grabbed her purse from a desk drawer. She reached in and removed her pack of Capri Indigo cigarettes.

"See there, Nicole. This woman pretends to have it together, but she is weak. She depends on cigarettes to cope. What's next, crack?"

Alexis merely ignored the comment.

"The only ring Alexis McNeil can get . . . is a smoke ring." Nicole pretended to hold a cigarette, inhale, and blow invisible smoke rings. Shyla burst into giggles.

Alexis knew that someday, somehow she was going to make these women regret ever fucking with her.

The next day was Hump Day. And Rashad blew off Alexis for lunch. She knew she wouldn't have sex with him, but she still needed to see and talk to him.

"Busy. Can't do it. I'm working hard. But I will see you again soon. I promise."

"You know what you can do with your promises."

"You sound so cute when you're mad."

She hung up on him. Then she went to the bathroom. She made sure no one else was in there. She entered the last stall. She wouldn't be long; she just wanted to have a ten-minute moment to herself before she went back to her desk.

While Alexis sat on the commode, she heard a voice as someone entered the ladies' room.

"Hey, sexy." The voice was Rashad's. He was on speaker phone. She figured he was checking in with Kiara and that she had come to use the restroom just then.

"Hiiiiii."

That woman didn't sound like Kiara.

"What you doing for lunch today?" she heard Rashad say.

"You asking me out to lunch? That's a first."

"I like to try new things."

"How we gone do this? I only get thirty minutes, re-member?"

"Tell her you had a little emergency and had to take thirty minutes extra."

"You sure that's okay? I'm still on probation."

"It'll be fine. Kiara will approve it."

"Okay."

Alexis covered her mouth with her hands as she shook uncontrollably. She couldn't believe her lover was on the phone making plans with a coworker that she couldn't stand.

Nicole giggled and laughed as Rashad flirted with her. She told him she had to go. But before she hung up, she made kissing noises as she left the restroom.

Alexis remained on the commode. When she could think clearly, she made up her mind.

Alexis washed her hands and went back to her desk. Lunch would begin in thirty minutes.

She checked her boss's schedule. Kiara was away at a meeting and also had a lunch meeting directly after it. She'd never know she was gone.

Alexis discreetly left the office and drove to the spot.

Her and Rashad's spot. She slid her body way down in the front seat of her car so no one could see her.

She saw Rashad arrive first. But he wasn't in his van. He was in his black sedan. It was a new Honda Accord that he had recently purchased.

Alexis began to perspire under her arms. She'd never want Rashad to know what she was doing. But she hated to assume. Evidence would give her what a lying mouth wouldn't.

Rashad entered the restaurant without noticing Alexis. She sat up in her seat and took out her phone. She felt foolish, but she opened the camera app, aimed the phone at his car, and took a few pictures.

And five minutes later, Nicole slinked into the restaurant. Alexis snapped a couple shots of her, too.

She popped the locks and got out of the car. She walked toward the restaurant entrance, grabbed the door handle, changed her mind, and started walking back toward her car. She reached her car and turned around and went back to the restaurant.

She stepped inside and saw the back of Rashad's head. He was standing next to Nicole as they waited for the hostess. Nicole was gazing up at him and laughing. They posed for a picture that Nicole took with her camera.

Alexis was infuriated. She texted Rashad.

We need a face-to-face.

He looked at his wrist but didn't respond.

Seeing him with another woman made Alexis feel an indescribable sadness. She was used to being the object of his attention. It felt different when she knew he had to give time to his wife.

Alexis decided not to return to work after lunch. Instead, she texted her boss, then drove all the way to the house on the north side. She parked her car and hurried up the walk to the front door. After she knocked, Glynis answered and said, "What are you doing here? It's not Sunday." Alexis pushed past her and went inside until she reached the breakfast room. Hayley played with her food. Four little boys were eating their afternoon snack.

"Lessie, Lessie," the girl chirped.

"How's my little sweetheart?" Alexis picked Hayley up and kissed her cheeks.

"I love you so much. You have no idea how much I love you."

"What's this about?" Glynis asked.

"I-I just had to see her."

"Oh, y'all must be on the outs."

"Why would you say that?"

"Because I know how it works. I've seen it plenty of times. When a man pisses off a woman, she either don't wanna see the child to punish the man, or she really wants to be with that child . . . and turns it against the daddy."

"I'm not trying to do that, if that's what you're thinking. I just miss her."

Glynis came and seized Hayley from Alexis. Hayley started kicking her legs and screaming. Alexis gave Glynis a smug look and took the little girl back from her. She placed her on her hip and glanced around. "You only got seven kids today, huh?"

"Yeah, one mother heard a rumor about me, and unenrolled her two kids. That really messed me up. But I'll be fine."

"What's the rumor that she heard?"

"I don't want to talk about it."

"Miss Glynn left us by ourselves one time."

Glynis shushed the child. "Stop lying. I did no such thing. Hazel was here."

"You leave the kids alone? You could get in a lot of trouble."

"I told you Hazel was here."

"You probably did it that day you were trying to spy on me and Rashad. You gotta do better, Glynn."

"Don't judge me. I just got out the hospital, for your information. I'm doing the best I can."

"Oh yeah? What happened?"

"I had an issue with my blood sugar. I'm better now."

"Glad to hear that."

Alexis went to sit in the living room on the lumpy sofa that had books and tops lying stuffed between the cushions.

"You could stand to clean up around here."

"Unless you're willing to grab a broom and a dust pan, don't tell me how to run my business."

"Don't be so sensitive. I'm just saying—"

"The custodian will be here this afternoon."

"Thank God for that."

Glynis looked her sister up and down. "You always did think you were better than me even though I was Daddy's favorite."

"I've had a rough day and I don't want to hear all that negativity."

"Well, you're about to hear it. Your mama was something else, back in the day."

"Leave my mother out of it."

"She tried her best to get my daddy to leave us . . . and she was successful . . . except he ended up with another whore and left us broke and forgotten. It seems like you turned out just like her."

"Glynis, please stop. Why bring up old news? And my mother isn't here to defend herself."

"Ain't nothing to defend. She was a 'CU Next Tuesday' type of woman."

"Are you trying to call my mother a cunt?"

"If the pussy fit . . ."

"That's it. I'm about to take Hayley with me. This is a bad environment for her."

"It can't be any worse than the one you created for her."

"Glynis, you're a hot mess. I regret—"

"You regret what? You regret having Hayley for a married jackass named Rashad?"

"Shhhh!" Alexis covered Hayley's ears.

"You're a fool. You're the mess. And you need to get on up outta here right now." Glynis's voice was loud and harsh.

"I will leave as soon as you pack her bag. I want her to spend the night."

"Nope, not today. You gone give me more than a five-minute notice, I know that much. That's what your problem is. You so used to snapping your fingers and getting weak men to bow down and kiss your stuck-up ass. But I ain't the one. I got standards. I can say 'no' as fast as I can say 'hell no.' And you won't be coming over here any time you please without calling and acting like you can disrespect my place of business."

Glynis went on and on and on.

Alexis wanted to lash out at her sister, but she knew that would have been the wrong thing to do. She had her child to think about. So while Glynis rattled on, cussing and sputtering herself into some high blood pressure, Alexis raised her hand and begged her to "give me a minute."

Alexis saw the back of Glynis's head as she took her time leaving the room, but she heard her cussing all the while.

Her daughter grew alarmed by all the yelling and ar-guing. Little Hayley was sniffling, coughing, and weeping, all at the same time. Alexis rocked the baby in her arms and softly sang a little song that she made up:

> *Hush, little baby*
> *Don't you cry*
> *Mama's gonna make everything all right.*

She couldn't think of a new line to sing. So she just repeated the words:

> *Mama's gonna make everything all right.*

Chapter 11

"Mama Flora, is the divorce still on?"

"Well, miracles can happen."

"Grandma, stop playing. Tell me the facts. I want to know how things are. And if you don't tell me, I'll just call Grand Pop."

"Don't call that fool."

"Oh, it's still on!"

It had been a while since she'd seen her grandmother, so Kiara decided to visit her on a Sunday afternoon. The streets of Houston were so hot if an egg got cracked and poured on the sidewalk, a fried egg would appear in seconds. Kiara had to get out of the house. So she and Myles ended up at her grandmother's sitting in the kitchen, and helping her to fold the clothes that had just come out the dryer.

"I wish you would've told me that you spent the Fourth by yourself, Grandma. If I'd known, I would have picked you up and we could've gone to see the fireworks."

"It's all right, sweetie. I'm fine. I'm here."

Kiara wanted to wrap her arms around the fragile woman and take away all her pain. Grandma wasn't fooling anyone. Kiara could tell the way the woman walked from one room to another, holding an empty mug, sitting down and standing up. And started the process all over again.

Kiara slid a round plastic laundry basket next to her feet. She lifted up some bath towels.

"C'mon, you can tell me. What's happening with y'all?"

"Well, he is gone, yet he's still here, if that's what you asking."

"What's that supposed to mean?"

"John calls himself quitting me but he still has a room in this house that he comes to whenever he gets ready."

"What type of crap is that?"

"I dunno."

"Well, how do you feel about it?"

Her grandmother was silent.

Kiara couldn't understand why her grandmother wasn't throwing dishes and breaking glasses. It was like her emotions were trapped deep inside a long, dark pipe.

"Are you hungry, Grandma? We can go out and eat some crawfish."

"I don't want no crawfish."

"For real? I know you lying 'cause that's your favorite thing to do on a Sunday afternoon."

"Yeah, I know, but I'm not hungry."

"Oh, you know Grand Pop may be family, Lord forgive me, but I can't stand him right now."

"Oh, baby, I don't mean to pull you into this. You have your own family to worry about. How is Rashad?"

Kiara wished she could pour out her heart to her grandmother, to tell her how Rashad was acting and to admit to her all the things that made her feel depressed and confused, but she just couldn't. She was a proud young woman who didn't want her family to know all her dirty secrets.

"How's Rashad? He's great," she chirped. "Just busy. And we are getting excited about the cruise. We plan to go snorkeling. We'll be gambling like crazy on the ship. And I've been trying to consistently work out so I can buy me some pretty swimwear real soon."

"You're saying the right words, but your voice don't sound right."

"Um, Mama Flora, honestly, on the real. My husband and I are having a few issues, but I'm positive things will work out for the better."

"If you insist, then I'm glad for you," Grandma said in a light voice. "Keep it up. Invest in him."

"Invest in him? Isn't that what *you* did?"

"Yes, I did. So what? You do it anyway because *you* might get a different outcome."

"Grandma, that sounds crazy."

"I'm sure it does. But it's because you don't understand. I can't look with regrets. Do I wish things were done differently? I believe no matter what I would have done, there were no guarantees."

"That sounds scary to me."

"That's what taking a risk is about. When you walk down that aisle, you are filled with joy. It's all about that special day. But there is a long, uncertain road ahead of you. You take the good days, mix them with the bad, and if you stay together through it all, you've done well."

Suddenly her grandmother rose to her feet.

"Tell you what. You finish up the laundry and I will bake us some vegan cupcakes. How's that sound?"

"Sounds like a winner."

The elderly woman started banging pots and pans and gathering the utensils and ingredients. She even started to hum. She grabbed a spatula and pretended like it was a microphone. She spun in a circle and whipped back her hair.

"Are you all right?" Kiara asked.

"I'm fine. I may have a moment now and then. But that's all it is. A moment. Just like bad times come our way, good times will return, too."

"I guess I hadn't looked at it that way."

"Listen, baby, John and I were together and happy for a good minute. And believe it or not, I still have hope. You never know what can happen even when things look real dark and bleak."

"I guess so."

"I know so. The other day I was sitting out in the backyard patio. I couldn't sleep. It was five something in the morning. And it was very dark. But the birds started to sing. Their voices sounded sweet and happy. Before I knew it, the sun was rising. Within seconds, light swallowed up darkness. And let me know how fast things can change. Just because they're one way today don't mean they'll be that way tomorrow."

Chapter 12

It was a Tuesday in mid-July. Kiara woke up, showered, got dressed, and packed her lunch. By this time she was on marriage autopilot. She did everything without feeling. It was because she'd done certain routine tasks a thousand times before. So without thinking about it, she said, "Bye, I love you" before she drove off to work. She knew that Rashad would get up and take Myles to school. She knew he'd probably go to pick up some tools and start all his jobs for the day. Nothing out of the ordinary. But when she got to work, the first person she saw was Nicole. It was six-thirty in the morning.

"You're here early," Kiara told her as she passed the girl in the hallway. Kiara inhaled and took in the flowery fragrance. Nicole was saturated in perfume. She wore a mint-colored belted dress that was very flattering to her shape. She even wore some chic-looking slinky sandals.

Kiara glanced at Nicole's nails. "Green nail polish?"

"Yes, is that all right?"

"Of course it is. It's your hands. Cute." She noticed the girl's toes. "Green pedicure. You've really been stepping it up. Hmmm."

Kiara proceeded to her office. But she stole one final look at Nicole. Her head was perfectly straight as she walked. The swivel in her hips said, "I am here." Her face looked brighter, more alive. And she wore no eyeglasses.

When Kiara got settled in her own office and booted up her computer, she noticed an email Nicole had initiated. She clicked on it.

"Emergency vacation. Leaving at noon today. Okay with you?"

A nagging feeling streaked through Kiara's belly.

She typed back, "Sure. No problem."

Later on, Kiara overheard Shyla and Nicole talking. She could hear them but they couldn't hear her because she was around the corner at the copier and totally out of their view.

"Yeah, so he's going to do something special for me for my birthday because he has to work on my real birthday."

Kiara wondered what man they were referring to. She hadn't heard that Nicole had caught a man.

"Celebrating early, huh?" Shyla said. "You go, girl. I can tell you been getting worked on."

"I don't know what you talkin' 'bout."

"You know if you got fucked last night. Answer me."

"Shhh, Shyla." Nicole hushed up when she saw Tony Fu quietly walk up to them.

"Who did what last night? What y'all talking about?"

"No, Tony, see, I was asking Nicole when's the last time she inserted a floppy disk inside her hard drive."

"And I told her I don't mess around with floppy disks. Never have. Never will." The two women cackled. "Tony, you're too nosy. Get some business."

"You two are nuts. I think I will leave y'all alone."
Tony left them to continue their conversation.

"Anyway, Nicole, I can tell you got some."

"No, you cannot."

"Girl, you walked in this place with that 'I just got me some dick' walk."

Nicole laughed out loud. "You're tripping, Shyla."

"But girl, a woman always senses when another woman is getting sex on the regular."

The two women cackled and started whispering. Kiara couldn't hear anymore. Yet the words the women exchanged flipped in her mind like somersaults.

As soon as Nicole left for the day, Kiara called Rashad. His phone rang and rang and went into voice mail. She waited for her husband to call her back. She thought. And wondered. She looked up Nicole's résumé. The address on the document was the old address that she had when she first applied for the job. Kiara had no idea where Nicole's current house was actually located, because she never updated her physical address when she moved.

She called Tony into her office.

"Hello, boss. What can I do for you?"

"I want you to find out Nicole Greene's current address for me. Send out an email to the entire staff and make sure everyone updates their home address and emergency contact info."

"Anything for you."

Around two o'clock, Kiara locked up her office. She came to a stop at Alexis's desk.

"Going to a meeting?" Alexis asked.

"Yes. A long meeting. I won't be back for the rest of the day."

"All righty then. See you tomorrow, Kiara."

"Thanks."

"Um, before you go, I want to show you something." Alexis retrieved her BlackBerry. She had forwarded and saved the photos she took of Rashad and Nicole.

"Take a look at this and draw your own conclusions."

Kiara examined the picture. It felt like someone kicked her in the stomach. "He's standing cheek to cheek with her?"

"Looks that way to me."

Her heart sank within her. This was so humiliating. The truth did more than just hurt; it devastated.

"Thanks for letting me know."

She thought about how she had wondered if Rashad would ever hit on Nicole. The photo could be innocent, but she wasn't sure what it meant.

Kiara walked down the hall and tried Rashad one more time. Again, the call went straight into voice mail.

When a wife thinks her spouse is unfaithful, she sometimes imagines that he is having sex with just about any woman, even if she has little proof. The darkness of her mind whispers words that cause her to imagine all kinds of scenarios. And her greatest fear is to believe him just to find out he's lying.

Kiara couldn't deal anymore. She dialed up Eddison when she got in her car. "Look, we need to talk. This is very last-minute. But I am hoping we can meet up."

"Sure, I can arrange that. When you want to meet?"

"In a couple hours. I have to make a stop first."

"Where you want to meet?"

"Your place."

"I'll be there."

Kiara didn't actually know where Eddison lived. She had to ask him to give her the address and directions.

She didn't want him to text the info, even though he volunteered. She didn't need a record of that on her phone.

"That won't be necessary. Just tell me real quick."

Tell me before I change my mind.

She memorized his address. Then she decided to pay a visit to Adina Davis.

Kiara texted Adina to let her know she was popping by her hair salon. When she arrived, she was happy to see that her friend was waiting for her as soon as she pulled into a parking spot outside the salon.

"Hey, girl." Adina hugged her. "I got one customer who just sat under the dryer so you can come on in my room and we can talk."

"Thanks."

Adina styled hair in a complex that housed seventy beauty professionals all under one roof. She led her friend down the long hallway and into her own separate little suite and closed the door.

"Well, Adina. The shit has hit the fan."

"Oh, girl, what happened?"

"I think Rashad is fucking a new chick I hired at the job."

"You *think* he is? Can you find out for sure?"

"If I ask him, all he'll do is deny. No unfaithful man will confess to anything unless you catch him with his pants down."

"Even if that was true, I don't think you need to worry about a new chick. You got the upper hand on that one, Ki. You have no history with her and you can shut that down easy. But still, girl, get your receipts first. You don't want to act salty over a bitch then find a lawsuit on your hands. I know your job is way too important to you."

"I'm not concerned about her. I'm more concerned about him. Did you not tell me that if it walks like a rat, it is a rat?"

"Yeah, but sometimes it looks like a rat, but it's really a mouse."

"Adina, please. I know my man. He loves sex. And when I can't give it to him, there will always be another woman who will. And I know he's not stupid enough to still be kicking it with Alexis."

"If that's true, he is getting ridiculous. Is he a sex addict or something?"

"I don't know what his problem is. He's becoming a whole different person."

"Oh, now that's where you're wrong. When a woman meets a man, all the signs of his true character are already evident, unless he's a con artist. But your man's ways were always obvious, Kiara."

"But I was too blind to see."

"And it sounds like you refuse to be Stevie Wonder anymore. So what's next?"

"Kiara Eason is about to do something she never thought she'd do."

"I feel you, baby girl, but please think long and hard before you do anything you regret." Adina sounded serious. "Women take a lot of shit off their men, but make sure whatever you decide that it's worth it, whatever it is. Don't be dumb and don't be weak."

"I'm not weak. I'm human. I'll let you go now. Just needed to vent. Bye, Adina."

And she left.

Kiara arrived at Eddison's house long before he did. Just as she expected, he lived in a classy, well-established neighborhood with stucco houses that had pretty green vines climbing the sides of the homes. His property was so big he had a horseshoe driveway. But she decided not to park there. Instead she did a U-turn and found an empty spot in front of a house several doors down. She waited in the car and thought about her life.

It was difficult for Kiara to breathe. The more she thought of Nicole and Rashad, the less normal she felt. It was one thing to test a man's faithfulness, another thing if he accepted the bait. She then knew that she was dealing with a deeper issue that might be irreparable.

Kiara and Rashad had just gotten engaged. She was ecstatic. She'd never been so in love before. And she felt pleased that the man she desired wanted her enough to put a ring on it.

They were out together on a Saturday evening having dinner.

She beamed at him when he stuck her straw in his mouth and slurped up some of her cocktail.

"I love you, Rashad."

"I love you back."

"I want to ask you something. Are you really going to be able to stay faithful to one woman the rest of your life?"

"I will damn sure try."

"Try?"

"Kiara, I'm used to getting a lot of pussy. I already told you that."

And he did. He never gave her actual figures about how many women he'd laid. Only a fool would confess that. But he never hid the fact that he had had ample sexual experience.

"So, Rashad, if you love pussy so much, why did you decide we should get married?"

"You are the future mother of my kids, Kiara. I want to leave an heir on this earth. I want to have a family. And I want a pretty, sweet, and ambitious woman by

*my side. You fit that description perfectly. Plus I've
never loved any other woman like I love you."*

*She smiled and her insides melted. Kiara decided
she'd give her man all the sex he wanted and felt that by
doing so she would make sure he never had a reason to
stray. Every single day she'd strive to be Super Woman
for Rashad and that alone would be enough.*

Kiara sat in her car and thought back on those early
years. She felt alarmed at how drastically things in her
marriage had changed. She wiped the tears from her eyes
and wished she had clarity.

Kiara's heart was hurting, which meant she could
feel. And if she could feel, that meant she was still alive.
And if she was still alive, that meant she could do something to help her situation.

As soon as Eddison drove past her vehicle, she waited
a few minutes then calmly stepped out of the car and
walked to his place. She was carrying her briefcase and
her laptop and felt self-conscious.

*The eyes of camera phones are in every place, be-
holding the evil and the good.*

Eddison warmly greeted Kiara and welcomed her
into the house. It smelled fresh and clean and was taste-
fully decorated.

"Make yourself at home." Kiara took a seat on the
sofa in his huge family room while he puttered around
in the kitchen.

"It's been one of those days. So thanks for your understanding. I had to get out of that office."

"What's going on?" he returned and handed her a
glass of red wine. "This may calm your nerves."

"Thanks, but do you have a drink from a bottle that
hasn't been opened yet?"

"Uh, I have flavored vodka."

"I appreciate that."

He brought her a watermelon Smirnoff, knelt at her feet, and removed both of her pumps.

While she talked, he rubbed her shoulders. "You are tense. What happened?"

She told him, "I have a confession. I feel like an idiot and I blame myself. But you know Nicole Greene?"

Kiara proceeded to tell Eddison everything. The way the woman was dressing these days, the way her husband behaved after working at Nicole's house. The way he was never hungry after he left her house; and how he seemed more distant than usual. She even told him about the photo of him smiling for the camera while he was with her. "Every little thing he does is adding up to something that doesn't sit well with me. His mood swings vary. Sometimes Rashad is warm and like his old self. Other times there is this invisible wall that I can't seem to climb. And I'm tired. So tired."

"So have you thought about what you're going to do?"

"I don't want to be pressured, I know that much."

"Sorry," he said sympathetically. "It'll be all right, Kiara. You're going through a lot. You need some peace of mind."

She appreciated how good Eddison's warm hands felt on her back, but when he started lowering his hands toward her butt, she stopped him. He was sensual and fine, but she was too distracted to enjoy his attention.

"Thanks, Eddy. But that's enough. I feel a little better."

"You sure? I can give you a full-body massage."

"Yeah, right. What good will that do?"

"Are you serious? What has my man been doing all this time? You've been living beneath your privileges."

"You're funny. I'm fine. I just want to figure out my life, that's all."

"Have you talked to him about how you feel?"

"How many times . . . I sense that he's holding back. And I want to know why, yet I don't want to know why."

"Because you'd—"

"I'd be devastated. Just about everyone knows us as a model couple. How can I face them if they know we're not?"

"Truthfully, all married people are probably going through their own problems."

"Did you have them with Nina?"

"They weren't big enough to cause a breakup. But when I lost her, it made me learn that life isn't guaranteed. You have to live every day like it's your last."

"Well, I certainly hope that's not what Rashad is doing."

Eddison smiled. "It could be a temporary crisis."

"Yeah, right."

"So, Kiara, do you feel that your husband is messing around with the secretary?"

"She's not a secretary. But her title could be marketing assistant to Jesus Christ and his twelve disciples. It doesn't matter. Rashad is slinging his dick in another woman."

She would die of embarrassment if Eddison knew about Alexis too, so she decided not to tell him about her.

"You have no solid proof. But you feel something's just not right."

"Exactly. In fact, she's already paid him for the work so he should be done. I deposited the check myself. And she gave him a check with an Alabama address."

"He accepts out-of-state checks?"

"That's what I'm talking about. So if he's finished and is still visiting her, that means he's over there because he wants to be there."

"Maybe he's tying up some loose ends. Oops, sorry."

"Oh, Eddison!"

He wanted to comfort her so badly, so he silently took her hand. He played with her fingers. He toyed with her hair. She smacked at his hand so he'd stop. Eddison picked up her legs and swung them onto his lap. He grabbed a bottle of lotion off the coffee table and dabbed some into the palm of his hand and started to gently massage her.

"That feels good," she murmured. She closed her eyes.

Eddy started caressing the base of her feet, then he rubbed her ankles, then stroked her thighs.

"Oh, my goodness," she gasped, wondering if her vivid dream was about to come true. She held her breath and was glad she'd worn a fresh new pair of bikini underwear.

Eddison stared at Kiara with a tenderness that said he adored her. He moved his fingers up her thighs to her groin. He started rubbing her and her eyes rolled around.

"Eddison."

"Yes, Kiara."

"That's my spot. That feels really good."

His fingers were strong and she felt herself getting weak and wet. Soon his lips were on her hair. He kissed her forehead and she couldn't believe how loving that felt. This was it. She wanted this. She deserved it. It had been so long since she'd really felt loved. She opened her eyes and smiled up at him.

"Kiara, I've been waiting to have you for a long time."

Their lips came together in a sensuous kiss. She was amazed at how hot she was getting. He scooped Kiara in his arms and carried her to his bedroom. He carefully laid her down like she was precious and valuable. She loved the way he stared into her eyes and the sexy thing he did when he licked his lips.

"Kiara, do you want me?"

She hesitated, then nodded. He removed his shirt and she helped him. She almost lost it when she saw the long shape in the front of his briefs. She reached out and squeezed him. He moaned. He stood in front of her and undid her bra. His hands were hot like flaming coals. He bent over and sucked on her erect nipples. She nodded and laughed and moaned and enjoyed how loving he felt. She kissed his hair and inhaled the good smell of his locs.

They were so into each other. She licked his ears and sucked on them. He told her to get on her knees and she did. Once he rolled on a condom, Eddison was like a field slave that got set free. This is what he had wanted for so long. He kissed her on her ass as she bent over. He entered her from behind and she heard him pump and grunt his pleasure. Kiara loved how it felt to feel his thrusts. She felt one with Eddison. And when he hit it from the back one final time and climaxed, she felt exhausted but satisfied.

"Let's go one more round."

"You making up for lost time, huh?" she gasped.

He got up and tossed the condom in the trash can. And when he returned, she ordered him to lie on the floor on his back.

He obeyed and waited on this gorgeous woman. She straddled his body, held his penis in her hands and took him in her mouth. She sucked him till he became rock hard. Then she eased herself on top of his shaft and rode him. The line between pleasure and pain was so thin, but she felt so good, she just kept on going. She flipped him so that he was on top. Eddison kept pounding her over and over. He groaned and arched his neck. She moaned with him and loved how he felt inside of her.

After they both exploded with an orgasm and they were lying on the bed spent, a thought popped into her mind.

Kiara tensed up. "Uh, did you use a condom?"

"Oh, shit. No. I didn't."

"Dammit."

What am I doing? My husband and I haven't had sex in a minute. What if . . . ?

Kiara shoved Eddison off of her and covered herself with a blanket. "I can't believe it. What the hell was I thinking?"

"You weren't thinking about Rashad, and for good reason. But don't worry. Nothing bad is going to happen. That was beautiful. Didn't you enjoy it?"

"Yes, of course, Eddy."

He uncovered Kiara's body and slowly started to kiss her neck. He jumped on top of Kiara and kissed her all over her body.

"What are we doing?" Kiara whispered.

"I don't know what you're doing, but I'm having a good time. I've wanted you for so long."

He stopped kissing her and stared into her eyes. "I love you inside and out."

What he said sounded so ridiculous yet made Kiara feel so good, she started laughing.

It was almost five o'clock. Kiara had gotten dressed and so had Eddison. Now she was pacing back and forth in his bedroom. "I need to talk to Rashad. I gotta hear from him. Soon."

"Why would he even care? He's screwing everything that moves."

"It doesn't matter, Eddison. I'm not trying to make things worse. I just want to touch base. I hate to leave you like this. But I'll hit you up when I can."

She wanted to get home and take a quick shower. She got in her car and called Rashad. He didn't answer. She left him a voice mail.

"Hey, bae. What you doing? I haven't heard from you all day. I—um, call me." She wanted to say more but didn't. It was her day to pick up Myles from the after-school day care. She made a U-turn and drove to the school and collected her son and rushed home. When she saw her husband's car in the driveway, but not his work van, she felt a little better.

Once she got Myles settled, the first thing she did was hop in the shower. She squirted lots of liquid soap on her body and scrubbed herself from head to toe.

"I can't believe I did that. Doing dumb stuff like cheating isn't even in my DNA."

She got dressed and couldn't help but notice the new clothes from Nordstrom hanging in her closet. She stared at them and felt sick to her stomach.

Rashad walked through the door earlier than she expected.

She greeted him with a hug but failed to look him in the eyes. He avoided eye contact with her as well.

"Hey," she said, "how was your day?"

"Busy man. Working hard."

"Um, have you ever taken Nicole to lunch?"

"Yes, but only as a client; nothing more."

"Are you sure?"

"Of course I'm sure. Why?"

If what he said was true, did she actually have revenge sex with Eddison? Did she really have it in her to stoop that low?

"Never mind."

She was dressed in a negligee. A red one that she knew

Rashad loved. On the drive back to her house, she had come up with a plan. Her plan was to seduce Rashad, but now she felt unsure. Using sex as a tool for any reason was a dangerous game.

"Hey, sexy. You look hot," he said.

"I do?"

"And you look exhausted. You had a hard day?"

"Uh, yeah. It was . . . very hard," she told him.

"What you got to eat in there?"

"What?"

"Are you all right? I asked what is there to eat."

"Rashad, trust me. I didn't have time to cook. I ate some leftovers."

"No biggie."

Rashad headed toward their room and she was right behind him.

"What are you about to do, Rashad?"

He looked at Kiara like she was insane. "What do I always do? I'm about to hit the shower."

"Good. I'll join you."

"That's cool."

"You know it's been a while. Too long," she said and felt like her dinner was about to rise up her throat and explode from her mouth.

He accepted her embrace, then peeled off his clothes and dumped them on the floor by the bed. While he was in the shower, she quietly found his pants and felt around in both pockets. She reached in one pocket and pulled out a single condom still in the wrapper.

Well, at least he's smart enough to use protection, she thought.

Kiara got undressed and slipped into the shower behind her husband. Water had already splattered on his back. She couldn't see any scratches, nothing. But it didn't matter. She grabbed Rashad's waist from behind and pressed her lips against him.

Inside she was trembling. Having sex with two men in one day wasn't part of her character. Yet Kiara felt that his cheating could not completely justify her having unprotected sex.

She made her way down the back of his legs, kissing his skin and not feeling aroused while she did it. When she worked long enough to hear him moaning and groaning, she still wasn't satisfied until she moved to his front.

He pushed her head toward his dick.

She said, "No way!"

"Why not?"

"I want you in me right now." But what she wanted to say was, *Two BJs in one day is a bit much.*

She gulped, grabbed his penis and tried to insert him inside of her.

"Kiara, hold up, I ain't trying to—"

"Shhh," she said and silenced him. "I'm not ovulating," she assured him. "I just really want to feel you inside me."

"You sure?"

"I'm a hundred percent sure, babe." She grabbed his plump dick and almost broke her hand trying to jam it into her.

He was hard enough for them to feel friction. Rashad moaned and pumped. She still felt raw from when Eddison ravished her. But Kiara stayed silent and rocked with her husband. Standing up and moving together like a ship rocking against the waves of an angry, savage ocean. Rashad pushed her back against the shower wall and lifted her leg.

"Please, please, please," Kiara gasped each time he rammed into her.

"I'm trying."

"Try harder," she said and started silently weeping. The water drops from the shower splattered across Kiara's face. Rashad never noticed all the tears sliding down her face as he smashed hard inside her over and over.

"Try harder."

Chapter 13

The day following her sexual indiscretion, Kiara woke up very early. It was hard to think clearly but she managed to grab her cell phone and sneak out of the bedroom. Rashad was spread out. She heard him snoring. Good. She ran upstairs to the guest bedroom and closed the door.

The room was dark. And it was pitch black outside. She powered up her cell phone, which had been turned off all night.

Four new texts loaded up. And she had two voice mail messages.

All of the messages were from Eddison.

Kiara glanced at each message:

R U all right?

Then,

Call me.

Then,

I hope everything is ok.

I'm here 4 u if u need 2 talk.

The fact that he sent four texts between nine o'clock and two in the morning made her nervous.

Even though it was five in the morning, Kiara decided to call. She would use the home phone line and dial star sixty-seven. She tiptoed to the media room down the hall and picked up the cordless phone. Then she called Eddison.

"Pick up, pick up," she prayed.

"Hello?"

"It's me. I'm calling from the home phone. I wanted to see if you'd answer. And now I will call you from my cell anonymously. I wouldn't want him to listen in on the home phone."

"All right," Eddison said and hung up.

It was completely quiet, but Kiara's heart beat so loud she wondered if Myles could hear her. His room was right next door.

"I gotta get it together for my baby," she said out loud.

Kiara was so distracted she absentmindedly called Eddison again from the home phone even though she was holding her cell in her hand. She put the phone to her ear and Eddison answered quickly.

"Are you all right?" he asked.

Suddenly the cordless phone she was holding got violently snatched from her hand.

Rashad stood before her in his boxers.

"What are you doing, Kiara?" he said in a loud voice. He turned on the overhead light. He looked at the cordless phone then at her.

"I-I was—"

"Hello?" he said into the phone. No one answered.

There was a dial tone.

"Rashad, I'm sorry, I-I—"

"You're full of shit. I know what you were doing."

He pressed the redial button, but the call went directly into voice mail. There was no greeting that identified the owner.

"You trying to call someone that you think I'm messing around with, right?"

Kiara blinked. Then she nodded. She had to think fast. "Are you messing around?" she asked.

"You need to quit. I ain't done nothing."

"I'm sorry."

"This is getting out of hand. You either listening in if I accidentally dial you or you making me drive to folks' house that you don't even know, or doing other stupid shit. This has to stop." He shook his head. "But I can't totally blame you. That wouldn't be dope."

She stared breathlessly at her husband.

He balled his hand into a fist and punched the wall.

"Kiara, I'm going through some things. Things that make me act crazy. I think I need help. But so do you. Maybe I'm driving you to act this way. You can't turn into a monster like I have."

She stared at Rashad and slowly nodded. *Monster.*

He's turning me into a monster.

Kiara decided to act normal right after that episode. She made Myles get up for school. She put on a dress and some pumps and grabbed her attaché case and floral lunch bag, even though it was empty.

"I'm going to work now." Kiara drove to a nearby gas station. She pulled alongside a pay phone and grabbed two quarters.

She got out of the car and dialed Eddison. He did not pick up.

She texted him.

Pls answer ur phone.

Then she called him again, and this time he answered.

"Oh, Eddison. I want to see you. Can I come by your place again?"

"Come on, sweetie."

"And please delete that text. I will delete mine."

The second Eddison opened his front door, she fell into his arms. They held each other for the longest time. He took Kiara by the hand and invited her to get in his bed. He fluffed the pillows for her and handed her one of his silk robes. He went and made her a cup of hot tea and brought it to her.

"Thanks." She looked calmer. Her thoughts were now collected. She'd gotten undressed and slipped on his robe and was comfortably settled under the covers.

"I called in today."

"I don't blame you," he said sympathetically.

"It's not what you think. I'm fine."

Eddison wanted to comfort Kiara. He wanted to protect her and let her know everything would work out for her. But as much as he cared about her, he realized that she really wasn't his, not like he wished she could be.

"I am here to support you in any way that I can. You may stay as long as you like. My home is your home."

His words soothed her tremendously. She heard him go in his bathroom and turn on the running water. She heard the sounds of his electric shaver. She closed her eyes and visualized a better life with a better man. She knew she wasn't there yet. But in Kiara's mind, she was well on her way.

Chapter 14

That Saturday morning, Alexis drove over to the Home Depot. She found a parking space and shut off the ignition. She sat in her car and stared out the window. It was about a twenty-minute wait, but she finally saw Rashad pull up in his new black sedan. She watched him emerge from his car. The other day he had finally texted her back and asked if everything was all right with Hayley. She told him yes. He responded that he was sorry for just getting back but if she could swing by the store, he could talk to her there in person.

Alexis observed Rashad like a cop on a stakeout. Before he could reach the front entrance, she hurriedly got out of her car and followed him inside the store. Rashad grabbed an orange cart and wheeled it down a long aisle, turned right, then made another right into the paint aisle. She caught up with him and tapped him on the shoulder. He spun around. His eyes widened. He broke out in a grin.

"Heyyy, babe." He grabbed Alexis around the waist and pulled her in for a hug.

Her body stiffened at his touch.

"Oh, it's like that, huh? I thought you were going to meet me here after I was done."

"No, I got here earlier than I thought. I'm anxious to talk to you."

He let her go and resumed looking at paint cans.

"Babe, you have rings under your eyes. Have you been getting enough sleep?"

"Rashad, we need to have a serious conversation." She took a deep breath and pulled out her phone. As she flashed the photo of him and Nicole, she observed his reaction. He looked confused.

"What's that?"

"You and my coworker."

"How'd you get that?" He paused. "Did my wife put you up to this? Are you on Team Kiara now?"

He turned away from her and pushed his basket.

Alexis felt stupid.

She ran up to him. "Rashad, I'm sorry. This doesn't look right. Common sense tells me—"

"Common sense tells me that you're beginning to act like Kiara. I thought we had something special. You've never been the type to roll up on me like that. Why now?"

"Because of what you're doing now. You are getting close to her."

"That's only because she is paying me to do some work."

"You don't have to take photos with your clients."

"I know. But she's all into that social media stuff. I fell for it."

"You're such a liar."

"I resent that," he told her.

He calmed himself down and caressed her cheek. "You of anybody should know how it is. I'm treating a client well and collecting checks. How do you think I can afford to buy you all those nice gifts you like?"

He grabbed her wrist.

"Where's the bracelet I gave you?"

"I-I don't wear it every day."

"Oh, I see. Anyway, you better stop having an attitude and let me do what I do. Hell, I know you wanna see a brother, but when I get off, the last thing I'm thinking about is hanging out. By the time I leave a work site, all I want to do is crash at the crib."

"So all you been doing is catching up on sleep?"

"That's it."

She knew he was lying, but what more could she expect.

"A successful businessman always gotta deal with all kinds of shit. It's bananas."

His eyes twinkled. She couldn't believe that he actually looked happy and like nothing bothered him.

Rashad glanced at his watch. "I was just killing time picking up a few supplies. I ain't gonna get much because I don't like carrying around paint in my car. My van is in the shop," he explained. "The A/C went out."

"Oh, okay. Sorry to hear that."

His phone chirped. He glanced at a text.

"Woman, it is your lucky day. I just got a cancellation, which frees me up till two. You wanna do something? Let's go to the beach and hang out."

Rashad had just purchased several cans of paint that he wanted to place in the trunk of his sedan. Alexis walked beside him and inhaled. His masculine scent was intoxicating. His presence was comparable to the lure of a strong magnet. She knew she should have said no, but her legs wouldn't stop. Rashad was her drug. He always had been.

"We can ride in my car."

"That's fine."

When they got to his car, she noticed the windows weren't rolled up all the way.

"You left your windows down. Anybody can reach in and take your valuables off the seat."

"Damn. I forgot."

Rashad opened Alexis's door for her and waited until she was seated.

"I see you're still a gentleman."

"Always. Ain't nothing changed."

She could only laugh.

Rashad settled in his seat and spoke aloud. "Engine start."

Rashad had one of those voice recognition devices in his new ride. The ignition automatically powered up.

He was getting ready to put the gear in reverse but the instrument panel indicated that his trunk was ajar.

"Be right back." He turned off the ignition and ran back out to slam the trunk tighter.

While he was gone, Alexis carefully took out her smartphone and activated its voice recorder. Rashad hopped back in his seat and said, "Engine start."

Alexis recorded his voice and saved it on her phone.

They ended up taking I-45 south to Galveston. Alexis tried to relax and just enjoy the ride. Once they reached the island, they drove past towering frame houses that were more than one hundred years old. He traveled down Harborside Drive until they reached the Port of Galveston.

She took in the sight of a Royal Caribbean cruise liner that was docked.

"I can't wait to get on that ship this fall," he told her.

"Oh, you're still going, huh?"

"Why wouldn't I?"

She didn't say anything.

They drove around until they reached the northeast end of the island.

"Let's get out." She agreed and they ended up sitting

on some giant slabs of concrete. They watched the ships creep across the ocean.

Alexis was so quiet that Rashad simply grabbed her hand and squeezed it. She squeezed back. Instead of letting go, he held on.

"Rashad, is there anyone else?"

"What you mean, is there anyone else?"

"Another woman."

"The only woman I've been with is the one that I'm married to."

"You sure?"

"What's with all the questions?"

"I know that if a man ain't spending time with me—"

"Oh, he automatically gotta be smashing someone else?"

"Pretty much."

"That ain't always true."

He let go of her hand.

"Rashad, you can tell me."

"Babe, don't do this."

Alexis wanted to say how she felt but she didn't think it was necessary. Rashad wasn't stupid. He knew her.

"You're hurt." He pulled her against him and kissed her hair. "I don't want you to feel that way. But I haven't smashed anyone else."

"Negro, you lying and you know it." At that moment, she felt like a wife, a married woman who has the guts to ask the question but wasn't buying the answer he gave her.

"You can believe what you wanna believe."

"I know that already."

"Anyway, what else you wanna talk about? You want to make plans to do something for real? 'Cause I want to do that to prove it to you."

In her head she didn't want to have sex with him

anymore but she found herself making him promise to take her and Hayley to SeaWorld in San Antonio. She'd never been to San Antonio and had always wanted to go.

"Okay. I got you. As soon as I can find the time, I'll try to coordinate that trip for us."

Suddenly, Alexis wanted to leave the island. She made him drive back to the Home Depot so she could get her car. She told him good-bye. Then she drove home completely lost in her thoughts.

She went straight upstairs to her bedroom and opened the top drawer of her nightstand. She found the pretty charm bracelet that Rashad gave her. She dropped it in her purse and scrounged through the drawer searching for more of his trinkets. She soon found the crystal-and-pearl bracelet that Rashad had given her on Valentine's Day. She dropped that in her purse, too. By the time she was done, Alexis's bag was weighed down with bracelets, necklaces, and a fancy watch.

She drove around until she saw a pawn shop. She got out the car, entered the store, and reached in to pull out all the items Rashad had given her that she wanted to unload.

"Looks like a nice sale," the man behind the counter told her.

"Yeah, I call it a Former Mistress Garage Sale."

He nodded as if he understood.

The man asked for her driver's license and gave her a quote for the things she wanted to get rid of.

"That's fine." He took the jewelry, printed a receipt, and handed her the cash. As Alexis left the shop, she wondered what other courageous steps she could take to make positive changes in her life.

That evening Alexis received a call from an unrecognizable number. She decided to pick up.

"Hello," she said with caution.

"Is this Alexis?"

"Yes, who's this?"

"This is Varnell."

"Who?"

"The man you met at the Kroger store in Fresno. The nice one." It had taken Varnell so long to call her that she'd deleted him from her address book. But now she was happy to hear from him.

"Oh yes, Mr. Nice Guy. What a nice surprise. I thought you'd forgotten about me."

"Naw, nothing like that. I just gave it a little time. I take my time when I'm thinking about doing something, that's all."

"Doesn't that mean you miss out on a lot of things?"

"Maybe. But if it ain't good for me and I missed out, then what was I really missing?"

"But you won't know if it's good or not unless you take the time to find out."

"True that, young lady. What have you been up to? How's life treating you?"

"Life wants to treat me bad, but I've decided that's not going to happen." She laughed. "I'm beginning to understand the things I want, and to recognize the stuff that isn't good for me."

"I'm intrigued. What do you want?"

"Oh wow, you're putting me on the spot, but it's cool." She paused and searched her heart. "I want . . . true happiness; happiness that comes from feeling safe and protected. And loved. All that good stuff. And, Varnell, I'm ready to have fun. I just want to enjoy each day. I feel like I do the same boring stuff over and over."

"Then you and I need to make time to see each other and do some fun things. I work for Continental Airlines and my hours are long and sporadic, but I've got some free time coming up."

"That sounds good." She relaxed as she listened to the sound of his soothing voice.

"Okay, bucket list time. You want to have fun. What do you like to do, Alexis?"

"I love the movies, I love entertainment—you know, concerts, outdoor fairs, amusement parks, basketball games."

"I like all of that, too. You ever been fishing?"

"Nope."

"We gotta do that. How about museums?"

"I've never been to one since I've been grown."

He burst out laughing. She liked that she could make him laugh. "We're going, then. I'm serious. Make a list. We are going to have a good time. It's time for us to stop letting life pass us by."

The more they talked, the more excited Alexis felt about the future. She hadn't felt that way in a long time. She and Varnell conversed for an hour. The only reason she ended the call was because her cell phone began overheating.

"I really do have to go but I must say that I've enjoyed you." She laughed then stopped. "How long has it been since I've enjoyed something simple like this. Oh, that came out totally wrong. I'm not calling you simple."

"I know what you meant. And I understand if you have to go. But next time we talk it will be face-to-face. How's that sound?"

She thought about Rashad. He was so busy he'd never even know about Varnell. And even if he did, and he got in his feelings, that wouldn't be her concern.

"That sounds good, Varnell." She opened up a notebook app in her phone and typed, "Relationship Goals."

"I am starting my list," she sweetly told him.

They made plans to meet up very soon.

Alexis and Regina, the chick she met at the outdoor café, kept in touch via text. The next Saturday afternoon, she picked up Regina in her Benz and drove to an exclusive spa in a ritzy part of town. Once they checked in, Alexis decided to explain herself after Regina kept giving her perplexed looks.

"I was your age once. The early twenties can be a tough and confusing time. And last time I saw you, you looked like you could use some good old-fashioned spoiling."

Warm feelings flooded through Regina.

"I-I can't believe this," she sputtered. "I barely know you. And you're being so nice to me. I've never had a damned body scrub exfol-exfo—"

"Exfoliation."

"Yeah, that." Regina's voice was filled with amazement as she read aloud their schedule.

"Never had a seaweed wrap, a French pedicure, a full-body hot stone massage, a fucking *Playboy* wax."

"Welcome to the Weekend Wives Club."

"And you don't need me to give you ten or twenty dollars?"

"You're funny. No, it's cool. When I get paid, someone else gets paid, too."

"Damn, this is crazy. It seems like my man should be doing this . . ."

"I was wondering if you were still with him. And you're right. He should be doing this. And that's exactly why I feel sorry for you."

"Excuse me?"

"Don't be offended. I'm not trying to make you feel

unworthy or bad. But I meant that as a side, you take a lot of shit you don't deserve."

"I'm not—"

"Regina, you are not his woman. Let's get that out of the way right now."

"I may not be his main woman, but I don't appreciate being called a side chick. That's way worse than a baby momma."

"He's a truck driver. They can make up to five g's a month. Has he ever given you money?"

"No, not really."

"Have you ever asked?"

"No, I got a job at the medical center. I make my own money."

"That's dumb. You're assuming all the risk of being with him. You're probably having unprotected sex. You don't know if he's married to a whack job that might come for you one day. And most importantly, you're giving up your most precious goodies from your treasure chest but you're not getting anything of value in return. Great sex can't pay bills."

Alexis studied Regina. "The sex is amazing, isn't it?"

"Hell yeah."

"I knew it. Hmm. All I can say is if you've got the good-good and you're giving it away for free, then that's on you."

"I don't know about that," Regina said angrily. "I don't want him to think I'm a gold digger."

"Oh, like me? Is that what you're saying?"

Regina whispered, "No."

"It's okay to say whatever you're thinking because I plan to say what I am thinking."

"I can see that."

"Look at this ring! See that one? I got those from a

well-off ex. These are my war medals . . . the ones I de-cided to keep . . . as a reminder."

"Those are nice," Regina said. "But you seem angry. If a man gave me money, or jewelry, and a car, I'd be doing the happy dance."

"You think I'm angry?" Alexis relaxed as her back was getting massaged. "You're right. I get mad at my guy at times. I love him, he knows it, and he can be full of shit. I even get mad at myself. Being about this life can cause drama, and it's hard to break things off. But more than anything, I'm angry at the wives because he doesn't deserve their trust. They should know their man. At home he is the happy husband. But once he's outside the door, he's Rico Suave. And he is lying to us. You can't have an affair and not tell lies. But if he told her the truth, he'd be dead. And he doesn't want that."

"Why is it about what he wants?"

"Because that's how the game is played. He knows he wants some drama-free pussy. A woman that strokes his ego. A woman with low self-esteem."

Regina frowned. "You got any more of them ciga-rettes you carry in your purse?"

"Yes. I do have them, but no, I won't let you start this nasty habit. We'll find a better way for you to handle what you're going through."

The ladies enjoyed their massages and continued chatting, providing mutual therapy to each other.

"Well, Alexis, if what you're saying is true, why wouldn't the wives just leave instead of sticking with these losers?"

"Oh, that's easy. When it comes to cheating husbands, there are four different types of wives: the ones that think he's not doing anything, but *he is*; the ones that think he's doing something, but *he's not*; the ones that don't think he's doing anything, and *he isn't*; and the ones that think he is doing something, and yes, she's on it, because *the bastard definitely is*."

"Damn shame. I'm starting to hate my man just listening to you."

"Don't hate him. Love yourself, Regina. We gotta learn to love ourselves."

"Yeah, you're right." She scratched her head. "I'm learning from you, Alexis."

"I have so much more to learn, too, girl. Especially now that his wife knows I exist."

"I wouldn't ever want to meet my man's wife."

"And trust me," Alexis assured her, "he's not trying to let that happen, either."

"I think I get it now. He's having his cake and eating it, too. And the man can't let those two worlds bump into each other. It would be too messy. Like an accident that shuts down the highway."

"If he doesn't want the accident to happen, then he needs to get out the driver's seat."

"Okay, but what about us?" Regina asked. "Don't we gotta get out the seat, too?"

"Oh, we will get out the seat when we get tired. But a woman that knowingly messes with a married man is a stubborn bitch. It's like Area Fifty-one. The more you're warned not to drive there, not to get out your car, and not to take photos, the more your ass wants to do it."

When they got their *Playboy* wax, and the hot liquid was poured on her vagina then ripped off, Regina thrashed her legs and squealed in pain.

"Damn, that hurt."

"Don't worry. It won't hurt for too long. Anyway, it's a good kind of pain. And we women must go through a lot to get what we really want. It's always been that way. So I have an assignment for you, Regina."

"You have a what?"

"I want you to confront your man, right now. Come on. Pick up the phone and call him."

"I knew there had to be a catch to all this expensive treatment."

Alexis laughed. "Look, I want you to enjoy your special day because, believe it or not, you deserve it. But stop putting off the inevitable. I see myself in you so much. I want you to do right now what I should have done a long fucking time ago."

"Whatever," Regina said, but she did what Alexis asked of her. The ladies were moved to another room where they sat in cushy lounge chairs so they could receive deluxe pedicures. Regina gave Alexis the full name of her boyfriend. She told her where he was born. His age. Date of birth and other identifiable family info. Then, looking scared to death, Regina got her man on the phone. She placed the call on speaker. She didn't care about the odd looks the manicurist gave her. She finally was ready to unload her heart of all the questions she'd wanted to ask him since the day they started having sex. While Regina was talking to him, Alexis was on her own phone doing all kinds of web searches.

"Um, Lance. I wanna ask you something."

"I'm driving. I'm bored. Go ahead."

"Why haven't you ever asked me over to your crib?"

"Huh? I-I already told you. I live with my crazy-ass family."

"I've met crazy-ass families before. It wouldn't be a big deal if you introduced us. Is it true that the real reason you've never invited me is because you stay with a woman?"

"I told you who I stay with. And they're female family members."

"Do you sleep with any of the women that you stay with?"

"What the fuck? What are you getting at?"

"Lance, you can tell me anything you think I want to hear. But until you can prove to me that your ass ain't married and living with a woman you're fucking, we are through. If I can't come to your house, then you can't come to mine."

Lance was silent.

"I know you heard me," Regina told him.

"You are spazzing big time. I'm single."

Alexis waved frantically at Regina. She handed over her cell phone and showed her the website she had located.

"Lance, if you're single, then why am I looking at a marriage record of a Lancelot Dewain Tyjon Perryman who was married in Montgomery County on February twelfth five years ago and who lives at 4023 Hummingbird Road which is the exact same address I've seen on your driver's license?"

Lance was silent.

"You and Shantay Francesca Jones were married by a Reverend Thomas Phillip Meriweather—"

He began yelling, "I never liked your weak ass anyway. You got a lot of nerve spying on me. You're a damned stalker. Lose my number, bitch. You better not come near my house, either."

Regina hung up.

"You're right, Alexis. I deserve better. And so does his stupid-ass wife."

Chapter 15

It was Saturday, August 2. The weather was picture perfect.

Rashad had a rare day off. And he was eager to do something spontaneous. He noticed how Alexis had been acting lately, and it made him feel uncomfortable. He loved the old Alexis, but the new one, it seemed, had become paranoid. He wondered if she'd ever be the same woman again.

So that morning, he stuck around the house until Kiara packed up her car and left. Last night, she'd told him that she was driving Myles and a couple of his friends to the outskirts of Austin. At the last minute, she had signed Myles up to attend a sports, music, and arts day camp that would be held from mid-morning to late afternoon.

"You are the dopest mother ever. This is how I like to see you behave. Bye, you two. Be safe and have fun." Rashad waved at his family as they told him good-bye.

As soon as they left, he went into his van, which had been returned from the repair shop. He retrieved a bag of new clothes he'd recently purchased. He got showered, dressed, and drove the sedan to Nicole's. When he pulled in front of her house, he reached down in the backseat and removed another plastic shopping bag.

Instead of using his key, Rashad rang the doorbell. She answered and greeted him with a happy smile.

"Happy birthday, Nicky."

She squealed in delight when he handed her a tiny box of chocolates and a greeting card.

"Wait, what's all this? You already took me out for my birthday."

"I know. But since today is your actual birthday, I thought I'd surprise you with a little present."

"You're too sweet. Come on in."

Rashad watched her booty jiggle like a hula dancer as she sashayed in front of him.

"Mmm mmm mmm. You are fine from behind."

"Oh, stop." She laughed. "No, don't stop. Keep going."

Nicole felt excited, like she was in a wonderful dream. He'd texted her last night and informed her he was popping over in the morning. The only thing he told her was to look cute and dress comfortably. So when she woke up and got ready, she meticulously applied eye liner, eye shadow, thick mascara, and dusted her cheeks with blush. And the orange-and-white summer dress she had on was from Nordstrom Rack. Her cute leather flats and studded cross-body purse completed her look.

Rashad admired her and nodded.

"Okay, number one, you look good from the front, too. And you rocking that hairstyle." He reached out and smoothed her curls. He gave her a light, friendly kiss on the cheek.

She said thanks but her face was punctuated with a frown.

"What's wrong?"

"Nothing. Never mind."

Nicole stared at every inch of Rashad. He made a simple black t-shirt, jeans, and hightops look sexy. She thought Kiara was a fool not to keep heavy tabs on her man. She couldn't believe it when Rashad had recently admitted to her that his wife didn't always meet his needs. He could be lying, she thought, but what if he's telling the truth.

"Now look at your card."

She tore open the envelope and glanced at her birthday card. She gasped when a fifty-dollar Macy's gift card fell out. "That's so nice of you." She read the card but noticed he didn't sign it. She didn't care. He'd never given her a gift before and she was pleasantly surprised.

"So, here's the deal. I have plans for us. But first I gotta do something."

Rashad reached inside the shopping bag and removed a purple silk scarf. It was pretty and lightweight.

"Um, don't judge me, but someone left this at one of the houses I am restoring. It still has the price tag on it. They never came and got it, so—"

"OMG, that's their loss. I'll take it. It's too hot to wear it but I can put it in my drawer."

"Actually, I have a better idea."

Rashad stepped behind Nicole. She smelled so good he was dying to kiss her neck, but he resisted. He wrapped the scarf around her eyes and tied it in the back.

"I can't see."

"That's the point."

"Oh, you're really getting me turnt up."

He led her out of the house and locked the door behind them. She took small, measured steps until she was safely seated in his car. He got in and they drove off.

"Where are you taking me?"

"You'll see when we get there."

"Literally!"

Nicole sat back and enjoyed the ride. XM Satellite radio was playing some romantic R & B music, which made her feel like Rashad was the type of man who was into details. She wanted to pinch herself. Even though she was happier than she'd been in a while, she still felt cautious on the inside. She enjoyed the feeling of meeting someone, connecting, and becoming a part of each other's lives. And now the same jittery butterflies snuck up in her stomach again.

Rashad decided to turn off the radio. He popped in a CD. The music of Faith Evans began playing.

"Oh, that's my jam. I can't believe you remembered how much I love her."

"I pay attention to what you tell me."

"Good. But why?"

She got scared when she didn't hear him answer right away. She wanted to remove the scarf so she could peep his facial expression.

"Just sit back and enjoy being chauffeured. We gonna be driving another forty minutes."

"That's fine."

After a while, Nicole felt Rashad casually place his hand on her bare thigh and let it rest there. She bit her bottom lip. Tears sprang into her eyelids. His touch made Nicole feel weak, like she was losing control.

"You're so sexy, Rashad."

"You think?"

When he fell silent again, she knew it was a good thing.

Just like he promised, she could feel the car's speed slowing down after an enjoyable forty-minute drive along the highway. Soon she could tell that her window was rolling down slightly.

"You smell anything, Nicky?"

She sniffed and breathed in grains of sand and the fragrance of the ocean. "I think I know where we are."

When their speed greatly decreased, the car began to idle. Rashad removed the scarf from Nicole's head. She squinted as her eyes adjusted to the sun's brightness.

"The Bolivar ferry?"

"You're a genius."

They pulled in line behind all the other vehicles and waited another half hour before they were able to board. Rashad carefully drove his car onto the ferry and after a while they were on their way, lazily drifting over the waterway. Their fellow passengers happily chatted and took generous numbers of photos. While they enjoyed the ride, Rashad handed Nicole a plastic bag filled with stale bread and corn chips.

"Here," he said. Together they tossed a handful of food over the side of the boat. They laughed as they watched the seagulls and pelicans circle the ship and swoop down to snatch the bread in their beaks. The birds squawked and flapped their wings and Nicole couldn't help but notice their freedom. To Nicole, the smell of fish, the breezy wind that caressed her cheeks, plus the dolphins gracefully swimming alongside the ship made the day feel romantic. Like the prelude to a honeymoon.

"I'm having such a good time; I can't even believe we're here."

"Glad you're enjoying yourself. You've been through a lot. It's about time you experienced fun in your life." Nicole realized that Rashad really did listen to her. When she recently divulged the ugly details of her past, she felt scared and insecure. She told him how her ex-boyfriend, Ajalon Cantu, got locked up for unlawful distribution of a controlled substance. And how at first she was loyal; she visited him in jail, deposited money on his account, and accepted his collect calls. But she grew weary of putting up money for his bonds. She despised the whole idea of an imprisoned boyfriend. It was expensive as hell. And the physical distance made her depressed. She got mad at Ajalon for being stupid enough to get caught selling drugs. In the beginning of their relationship, he made her feel safe, but later she felt lonely. He'd made foolish decisions just when she was starting to believe they'd get married and become a family. But his drug involvement made life scary and complicated. She decided to dump him and leave Alabama. That's how she ended up in Houston.

Being vulnerable about the tragedies of life, love, and broken relationships wasn't easy. But Rashad had been nothing but supportive after she shared her past.

Even so, she had questions.

"Rashad, I want to ask you something."

"Shoot."

"I'm happy about everything . . . all this. But I am shocked you brought me here . . . What if—?"

"She's far away from here today."

"Okay, I figured that. But what if you see anybody else you know? How would you explain . . . ?"

"I don't worry about that. I ain't doing nothing. Just taking a special client out for her birthday. That's all."

"Are you serious?"

"People need to mind they own business. Plus, do you see any black people on this boat?" They laughed.

"That's silly, but I get what you're trying to say. I want to make sure you're okay with being out here like this with me."

"Do you want to be with me out here?"

"There's no other place I'd want to be . . . except with you, Rashad."

"Then that's what's up."

Right before the ferry reached the Bolivar Peninsula, they climbed back into his sedan. After they docked at Seawolf Park, Rashad drove off and ended up settling at an area where people were casting fishing rods. He found a semi-private section on the beach and set up foldable travel chairs. He unfolded the chairs and invited her to sit down and relax.

"You think of everything, don't you?"

"Not all the time."

"Then this makes me feel even more special."

"That's 'cause you are."

"Are you blowing smoke up my ass?"

He couldn't do anything except laugh. It made Rashad feel good to treat her special on this day. He thought of himself as a good man, and his actions were just what a good man does.

Rashad surprised Nicole again when he opened his trunk and lifted out a small cooler filled with beer, bottled water, and ginger ale, Nicole's favorite. They feasted on deli sandwiches, a carton of strawberries, and tiny bags of chips, and talked for an hour.

Rashad decided to tell a joke.

"Did you ever hear about this Christian chick who always told everybody, 'It's just me and Jesus, it's just me and Jesus'? Well, early one morning, a fire broke out at this chick's house. Her neighbors gathered in the street watching the flames shoot from her roof. They worried. They prayed. And when they saw the woman running out the front door in her bathrobe, and noticed a butt-naked man following her, somebody said, 'Welp, there goes Jesus.'"

"Ah ha ha, Rashad. That was corny, but cute."

"Oh, here's another one. What did Jay-Z call his girl-friend before they got married? Feyoncé. Get it?"

"Ha ha, that wasn't very funny."

"But you're laughing. I like when I can make you laugh."

Nicole was having so much fun she didn't want their time together to end. At one point, she hopped on his back and placed her arms securely around his neck. He broke off into a sprint and she screamed when he ran around galloping like a wild horse and acting as if he was going to let her fall.

"Don't worry," he assured her. "I got you, Nicky."

Later on, Rashad stood up and stretched his legs. "Okay, I can tell you're getting bored. We should be headed back."

"I'm not bored with you, Rashad. I love everything about this day. We get along so well."

"I'm a good guy."

"I wish you were an available guy."

He raised one eyebrow. "Why is that?"

"The good ones are always taken. And it seems so un-fair. Seems like there are a lot more bad ones out there, the ones that don't mean a woman any good. They mainly just want a bump and grind, then they're done. I want more. All I want is my chance to have a man just like you."

Her words tugged at his heart. Even though her sin-gleness wasn't his problem, he knew if he had Nicole, she'd be loyal. He could tell she was the type of woman that rode for her man unless something horrifically tragic was going on, which obviously was the case with Ajalon.

He told Nicole they should get going. They packed up their things and headed back for the return ride on the ferry. She took a nap on the drive back and dreamt of Rashad and how happy he made her.

Once he dropped her off outside her house, she invited him inside, even though he had told her good-bye and that he'd try to call her later.

"Can you stay a little longer, please, Rashad?"

Nicole's sweet pleading voice moved his heart. He found himself floating behind this woman, effortlessly following her up the sidewalk, through the front door, and into her living room. He flopped on the couch and remained there deep in thought as she put away the scarf he had given her.

"Damn, this feels weird."

"Why is that?" She went to the kitchen and returned with a chilled can of Colt 45 that he'd bought and kept stored in her refrigerator.

She popped the top off and handed it to him. Their hands touched and she shivered.

Usually whenever Rashad was at her house working, they never sat in the living room, but that day Nicole wanted to be close to him. When she sat down, the hem of her dress rose; her thighs were exposed. She felt self-conscious and abruptly grabbed some oversize throw pillows. Rashad stopped her.

"Never cover up all that beauty. You're dope, Nicky."

"Thanks, Rashad." Her voice trembled. "You're amazing. You make me so happy. I'm glad we met." She grabbed his hand, clenched her eyes shut, and pulled his fingers inside her panties. She released his hand, and he began stroking her. Nicole moaned when she felt

Rashad's fingers stroke her mound like a skilled guitarist. She bit her bottom lip and shuddered. Together they rubbed her until she climaxed. Nicole slipped out of her dress. Rashad unhooked her bra. She slid off her thong. She helped him pull off his t-shirt, blue jeans, and underwear.

Rashad was instantly into Nicole, kissing her and savoring her restrained sensuality. Her deep desire exploded for him, and her love for him, the love that drizzled from her soul, completely turned him on. She hooked her hands around his neck and kissed him all over his face, his ears, his lips. He loved it, for Rashad had a need to be admired, wanted, and treated like he was everything to a woman.

Rashad's dick was rock-hard as Nicole kissed it and then took it deeply into her mouth. She hungrily sucked, stroked, and licked him. He grabbed her head, twisted and turned, and yelled and hollered. The more he shouted, the more excited Nicole became. She knew this moment would go beyond some oral sex.

Nicole had to have this man completely inside of her.

They engaged in more vigorous foreplay until he got behind Nicole, grabbed her ass, eagerly plunged in, and pumped her over and over again.

He hit it from the back and made noises as his thighs slapped against her.

He cupped her breasts and she cried out to the Lord and gritted her teeth.

"Oh, Rashad, baby, I love this, I love this, God, I love you."

"Whose pussy is this?"

"It's yours. It's all Rashad's."

He heard her declaration and knew she meant it.

And in her young mind, Rashad coming inside of her

was his way of branding Nicole; an identification mark to declare she was his.

They climaxed simultaneously and fell together in an exhausted heap.

After they rested, Nicole begged for one more round.

Rashad and Nicole were at the point of no return.

Chapter 16

Four weeks later

Since the day Eddison and Kiara had unprotected sex, she knew her life was transitioning. It had nowhere else to go but in a different and radical direction.

Kiara tried to be normal and act like all was well in her life, but it was hard to do.

That night Rashad came home late.

She met her husband at the door. He almost stumbled across his suitcase. A few more shirts and pants were tossed in there. It was now three fourths full.

"Oh, we're doing this again?"

"We are doing this and will continue to do this as long as you stop communicating with me about things that are important."

"What, Kiara?"

"Tonight was our son's Cub Scouts meeting. You were supposed to take him. I called you. You failed to call me back."

"Oh, snap. Totally forgot. Dammit."

Rashad had been hanging out at Nicole's. Even though the work at her house was complete, she invited him over to celebrate. She sent him a naked photo of herself and told him, "Use your key." He was at her place within twenty minutes. They enjoyed a quickie and Rashad actually did forget his son's meeting.

"And that's why this steadily filled-up suitcase will serve as a reminder. Because as long as you keep hanging out with these hoes, you forget what you have at home."

"Why I gotta be hanging out with a hoe?"

"That's what I want to know."

Kiara smacked Rashad across his face.

He scowled and walked away.

"I thought you were so big and bad," she shouted. "But like a guilty person, all you can do is run away. You won't even deny anything. At least tell me the same old lie that you always tell me."

He twirled around. "I won't argue with you. I was taking care of some business. A client held a party and I came through there for a minute and forgot about the Cub Scout meeting. I got the days mixed up. Where is Myles?"

"I'm about to go pick him up."

"Where is he?"

"H-he's with one of his friends."

"Oh, okay. I can go with you to get him. I need to apologize to little man."

"Nope, if you weren't worried about him before, please don't give a damn now."

"Kiara, I don't wanna hear that. Let's go."

She felt nervous. Myles was with Eddison. And there was no way she was taking Rashad with her. She had actually ended up driving Myles to the Scout activity. And since Eddison's house was along the way, she picked up her son and stopped by there to see him after Myles's meeting was over. She was angry that Rashad hadn't shown up. And it felt good she had somewhere else to go besides her empty house. Once Eddison gave Myles popsicles and then showed him the awesome model train collection in the game room, no amount of begging could get the boy to leave. She decided to let her son hang out at Eddison's. She trusted him enough to leave Myles at his place for a short while even though it was almost time for him to go to sleep. That gave her time to go home to confront Rashad.

During the drive home, she imagined what Rashad would do if he knew his son was hanging out with another man.

But right then Kiara knew Rashad was serious about going with her. She took a good look at him. His clothes were wrinkled. He looked different. Her mouth dropped open. He was wearing a green-and-white UAB Alumni t-shirt. She'd never seen it before. She knew he did not leave out the house with that strange-looking shirt.

"What in hell is that shirt you're wearing, Rashad?"

He glanced at his clothes. His face turned red.

"Huh? Answer me!" Kiara screamed.

"Um, it's a—"

"Rashad, you lie so fucking much. I know you probably got that shirt from some bitch you're laying up with. You don't even like UAB. That's why I'm glad I—"

He snatched her by her wrists. "You're so glad you what?" He looked frightened. "Kiara, what's really going on with you? Have you done something bad to Myles?"

"Hurt my own child? Are you crazy?" she screamed.

"No, but you are!" He squeezed her wrists.

"Ouch. Let me go. You're hurting me."

"What were you about to say, Kiara? What are you glad about?"

She tried to knee him in the groin. He jumped back. He twisted her arm even more. She began crying and struggled to get away.

"Rashad, that fucking hurts. Why do you continue to hurt me? You think I'm supposed to be happy living like this?" She looked at his luggage sprawled on the floor as she shrieked in pain. "You're physically assaulting me, yet you're the one who's done all the dirt; fucking my admin and probably half your damned clients."

"For the last time, where is my son? What'd you do to him?"

"Jesus Christ, I-I haven't done anything to Myles, you dumb fuck. And I know about UAB. It stands for University of Alabama. Where'd you get that shirt from?"

"Can't I buy a stupid shirt?"

"You are such a liar!"

He let her go and stormed away. She heard their bedroom door slam and the locks turned.

"Liar, liar, liar," she said. She was glad he fled to the room. It was her perfect chance to avoid his questions and pull herself together before she left to pick up Myles.

By the time she rang Eddison's doorbell, she had calmed down. He opened the door and she mouthed, "Thanks, baby."

He looked pleased to see her. She found Myles. He was watching the Lionel NASCAR trains zip around the tracks. He barely said hello to her.

"Hey, son. It's getting late. We have to go."

"You hear the choo choo sounds? Can you see the smoke coming out the train, Mommy? This is so much fun. Can I spend the night, please, Mommy?"

"Um, not tonight, Myles. Maybe some other time."

"Eddy is my new best friend."

She laughed out loud. Eddison did, too.

"Kiara, may I see you for a second?" She followed him into his kitchen. He knew Myles was preoccupied so he quickly swept the woman he adored into his arms.

"That little man is so smart, so engaged. He is amazing. We had a ball. And I fed him a turkey burger so he's good for the night."

"*You* are amazing. I feel so bad pulling you into all of this—"

"Shhh," he said and kissed her lips. "I'm here. I want to be here." He kissed her again. "If all goes well, you're going to be my lady one day."

He placed his hand on her flat belly and closed his eyes.

"Are you praying that I'm pregnant and that the baby will be yours?" she asked.

"It *is* mine."

She turned from him and wrung her hands. This was getting to be too much to deal with. And she felt confused.

She faced him and said softly, "I-I-I don't even know if I'm pregnant yet. Plus we wouldn't know until DNA tells us."

"But I can dream, can't I?"

She didn't want to dash his hopes. Ever since she had learned that her period was late, he and Adina were the only people she'd told. Kiara was in a daze. She knew that if she was pregnant, it would be because the Lord allowed it.

If Eddison turned out to be the father, Kiara would have to deal with that when the time came. She could envision Eddison being a good daddy. But the power of paternity wasn't in her hands. It was in God's hands. And that's what Kiara was afraid of.

Regardless of what happened, as long as there was a chance that Rashad was the father of her baby, Kiara knew that she had to take control in ways she never imagined.

Chapter 17

It was a Wednesday. A Hump Day. Alexis was at work using the women's restroom. As she sat there, Rashad texted her.

Where u been? R U ok?

She had been ignoring him for weeks. But for a moment she felt curious. She picked up her iPhone, the one she used to keep in touch with him, and she called him.

"Hey, Skillet. It's about time you answered my calls."

"I've been busy."

"What? You have never been too busy for me. What you been doing?"

"Living my life; just like you've been living yours."

Alexis heard some commotion and recognized Nicole and Shyla's voices as they entered the restroom. They were so busy cackling she figured they didn't know she was hidden away in a stall. She thought about how she had seen Nicole and him at the restaurant that day hugged up for a photo op, and how the basic chick was always talking trash to her for no reason. It infuriated her. She put Rashad on speaker and let him talk.

"I ain't been doing nothing out the ordinary," he said, his loud voice echoed against the walls.

"Shhh," Alexis heard one of the ladies say.

Alexis continued talking. "It's me. I know you. If you ain't fucking one bitch, then I know you'll be fucking another. That's how you do—with your fine ass."

A hush fell over the restroom.

"Skillet, you spazzing out." He laughed. "You ought to let me get some loving again. You act like your legs are closed up to me. You been letting anybody else hit that?"

"As a married man, you have zero jurisdiction over me, sweetie. You can't be asking me questions like that."

"You better not be fucking anybody but me," he said.

Alexis emerged from her stall. She whipped back her weave and stared Nicole dead in the face. The woman's mouth was all twisted up in anger and disgust.

"You don't run me, Rashad!"

He laughed. "Okay, sweetness. We'll see. Meanwhile, let's plan to go see Hayley and do something fun with her."

"Sure. Anything for your child . . . I mean anything for you with your childish self."

She hung up.

"Who is Hayley?" Nicole demanded.

"Mind your business."

"He is my business, bitch."

"If he was really your business, you'd already know."

Alexis washed her hands and ignored the two women as she calmly left the restroom.

A little while later, Alexis looked up from her desk. She saw Nicole emerging from Kiara's office. Then she saw Kiara walking down the hall in her direction. Her face looked distressed.

"I need to talk to you, Alexis."

"Yes, ma'am."

Alexis wanted to cry. She hated Nicole. The chick just didn't know when to stop.

Kiara closed the door behind her and watched Alexis take her seat.

"Um, this is an odd question, but what kinds of dealings do you still have with my husband?"

"Barely any, to be honest."

"Are you sure about that?"

"Yes! Why do you ask?"

"Nicole told me she overheard—"

"Shouldn't you be questioning Rashad? Isn't he more of your concern than me?"

Kiara looked taken aback. "Well, yes, but I always like to hear both sides of the story."

"My side is that there is no side. I've been doing my best to avoid him. Unless it's absolutely necessary."

"What would make it necessary for you to see Rashad?"

Alexis said nothing.

"Does it have to do with a child?"

"Excuse me?"

"Nicole seems to believe that a child is involved."

"Oh really? Nicole doesn't know what the fuck she's talking about!" Alexis was on the verge of tears. Kiara was standing over her. She felt like a trapped animal.

"Alexis, if there is a child, and I hope there isn't, you should come clean."

"There is no child!"

Kiara stared at her and said, "All right then. You may return to your desk." Alexis left Kiara's office.

As soon as she was gone, Kiara placed a call to Rashad. He answered on the first ring.

"Hey—"

"What's this I hear about you having a child with Alexis?"

"What?"

"People overheard conversations, so there are rumors going around."

"People don't know what they heard."

"But you don't know what they heard either, so how can you even assume? Either you do or you don't."

"I don't."

She stared at the phone and fell into silence. And then she hung up.

Alexis couldn't wait till lunchtime. For the first time in a long time, she was ecstatic to meet up with a man on Hump Day and she was so happy that it wasn't Rashad.

She tried to hide her grin as she stood out in the employee parking lot next to her building. She could see Varnell approaching her. This felt good. This was how a woman ought to be treated.

He carefully parked next to her. Hopped out the car and opened her door for her.

"Thank you," she said. "You are a rare one."

He laughed and told her, "I've been out of practice for a minute so forgive me if I'm rusty."

Varnell asked her what she had a taste for.

"I love Cajun food."

"You got it."

She directed him to a downtown diner that she'd always heard about. Once they parked, got in line to order their meals, and took their seats, Alexis couldn't stop smiling.

"Why you look like that?" he asked.

"I'm glad we finally got to meet up. This is a nice way to break up my day, which has been pretty hectic so far."

"Oh, then I'll make sure that you have a good lunch, how about that?"

He sat across from her and, from the way he wolfed down his food, she liked that he appreciated a good, solid meal. The more she discreetly observed Varnell, the more she liked him. His skin was the color of a walnut. He had strong hands, twinkling eyes that were filled with compassion, and a gentle way about him that reminded her of her daddy.

"You know, Alexis, if anything, I must thank you for having patience. I know most women don't like to wait on guys."

"Tell me about it," she said. "It is hard for me to be patient. I like for things to stay popping."

"Well, thanks for the last-minute casual lunch. I was in the area and I just wanted to see you. Make sure you're okay. And let you know that I hadn't forgotten about you. I don't like to tell people one thing and do something else. So get ready for the first of many dates that I want us to have."

Alexis grinned and nodded. She sat and enjoyed her stuffed pork chop and jambalaya, and she daydreamed about a better future. A more realistic life that didn't depend on married men who played games. Alexis didn't want to be a mistress forever who had to hide. She wanted the best that life could offer to her and Hayley, and she could only hope that she was on her way to getting it.

Alexis sat on the edge of her seat in the darkness of the Hobby Center. She mouthed the lines to the Broadway musical as she watched the actress playing Sofia in *The Color Purple*.

She clutched the program tightly in her hands. She heard the tittered laughter of the audience that surrounded her on both sides. She sat smack in the middle of the aisle with a perfect view of the actors.

"You enjoying yourself?"

Alexis gently nodded, her eyes steadfast on the breathtaking production, her ears taking in the dialogue, the heightened sounds of the auditorium. She was moved to tears, thinking of the need to fight, and how you must battle in order to win.

When it was all over, and the audience rose to its feet in loud and enthusiastic applause, Alexis finally exhaled. The lights went up. Varnell grabbed her by the hand and escorted her to the crowded lobby where theatergoers were purchasing gift items and mementos from the popular musical.

She was so grateful that her mother had agreed to watch Hayley that Saturday afternoon. Earlier she told her mom she had a date with a single man. And thankfully, for the first time in a long time, her mother was excited for Alexis.

They went down the escalator, through the exits, and walked on the sidewalks amidst the crowds.

"I see you have a huge smile on your face," Varnell said. "I hope that means you were okay with this official first date."

"I am. It's just what I needed." She was thinking, *Maybe you're just what I needed*, but her cautious heart kept those words from escaping her mouth.

They took a leisurely stroll to a downtown Houston outdoor café. When Varnell pulled out her chair for her to sit down, Alexis fought hard to act calm and like she was used to good treatment. She relished how good it felt to be with this man.

"Let it out. Your facial expressions are saying all kinds of things . . . things I'd like to hear."

Alexis felt self-conscious when a blush spread across

her cheeks. Varnell was so different from Rashad. He was polite, strong yet gentle, and a teensy bit shy mixed with humbleness.

"No, really. I'm just having a great time. It's been awhile."

"Really? A pretty woman like you ain't used to having a good time every day?"

She shrugged. "Story of my life. Everything that glitters isn't gold."

"Well, somehow I knew that. From the first time I laid eyes on you in that grocery store, I knew there was a story underneath those beautifully sad eyes."

She didn't know how to respond.

"I'm glad we met, though. You are more chill than I thought."

"Oh, really?"

"You look high maintenance—"

"I can be," she admitted.

"I knew that, too, but I decided to take a chance. To not judge you by your pretty face, your nice clothes, your perfect hair."

"It's not all real. But I like it," she replied, sifting her fingers through her long strands.

"I know that. Some women these days think you gotta wear all this weave and . . . silicone booty and five-thousand-dollar boob jobs."

She laughed. "I know what you mean. It seems like you're not getting the real woman, right?"

"Correct."

"And I completely understand that, Varnell. It's just that when you give someone the real you, and you still get rejected, well, a little bit of Indian hair doesn't seem to matter that much. Some women do what they think they need to do to make themselves feel and look good."

"I know, but it always seems like it's something you

slap on yourself. On your head. On your body. On you. Over you. Covering you. Men just like to know what they actually getting, that's all."

"I hear you. And I hope my weave doesn't make you want to stop seeing me."

It was his turn to be surprised. "You want to see me again?"

"Why not? Don't sell yourself so short, boo."

"Oh, it ain't that. I just thought I moved a little too slow for you."

"Slow is good sometimes. I've done fast. Fast only speeds up heartbreak."

"Tell me about it."

They ordered seared salmon with mashed potatoes and broccoli. By this time, if she'd been with anybody else, she'd had retrieved a cigarette by now, lit it up and smoked away her nerves. But Alexis wasn't really nervous right then. She enjoyed her date's company so much she felt she didn't want to ruin anything. She wasn't sure what their new relationship would lead to, and God knows she didn't want to scare the man away.

"You got a man?"

"Whoa, I did not expect that abrupt question." She paused to take a long sip of green tea.

"What's your answer?"

"I have a . . . I have a situation."

"A situation."

"Yeah, you know one of those things where it's hard to explain exactly what it is and even if you do know what it is, you still aren't ready to explain it? One of those."

"One of those. Well, it happens, especially if you live in this world long enough."

"How about you?"

"Never married. I've had some long-term relationships. They were good . . . in the beginning. Now I'm kind
of chilling. When you've been there and done that, you
feel you already know what's going to happen. I'm waiting for a nice surprise to come my way."

"I love how that sounds. Nice surprises instead of the
normal B.S."

He concentrated on eating his food then asked,
"What do you want out of life, Alexis McNeil?"

"I-I just want to . . . um. I just want."

"You don't have to answer now. We have plenty of
time to figure it out. Together."

She offered Varnell a grateful smile. She knew what
she wanted to say, but right then she lacked the courage
to tell him that her life was a mess and she was in the
process of fixing her "situation"; that she wanted Varnell
to meet Hayley, and how she wanted a true, authentic relationship that was acceptable to her mother.

Alexis hoped that one day the fragmented pieces of
her life would eventually click together and make perfect, happy, unsurprising sense.

When the following weekend arrived, Alexis made a
random decision to go to the Home Depot. She needed
to get some fertilizer for the backyard. She found a parking place, got out of the car and started walking toward
the entrance. But as she passed through the lot, she saw
Rashad's new sedan. She knew his license plate number.
The windows were rolled down. Alexis peeped inside.
The car was empty. The key was in the ignition. She
knew Rashad had a bad habit of leaving his windows
open. And apparently now he was forgetting and leaving keys in the car too. She reached inside, removed his
key, and hid it in her hand.

She decided to go in the store and look for Rashad. Alexis quietly walked around the huge store until she saw the back of his head. He was in the appliance department. Nicole Greene stood next to him pointing at a refrigerator. They stood close together and were talking.

Alexis walked up to Rashad. He didn't see her. But Nicole stopped talking the second she saw Alexis.

"We have a visitor."

"What you mean?"

"Turn around."

Rashad slowly turned around. His face turned white when he saw Alexis.

"Yo, what's up?"

"Yo, what's up?" Alexis said.

"Yeah, I am saying hi. What's up?"

Alexis glared while Nicole grinned. "He and I are busy right now. He's helping me pick out an appliance." Nicole grabbed Rashad by his hand. He hesitated but let her pull him away from Alexis.

No wonder he can't keep his mind on what he's doing, Alexis thought as she discreetly placed his car key in her purse.

"Rashad, are you seriously letting her hold your hand too? Oh, hell no."

"What you mean 'hell no'? This man ain't yours."

Alexis was sick of Nicole. It was time to pay Rashad back.

"He's my child's father. That's what he is."

Nicole dropped Rashad's hand. "What did you say?"

"Ask him yourself."

"I thought you told our boss that there is no child. She came back and told me you denied it and that I need to stop spreading rumors before something bad happens. What the hell is going on? Rashad?"

"So you never told her, either?" Alexis asked. "Are you honest with any woman that's in your life?"

"Alexis, look. This is not the time or place. I'm with my client."

"She's way more than a client. It's obvious y'all two got something going on." Alexis whipped out the photo of them at the restaurant. "You do not pose like this with all your clients. Stop playing us for a fool. And tell the truth for once in your life."

"Rashad, baby, it's okay. We cool like that. You can tell me anything. It doesn't matter. I'm riding with you regardless."

"Alexis, I don't need you to dictate when I should tell Nicky what I want her to know. Now, if you don't mind, we got some business to take care of. I'll hit you up later, okay?"

Alexis felt sick to her stomach. She couldn't believe Rashad as he protectively placed his arm around Nicole right in front of her.

"Fool, you are not going to disrespect me in front of this ugly-ass bitch."

Nicole laughed. "It's funny that he spends a lot of time with this ugly-ass bitch. He don't want you. That's why he's always with me. A long, pretty weave is not enough to keep a man. And apparently a baby with you isn't enough, either."

Alexis rolled her eyes. "I don't have to fight over this Negro or any other one. Bye, Rashad. You are a bigger fool than I thought you were."

Nicole gave Alexis a triumphant look the second she saw her backing away from them.

Alexis stormed out of the store. She began walking toward her car. But when she saw Rashad's sedan, she went and jerked open the door handle. She got in the car, retrieved the key, and started the engine. Alexis backed Rashad's car out of the parking space. She quickly sped away from the Home Depot. She kept wiping hot tears from her eyes as she drove down the street and ignored the calls that began making her cell phone beep.

The texts started pouring in.

Forget what just happened. Little Shorty feeling me, that's all.

Answer ur phone. She in the ladies room. I only got 5 mins.

We can talk.

Alexis drove and drove. Each time she saw a police car, she held her breath and her stomach felt tense. "He can't call the police on me. He doesn't know I have his car. But what if he finds out? Could I go to jail?"

She drove until she reached a corner gas station. She pulled next to a pay phone. She stepped out, put money in the slot, and dialed Rashad's number. He didn't pick up the first time, but he answered the second time.

"Hello?"

"I can't believe you are fucking that psycho—"

"Alexis, I wanna tell you all about that, but I got an emergency right now. Somebody stole my car."

"What? Are you kidding me?"

"No. It's fucked up. I came out here and the car was gone."

"Wow, karma is a nasty bitch."

"Did you do something to my car?"

"Nope."

"Please don't lie to me."

"Please don't lie to you? That's funny, Rashad."

"You sure you didn't do anything to my car?"

"I haven't done anything to your car."

She hung up. He called her cell phone. She didn't answer. Logic and sensibility had no place in her head. She thought about herself, then thought about Nicole.

"Filet mignon versus a hot dog. J. W. Marriott versus Motel Six. Neiman Marcus versus Walmart. Hell, not even Walmart. More like the Salvation Army. He must be out his mind."

Alexis decided to drive to Glynis's. She couldn't think of any other place to go. Once she arrived, it took Alexis longer than normal to locate a parking space. The street that was typically clear from traffic was now filled with parked vehicles up and down the block. Alexis found an available spot at the very end and briskly walked until she reached her sister's house. The door of the fence was wide open. Alexis timidly went up to the front door. Before she could knock, Hazel, the center's co-operator, answered. Hazel looked a hot mess, sweaty and funky like she'd been running from the police.

"I'm shocked you got here so fast. News spreads fast."

"What are you talking about? What news?"

"Your sister. She's dead. She passed away an hour ago."

Alexis's knees buckled. She sunk to the ground, her head hitting the concrete.

Rashad and Nicole took a taxi to her house. Once he paid the driver, he impatiently asked Nicole if he could drive her car.

"I need to report that my ride's been jacked. I would let you drive but you drive too slow."

"Okay then." She handed him the keys and smiled while he took the wheel. He hadn't driven too far when he got another call from an unrecognized number.

Hazel identified herself and told Rashad about Glynis.

"Aw, damn. I'm sorry to hear that. Where's my baby?"

Nicole gave him the side-eye.

"I'm on my way."

Nicole was silent for the majority of the ride over to the north side.

"So you really do have a baby?"

"Yeah, I do. Her name is Hayley. What about it?"

"Oh, so it is true. Damn. We been rolling a long time and you could have told me that."

"I didn't want to tell you. I still don't. That's my private business. I just didn't know when to tell you."

"But what man denies his child?"

"I've never denied my kid."

"I'm just saying. We tight. You can trust me."

"I can trust you to do what?"

"I won't tell a soul."

Rashad didn't say another word until they pulled up on the block and ended up having to park the next street over.

By the time they walked into Glynis's house and Rashad saw Alexis nursing her head injury, he went and knelt beside her. "I heard what happened. You all right? You gone be okay?"

He grabbed Alexis in a bear hug. She let him hold her. Nicole stood to the side with her arms folded. Alexis didn't care about the hateful looks Nicole shot at her. When Hayley stumbled into the room with her arms outstretched saying, "Mama," Alexis scooped the precious little girl into her arms. She squeezed her tight. She knew Hayley was looking for the woman who had always acted as her mother.

"Mama," she cried out as she squirmed and curiously stared at all the people that began to congregate throughout the house.

As the house started to fill up with family, friends, and associates, Alexis heard in bits and pieces the details about her sister's passing.

"She was driving to the store and she passed out at the wheel and crashed through the front of a Starbucks. Her blood sugar dropped too low and she blacked out. She died instantly."

Alexis felt so sad and dry inside, she had no tears. She and Glynis had butted heads off and on for years, but she'd never wish death upon anyone.

"This is shocking and so unexpected," Alexis said. "I knew she had seen the doctor about her blood sugar and she was on insulin. I thought she could beat this disease. Now this."

"Thank God the baby wasn't in the car with her," another person said.

"Speaking of cars . . ." Alexis told Rashad. "Did you find yours?"

"No. I was on my way to the police station when I got the phone call about this."

"Thank you for making this a priority."

"No problem."

"And I know where your car is."

"You do?"

"Follow me."

Nicole tightly held onto Rashad's arm as he rose to his feet. Alexis told her, "This has nothing to do with you. It's just me and him. Have a seat."

Nicole defiantly kept standing.

When Rashad proceeded to walk out of the house, Nicole was right behind him.

Alexis told him, "Please handle this."

"Chill, Nicky. I got to take care of my business real quick. And I'm warning you, don't ever tell anyone about my child. She's innocent and doesn't deserve to be in the middle of a scandal. If you tell anyone, especially Kiara, we are through, you got that?"

"Okay, I won't tell a soul. I love you, Rashad."

"Good. Now go get something to eat. I'll be back."

Nicole gave Alexis a hostile look but she smiled at Rashad and said, "Okay, babe."

Most women wouldn't put up with Rashad's reckless ways, but Nicole wasn't most women. She knew he wasn't a perfect man, but she could sense he was a man who tried to act like he had it all together. But she knew he had his fears about life, yet he tried anyway. He had a strong work ethic. And he was generous and thoughtful. Nicole felt she understood him. When he previously told her about the clashes he had with his own mother, and how disappointed he was at not receiving his mom's full support when he became a young man, Nicole wanted to hold him in her arms and let him know that she would ride for him no matter what. She believed in his potential. She knew that, if he had the right woman, he could excel. She felt he lied because of fear, and fear was something Nicole understood well.

Once Nicole left them alone, Alexis and Rashad stepped outside the house and walked down the block. Alexis cleared her throat. "What the hell is going on?"

"I told you, she's my client."

"Cut the bullshit. I can tell by y'all's body language that you're fucking her."

He scratched his head and looked away in the distance.

"It is only because you had a death in the family that I will ignore that accusation. Meanwhile, we got something serious on our hands. I am assuming you will take Hayley with you at some point till I figure out what to do."

"Rashad—"

"Here, take this." He handed her a wad of cash. She tossed the bills in the air.

"This is what you can do with your guilt money."

She proceeded to head back toward the house but he grabbed her.

"Okay." He couldn't look her in the eyes. "I messed up. I messed up."

"That's all I ask is that you be real with me. I know you too well for you to try anything else."

"We kind of fell into a little thing; before I knew it, I was in deep. It wasn't planned."

"No wonder you disappeared on me. But it's cool. Hayley and I will be just fine."

"This does not mean I have abandoned you, nor Hayley."

"Save it, Rashad."

He apologized again and reached down to pick up the money. When she turned around to walk back to the house, he called out after her, "What did you want to tell me about my ride?"

"Nothing, Rashad. I know nothing about your ride."

She started to walk away but she turned back around and looked him in the eye. "Except that you can find it parked all the way down the street on the right-hand side. Next time roll up your windows, lock your damn doors, and remember to take this with you." Then she reached in her purse and retrieved his key.

Alexis returned to the house where her relatives were grieving and swapping stories about her sister. By the time evening arrived, Alexis grew completely exhausted from all the talking and asking questions. Rashad told her, "Come on. We'll take you to Home Depot."

"We?"

"I meant me. Alexis, go and get Hayley's things so she can spend the night with you."

"She's not just spending the night. She's going to live where she always belonged."

While Alexis packed, Rashad fielded calls from Kiara, who'd been trying to reach him all day. Nicole stood around trying to listen to his conversation but he ducked inside another room. Alexis and Nicole were left alone.

"Sorry about your sister."

"Shut up, Nicole."

"You know what, I'm trying to be nice to you."

"I don't need you to be nice to me."

"You are one stupid ass—"

Alexis shoved Nicole up against a wall and held her by her wrists. "You and I are not friends. Got it? We have nothing in common. Nothing!" Alexis was close enough to spit on her.

"What are you doing? Get your hands off me. I'm gonna scream for Rashad, you better stop."

"Trust me. That man can't even save himself let alone you."

Alexis let her go. She had more important things to deal with.

Glynis's funeral was held a few days later. Rashad insisted on driving Alexis. She hadn't seen the family since Tandy had died a few years ago, but everyone in the family was happy to talk to her. Hayley sat perfectly still until she noticed the blown-up poster of Glynis stationed close to the casket. She pointed and yelled, "Mama," but Alexis didn't mind. She got up and carried her daughter to the open casket. As instructed, Hayley dropped a pack of Starbursts on top of the corpse, Glynis's favorite candy.

When the memorial service ended, Rashad drove them home. They were silent during the ride. Hayley was leaning all the way out of her car seat, snoring like a hundred-year-old woman.

Even though Alexis and her sister hadn't been particularly close, she still felt the loss. She wished she could hear Glynis's voice again . . . and wished she could say all the things that division and pride kept her from voicing during the times that she could.

Finally Rashad spoke. "I told myself I'd never let you ride in my car again, yet look at what I'm doing."

Alexis gave a small smile. "We always gotta try and do right by family, no matter how mad we get at them."

"Yeah. I guess . . . Fam."

"And, Rashad. I-I am sorry for getting pissed off at you . . . and taking off in your ride. I've never done anything like that before. But, hey. It was fun."

"You ain't right, Skillet."

She could tell from the sound of his voice that he wouldn't hold a grudge. He never had.

"I learned you never know what you'll do when you're in a certain situation. You only know when that thing is right in your face, when you're in the moment." Death always made Alexis think about life. And making sure life was right before it shifted into death. She paused and searched for the words she wanted to say. "You may not want to hear this, but I think two years is long enough to keep this situation from her. The longer you wait, the worse it's going to be, Rashad."

"Tell me about it. Lately, I've been thinking a lot about my life, my daddy, my son, Hayley, you, Kiara. I kind of wish I was a Mormon."

"You sound crazy."

"Who says I'm not? Seriously, you may not believe this, but I don't know what I'd do if I lost the most important things in my life. I wonder why things can't be the way I want them to be."

"But that's not fair, Rashad. There's something called 'order' that is supposed to rule everything in this world. And if you don't live life in the right order, well, things will be messed up. I sure wish our daughter had been born under better circumstances . . ."

"Hell, I do, too. But what's done is done. I've already hurt enough people. You really think I want to hurt her?"

"Think about it, Rashad. With everything that's happened, you already have."

Chapter 18

Kiara and Eddison were standing in a stairwell between the first and second floor of her office facility. Their voices were low, but they still echoed against the walls of the corridor.

"I had to see you. How are you doing?"

"I have moments when I feel great. And other times, I want to pinch myself just to make sure I'm not in a dream. But work . . . work helps me to keep it together. This is where I know my role. Where I'm in control. So it's coming along."

Kiara was indeed expecting, but she wasn't showing yet. She was wearing layered tops, a style that she'd usually wear during the late summer.

"Well, I'm sure you already know this, but you're glowing."

"I'll bet I am."

"Anyway, Kiara. Just checking on you. But I wanted to thank you for meeting with Collette and Gherman the other day. Because of you, the kids are going to make restitution. They'll bounce back and this whole thing will be behind them. And the university will be better off as well as the families."

"Yeah. It's funny how that works out. Glad I could help."

"One more thing. Did you find out . . . ?"

"The due date is April seventh. I don't know the gender. I don't think I want to know. I feel like I'm in an episode of Bill Cunningham."

"When will you know if it's mine or not?"

She could only smile at him. She knew he was as anxious as she was.

"When I know, you will know."

They said good-bye. It was eerily quiet as Eddison reached out to hug her.

Kiara noticed the sound of someone's footsteps running up the stairwell. When she tried to see who it could be, that person was already gone.

Later on, Tony Fu swung by Kiara's office.

"Hey, Tony, how are things going?"

"Cool. I just wanted to follow up with you about something. All the staff complied with the request to get their home addresses updated, except for one person."

"Let me guess. Nicole?"

"Yes! She wouldn't respond to all my emails so when I asked her for her driver's license so I could make a copy, she refused to hand it over. You think she's hiding something?"

"Something is definitely up. But don't worry. There are still other ways to find out where she lives . . . Not that I personally care. But we need updated info . . ."

"In case of an emergency," Tony said, and gave Kiara a knowing look.

Kiara got off work a couple hours early that day. She went to see her physician. After she received a full examination, Kiara knew her fate was sealed in terms of having a baby; but other parts of her life were still uncertain.

Afterward, Kiara decided to visit the woman she loved and trusted the most in the world. She held Mama Flora's hand as she finally admitted to her that she had had sex with two men in one day. And that a child would be the result of her rash behavior.

"Mama Flora, I have very mixed feelings. A part of me is excited. Another part is scared. I never thought this ratchet drama would be my life."

"It's okay, baby. And believe it or not, the Lord understands."

"He understands I'm a fool. I'm not his best child. I'm not as perfect as folks think I am." At that moment she felt a bit of despair. "I wouldn't mind if it's not Rashad's, but the court of public opinion may feel differently."

"Baby girl, horrible things happen to basically good people, and they still turn out OK."

"Who, Grandma? These days when people realize they mess up, they—" She swallowed deeply and shook her head.

"No. Wait one minute, young lady, I know you not thinking about—"

"But I hurt so bad. The pain is so deep. I don't want to face the day anymore." She buried her face in her hands and wept. "And my marriage is getting worse. I don't know if having a baby will save our relationship. Who am I kidding? I can't have this baby."

"You can have it and you will. Your child deserves a good life and if God didn't have a purpose for it, you never would have conceived."

"Thanks for saying that. If things were really great between us, I'd be super excited, Mama Flora. Sometimes I think back to our good old days, and I pray that they will return. If the old Rashad came back, that would give me hope. Back in the day, he was totally into my pregnancy; he rubbed my feet, he cooked the meals, made sure I ate healthy. He was everything."

"It seemed he understood his purpose back then, but somehow he lost his way."

"If only we can find it again," Kiara responded. "The bottom line is I'm scared. And I don't know how to properly handle this situation."

Kiara collapsed again in her grandmother's arms. She despised herself for thinking she could handle a situation that was clearly more complicated than what it seemed.

"Look, young lady, you may feel hopeless and regretful right now . . . but it's not the end of the world."

"How can you say that?"

"Because I've been through what you're going through."

"Huh? What did you say?"

"Everybody's got secrets. And only a privileged few know what married folk really go through behind closed doors."

"What on earth are you talking about?"

"Long ago when you were just a child, I thought John was doing something devious behind my back. There was a flirty lady that lived down the street from us. Her name was Billie Fay. One day I saw her leaving our house, coming through our front door as I was pulling up. I saw her with her red tinted scraggly hair, her wide hips, and her cleavage popping out her blouse. It was the middle of summer and, boy, was I hot. I ran up to her and smacked her hard across her face. She screamed and told me to stop. I hit her again. Billie Fay ran and got in her car. I ran and got in mine. John stormed out the house waving his arms and asking what's wrong. She sped down the street like she robbed a bank but I caught up with her. I rolled down my window and cursed her something good. Then I turned my steering wheel and side-scraped her. I heard that metal screeching. She gave me a horrified look and drove till she reached her house. That's when I saw an ambulance pull up. They went into my neighbor's house and . . ." Grandma hung her head. "They rolled out her husband on a gurney. He'd had a stroke. He died later that day. I found out that Billie Fay drove down to our house because their phone service was cut off. All she wanted to do was use the phone."

"Mama Flora, you didn't know. I'm so sorry."

"John said I made us look like countrified fools. He told me I made myself look real insecure and dumb. I couldn't argue. He was too ashamed to go to the man's funeral. And I just had to endure that time period and wait till John started talking to me again."

"Going off on the lady was pretty bad. I didn't know you had it in you."

"I didn't either. That was my one and only TKO. I retired after that."

Kiara managed to smile. "And you survived that one incident?"

"My situation wasn't yours, but it shows you that a couple that's dedicated can get over the biggest mistakes of their marriage. I eventually forgave myself. John got over it. But my point is, the thing you're most afraid of is the thing you can survive, even if you've done the worst thing ever."

"Are you saying that Grand Pop was the angel of your relationship and you were the devil?"

"Neither he nor I are perfect. But truth be told, when it came to him and what he was possibly doing behind my back, I never asked John any questions. So he couldn't tell me any lies."

Kiara couldn't begin to count the number of lies Rashad may have told. And she was no better than him now that she'd had her own affair. They were both guilty of sugar-coating the truth.

"You told me you try to get into his phone account, find out who he's calling and where he's going. Stop all that nonsense. It'll only make you feel sicker and crazier. This too shall pass."

"I wish I could take back every unwise thing that I've done since May; because right now I feel real low; like knocked-down-to-the-ground-can't-get-up type of low."

"That means there's nowhere else to go but up. And God will lift you like he lifts the birds he created. Kiara, one day you will soar again. He'll give you wings to help you fly, and feet to help you land."

Immediately after her visit with Mama Flora, Kiara had one last important trip to make. Moments later, she was standing at Eddison's front door. He looked surprised and happy to see her. He invited her in, but she declined.

She pointed to her nearby car, which still had the motor running.

"Eddison, this won't take long." She took a deep breath and let the words spill.

"I made a mistake. We shouldn't have gotten involved—"

"Kiara, no need to apologize—"

"Wait, let me explain. I gotta clean up my side of the street, really clean it up. God is looking at me, my actions, he knows my thoughts. I must do everything I can to be good to the man I married, instead of putting all my hope in a man who I didn't marry. I hope you understand."

Eddison looked crushed. "But what about the child?"

"As far as I'm concerned," she said firmly, "this baby will be Rashad's. It will have his name on the birth certificate. That's my story and I'm sticking with it."

"But Kiara, with all due respect, if it's mine, I'd want to know that it is. And I'd want to be involved."

"I understand but—"

"Do you understand that I love and care about you . . . and this child?"

"You're making this hard for me."

"It doesn't have to be hard."

"I need time to process, okay? I'm in a difficult situation. I put myself in it."

"We did it together."

She nodded unable to deny Eddison's truth.

She told him, "If it's meant to be, I will see you again. I gotta go." She turned around to leave.

"Kiara, please. Wait a minute."

"I wish I could, but I can't. Good-bye for now."

Her legs felt like sticks of lead as she walked to her car, waved at him, got in and drove away.

The time had come.

Kiara prayed that her marriage would be given one more chance. She wanted to act more civil and loving with Rashad. So that very night she prepared a delicious steak and potatoes dinner for her family. She cooked homemade gravy and cut up some green beans in a pot. She even baked some homemade rolls, something she hadn't done in three years.

Rashad's eyes enlarged when he got home from work and his nose led him to the kitchen.

"What's all this for?"

She took a deep breath. "Hello, Rashad. I just wanted

you to know that I love you. I do. I'm sorry for my insecure ways and crazy behavior, and I really want us to make it to our forty."

"You do?"

"Yes. I mean, that's my biggest hope, and it can only happen if we both are on the same page. And I know it can't happen if I keep acting like you're the devil, and if I keep being spiteful."

Rashad was stunned. She hadn't ever blamed herself for any of the problems in their marriage. A marriage never disintegrated as the result of one partner's actions.

He felt touched and could see the sincerity in her eyes.

He reached out and hugged her. "Thanks. Um, and if I have acted like the devil, and sometimes I do, I swear I don't mean it. I can't explain it. I guess I am just a fool sometimes. But it's only because I don't want to lose you."

"Are you serious?"

"I am."

"Thanks for saying that. I have to process it." She nervously laughed. "But later for that. I've got a big announcement to make."

"What's that?"

"Have a seat. Here's your beer. Um, Myles, come on and wash your hands for dinner. Your daddy's home."

Rashad beamed at her and winked. He made her feel twenty-something years old. He still looked so handsome. Things felt good for the first time in a long time.

Once they were all seated, Kiara stood at the head of the table.

"We are a family. And we need to start acting like one. Loving and trusting each other. And doing all we can to be a strong family unit."

"Can we eat, please?"

"Myles, hush. I need to say the blessing. Y'all bow your heads and close your big ole eyes."

Then she said, "Lord, thank You for this food we are about to receive. Let it nourish and strengthen our bodies. And let it especially strengthen me. Now that I know we are about to add a precious new addition to our little family."

Rashad's eyes popped open.

"You pregnant?"

"Amen. Yes!"

"How long have you known?"

"I just wanted to make sure it was really happening before I told you."

"How far along are you?"

"Um, about nine weeks now."

"Nine weeks, huh?"

Rashad was stunned. He remembered telling his wife that he didn't want to have another child.

"This is why I wanted us to use protection that time. Remember?"

"Yes, but I didn't think I could get pregnant back then. Remember?"

He nodded. Feeling dazed he repeated, "Nine weeks."

"Yeah, so that's my little breaking news."

"I wasn't expecting this at all. And I still can't believe it."

"Trust me, Rashad. I can't believe it, either."

Chapter 19

Kiara was getting a little excited. After her husband got over the initial shock, he seemed to accept that the baby was on the way. He even surprised Kiara and brought home a teddy bear bouquet. She was pleased that Rashad accepted the news of her pregnancy so well. She had hope. Maybe it would be a new beginning.

It was almost time for them to get away for their anniversary vacation. Kiara couldn't wait. All she did was work most of the time, and she stressed the rest of the time. She deserved some relaxation.

Rashad was just as hyped. He told her that he paid the remaining balance of their cruise including adding the AT&T cruise ship package so they could stay connected in case of an emergency. Myles would be cared for by Mama Flora. All the preparations were set.

In early October, a few days before their trip, Kiara was in their bedroom partially naked after having just taken a soothing bubble bath that Rashad drew for her.

She stared at herself in the mirror. "How do I look? Do I look fat?"

"You look fine."

"I wonder if I'll be able to get rid of the baby weight this time."

"It won't matter, you will still look hot, Kiara."

"For real, Rashad?"

"Of course; there's nothing ugly about you. Hey, I know you think I'm an ass. That's what you always say, 'I love you, but you're an ass.'"

She laughed. "True."

"I know this sounds strange, but maybe instead of calling me one, because that could be why I've acted the way I do, how about calling me a name that you really want me to be? Words have power, right?"

"Oh, I know you did not say that."

He grinned at Kiara, relieved that she didn't look like she wanted to punch him. "I'm just saying that if you want positive things, it may help both of us if we both started speaking the same language."

"I cannot believe what I'm hearing. Are you a changed man already? Just because I announced I'm pregnant?"

"Kiara, I've been thinking." He lifted her chin and stared into her eyes. "You've been through a lot of shit. And I know I'm responsible for most of it. I guess I shouldn't have acted so surprised, considering. But, I am willing to try and do better, really try. I gotta clear some things up first—"

"Yes, you do," she told him. She thought about Eddison and hoped he was doing well since their last conversation. But even if he wasn't, she knew she had to let go. Her husband was her main concern now.

"I cannot tell you how happy this makes me, babe," she told him.

"I could never predict I'd be this hyped about Myles having a little sibling. I'm happier for him than you will ever imagine."

He told her that he looked forward to being with her during their getaway. They both agreed they needed to keep the home fires burning.

* * *

Finally, the time had come for the Easons to celebrate their ten-year anniversary with a week-long visit to the Western Caribbean. They had just gotten onboard their ship at the Port of Galveston. The atmosphere was filled with energy. Some first-time cruisers were walking around and exploring the ship. But Kiara and Rashad bypassed the tour and went directly to their cabin. They were issued their identification cards and couldn't wait to settle in their mini suite.

Once they found their room and got comfortable, Kiara rolled her big brown eyes. Rashad was lying around on the couch, then hopping up every few minutes to look out the window to the balcony. He opened the sliding glass door and sat on the lounge chair and became lost in the view of the ocean. She joined him.

"So like I was saying, it makes me feel damned good to know that I can leave the business in the qualified hands of some of my workers. That means I trained them right. It doesn't make sense for a man to work so hard but rarely get to enjoy his coins. That's got to change."

"Everything will change now that we're having another child."

"Yeah, and I'm cool with that, but I've been thinking. What if I have to keep up the pace of my schedule? Babies cost way more now than they did when Myles was born."

"That's true. Every day these manufacturers coming up with something new that they trying to sell to us parents. But making yourself increase your hours? Nope. More work won't work."

"But what about the cost of diapers, equipment, child care?"

"You're getting ahead of yourself, Rashad. Where is your faith?"

He said nothing.

"Babe, I think we'll be still okay if you reduce some of your projects. Just think, Rashad. Now is our time to prove that love and family are what's most important. Chasing money? Not so much."

Rashad, unable to keep still, got up and Kiara followed him inside their cabin. He walked with a confident bounce in his steps fueled by the pride he had in being a business owner and in carrying on the legacy started by his late father.

"But what I'm doing is more than about stacking coins or paying bills. I consider my work very important. That's what you don't understand."

"Help me to understand."

"Kiara, do you know how good it feels to know I don't have to punch a clock for 'the man'? The man who tells me I gotta work twelve hours a day and thinks he's doing me a favor by giving me a thirty-minute lunch and two fifteen-minute breaks? It feels hella good to know I can call my own shots, and know that every hour I work, that money is going towards me and mines. When you work for someone else, times moves slow. But when you work for yourself, there ain't enough hours in the day."

"Okay, great. Your paycheck has your name on it instead of the government, but at what price? By neglecting your family and not having enough time for them? By breaking your promises to your son and teaching him that lying is the way to go?"

"I don't care what you say. I love y'all, but I can't afford to let my business fail. I gotta take all the jobs I can get and hustle as hard as I can. Just like Fred Sanford and Lamont, I'm out there every day to make sure there will always be an Eason & Son. It's Myles's heritage, my new child's heritage, and I won't let anything, even a marriage, interfere with that. I'm going to do all I can to keep my kids off these streets and out of a white man's prison."

"That's cool. That's commendable."

"But?"

"We need your presence, babe."

"And you need my presents, too! P-R-E-S-E-N-T-S."

"Ha! Nice try."

"See, that right there lets me know you don't get me. You don't understand all I'm trying to do."

"I don't get you?"

"No! You don't."

"Thing is, I really want to," she said in a soft voice. She gave Rashad an encouraging smile. She loved that he was opening up to her. That's all she ever wanted: clear communication.

"You know what, I agree with you, Rashad. I agree that I don't allow you to be you. And that's not right. I am going to listen to you and stop trying to change you into the man I want you to be."

He shouted and yelped. "That's what I'm talking about. All I want you to do is hear me out. If we both agree the decision won't work, we'll find a better solution. Together."

"I'm all for that, my king!"

By the grin on his face, Kiara knew she had done the right amount of ego stroking that her man needed. If only she could remember to keep this up, then it was possible her marriage could be saved.

"Now," Rashad said, "we have seven freaking nights on this *Love Boat* wannabe. Let's start having some fun."

"Let's."

A knock could be heard on their cabin door.

Rashad answered. It was a smiling middle-aged man whom he and Kiara had met when they boarded the ship. They'd promised to eat together at the Windjammer buffet. The guy was recently divorced, and was taking the cruise to get his mind off his heartbreak.

"I didn't mean to disturb you."

"No problem, buddy. We weren't talking about anything."

"Cool. You ready to go do something?" the man asked.

"Yeah, let's get outta this cabin. From now on, I just want to concentrate on having a great time. The best time of my life. Let's go."

"When we're done eating, I want to chill on the lounge chairs by the pool and have lots and lots of drinks," said their new friend.

"I want to play Putt Putt golf," said Rashad.

"All right." Kiara shrugged. "But after that, we gotta go to the casino. I need to take a gamble that I know I can win."

"When you gonna put on those sexy swimsuits?"

"When I'm good and ready."

After they ate a fabulous meal at the buffet, Kiara found the courage to dress in her swimsuit, but she covered herself with a maxi robe. She left the room and found Rashad by the Flowrider, where he was standing on a surfboard. He held out his hands as he tried to maintain his balance.

"I'm the king of the world," he yelled.

"Yes, you are . . . my king."

They were more than halfway through their cruise, which took them to Cozumel and Grand Cayman. Kiara was feeling better than she had in a long time. She and Rashad seemed to bond on the first five days of the cruise. By the time the sixth day came, Kiara felt she could make it.

They were headed back to Galveston. The weather had suddenly changed for the worse. The Gulf of Mexico waters turned choppy. Kiara prayed they would make it back safely. It was nighttime. They were in their room after a long day of cruise-ship activities including watching a Broadway play, swimming, and getting in the Flowrider. Kiara and Rashad had several drinks with their new friend and were feeling tipsy. Once they told the man good-bye for the evening, Rashad decided to take a shower.

"You want to join me?"

"No, you go right ahead. I'm feeling tired and nauseous. I'm going to lie down for a minute."

"Okay."

Kiara went to rest on the bed. And she had fallen into a light sleep when she heard a beep. She looked at the night table. She saw an unrecognizable watch. She knew it wasn't hers. It had to be Rashad's. She picked it up. She realized it was a watch phone. A message popped on the screen:

Say hello to your newest child.

Then an ultrasound picture loaded: a grainy photo of an embryo.

"What the fuck?"

Her feet felt unsteady as a wave of nausea settled over her.

Kiara threw the watch on the floor.

At the same time her own cell phone was beeping. She went and picked it up. A text came through from Alexis.

I hate to bother u but NG is telling ppl she's preggers. She told SP and SP of course told me. She showed me an ultrasound photo. This is so wack.

Kiara began hyperventilating. Her breath came in

spurts. She felt beside herself. All her hopes and dreams were swiftly disappearing. Did wanting love mean being eternally gullible? Her husband would never change.

Kiara went to her toiletry bag. She removed a tiny bottle of shampoo. She quietly went out to their balcony. She looked both ways and above the balcony. She saw no one. Then she twisted open the bottle. She squirted all the liquid on the floor of their balcony and watched it spread across the surface.

She went back inside their cabin and waited for Rashad to return from his shower.

He smiled at her when he emerged completely naked.

"You want to cuddle for a minute before we do something fun?"

"Um, cuddling sounds good, but no. I have something else in mind. Let's go out on the balcony."

"Cool. Let me get dressed."

"Just wrap a towel around your waist."

"Oh, okay," he said.

Kiara opened the door to the balcony. She invited him to go outside first.

She knew it was impossible for him to fall off the balcony, but maybe she could hurt him some other way. She wanted Rashad to feel pain, to suffer, to know what it felt like to be vulnerable and helpless.

When he stepped onto the balcony, he started out walking around normally. But he didn't notice the spill. And his bare feet stepped onto the slippery liquid. Rashad lost his balance. He crashed to the floor. He looked up at Kiara. She just stood there watching him with no expression on her face. He tried to stand up, but flipped over with a loud thump.

"Damn, my back." He pulled himself to his knees and tried crawling.

"Why aren't you helping me?"

Kiara stood and said not a word. Then her mouth opened wide. She stood horrified.

A sudden roar sounded. A wave of water hit the side of the cruise ship. It wasn't a horrific wave, but it caused a large amount of water to spill over the balcony rail and drench the deck floor.

Within seconds, Kiara's feet slipped from under her. She banged to the floor and landed on her thigh. The soapy watery mixture left her helpless; the pain made her want to cry.

"Kiara, are you all right?"

"Help me." She felt very frightened. "My baby." She held her stomach and her body started sliding around as she struggled to stand. She felt like she was drowning.

Somehow Rashad managed to crawl to a table where he was able to pull himself up. He threw his large towel on the floor. It was slightly damp but dry enough to give him good balance. And completely naked, he walked across it to reach his wife. He helped her up and they both hurried across the towel and ducked back inside their room.

"What happened out there? Why was the floor so wet?"

"Because of the rogue wave?"

"That wasn't just water. It was something more dangerous."

Kiara fumed. "Did you know that Nicole is pregnant by you?"

"What? What are you talking about?"

"She just texted you a photo of the unborn baby that is in her stomach. I'm assuming you put it there."

"How do you know this?"

"I saw it on your stupid watch phone."

"Oh, that can't be right. That has to be a joke."

"That is nothing to joke about. I'm so upset at you I don't know what to do."

Rashad stared at his wife then at the empty bottle of shampoo that was sitting on a table. "You tried to kill me, didn't you?"

"No, I did not."

"Kiara, don't lie. You're insane. And you want me dead without even knowing the full truth. Nicole has an ex. That baby could be his. You ever thought about that?"

"If that were true, she'd be texting her ex and not you, you big dummy." She was screaming. She beat his chest with her fists. "Tell the truth for once in your life."

Rashad was speechless. And he was scared. He stopped her from hitting him and forced her to sit.

Rashad was twelve years old. His daddy had just come in real late after being gone from the house the entire weekend. The first person his daddy saw was his son, Rashad.

"Shhh," his dad told him and winked. "If your mama asks where I was, tell her I fell asleep in the room above the garage."

"Oh, okay, Daddy." Rashad knew it was a lie. But he loved his father. He loved it when his dad let him sit in the driver's seat of his Eason & Son van. He had a ball when his dad brought him to work and explained to him all about nuts and bolts and hammers and wood.

His father was good with his hands and he told Rashad he had the same talent.

"You will always have a job when you can fix and build things, son."

Rashad nodded and stared at his hands.

"Protect them. They will make you a lot of money."

He'd follow his dad around the contracting firm,

watching him fill his toolkit with all kinds of metal objects.

But little Rashad also saw when his dad would wink and flirt with his secretary, Gloria.

Gloria had short hair and a nice shape. She liked to smoke and dance around the office playing her beat box real loud.

Rashad took it all in. His dad would wink at his son and take Gloria with him into one of the empty rooms at his office building. They'd be gone for an hour, leaving the boy alone to play.

And when he'd return home after being with his father, his mom, Beeva Reese, would corner him.

"Where were you?"

"At Daddy's job."

"Were other women there?"

He'd shrug, nod "yeah," and look around and ask to be excused because he was tired and hungry.

Beeva would explode at his daddy. She hit her husband with her fists. He'd pop her back in her jaw and push her off him. She'd fall to the ground, cower and scream as he kicked her.

That was when Rashad became afraid to tell the truth.

Truth caused pain.

Pain caused suffering.

Suffering caused a woman to cry.

Truth hurt.

Rashad thought about his mother and the fact she'd been married a few times since his daddy died. He wasn't very close to the woman. She seemed to be too busy with her own life. And their estrangement made him feel bad. Somehow he feared he may always have a horrible disconnect with a woman. And he just didn't know how to close in the gap.

He sighed and his shoulders felt heavy with fear.

"Okay, Kiara. I'll be honest with you. The baby could be mine. It's a strong possibility. But it was an accident. Everything was an unintentional accident."

"I don't want to hear it."

Kiara got up and went to lie on the couch. She pulled the covers over her head. All she wanted was for the cruise to be over so she could think clearly and plan her next move.

Chapter 20

The Easons returned home from the cruise. Kiara consulted an attorney the second week of October. She made Rashad sleep in the upstairs guest room. He hadn't left the house since; he was too afraid to leave, but he was also afraid to stay.

Kiara felt nervous and jittery. So she invited Adina over on the Monday after they returned.

"I feel this is all my fault, Ki."

"Stop it. You have no control over what he does."

"But if I hadn't brought your attention to all he was doing, this wouldn't be happening."

Kiara said nothing. She had mixed feelings. In some ways, she wished Adina had kept her mouth shut. Truth hurt. Bad. But she needed to know what was up and now she knew.

"Why is he still here?"

"He refuses to leave."

"What?"

"He is still begging me to hear him out. He feels he deserves that chance."

"You've given him a hundred chances, based on what you told me."

"Don't worry. He is out of here. I'm about to pull an Olivia Pope and fix his ass good."

On Tuesday, Kiara returned to the job after being on vacation. She picked up the phone and called Alexis into her office.

"Close the door and have a seat."

Alexis calmly sat down and crossed her legs.

In a low voice, Kiara said, "I just wanted to give you a heads-up that I will be sending you a termination letter—"

"Excuse me?"

"It's not for you. It's regarding someone else."

"Oh."

"It will be addressed to Nicole. A lot of things are happening around here that have made me conclude she isn't going to make her probation. She's very unprofessional and causes too many disturbances in this office."

Alexis nodded, knowing exactly what she was referring to: the big announcement with the worst timing. Alexis hated having to rat out Nicole but she was doing things way beyond what was necessary.

"Anyway, there is no way I can envision Nicole as being part of our team. So I'm firing her. Of course, no one else knows yet. This is highly confidential, Alexis."

"I do understand. And I'm sorry about how things went down. And please do not tell Nicole that I told you. I don't need her harassing me anymore."

"No, thanks for telling me. I never would have known, otherwise."

Alexis felt guilty about not admitting that Hayley was Rashad's. She wasn't sure how long she could keep that a secret.

"I will email you the letter. I want you to review it, print it on my letterhead and bring it to me in a sealed envelope. And I want you to schedule a meeting between myself and Nicole—"

"I see. When?"

"I'm not finished yet." Kiara studied Alexis, then remarked, "You two have never hit it off very well. Why is that?"

"I just don't like the bitch. Excuse my French."

"You don't have to like someone to respect them."

"I don't respect the bitch, either."

"Well, all righty then. Anyway, I need you to send her the meeting invite. Just title it 'Miscellaneous Communications' and blind copy yourself. I need you to be present."

"Really? Why?"

"You'll see."

Alexis walked back to her desk. She was happy Nicole was getting let go, but she really didn't want to be in the meeting. Yet it was like a dream. She couldn't believe her good luck.

She almost salivated when she received Kiara's email. She reviewed the attachment:

Dear Nicole Kelly Greene,

This is in reference to your employment dated May 28 which requires you to undergo a probationary period of six (6) months before full employment is offered. Based upon a recent evaluation by your supervisor, we regret to inform you that your work performance does not merit an offer of a permanent position. We feel our work environment may not be the best match to your work skills and work style. This is your termination notice, which is effective immediately. You will be paid for any unused accumulated vacation leave which is calculated to be 48 hours.

We wish you the best of luck in all your future endeavors.

>**Sincerely,**

>**Kiara M. Eason**
>**Senior Manager of Communications**

By signing this letter below, you are acknowledging receipt of this termination notice:

>**Date;**
>**cc: Human Resources**
>**Nicole K. Greene**

Alexis felt a strong sense of jubilation when she read the letter. In large bold italics she spontaneously typed at the bottom:

>*P.S. Don't let the doorknob hit your bitch ass . . .*

Alexis snickered, then deleted the last line. Nicole's firing would be sufficient.

"It's a shame we gotta pay this woman to leave out the door. But even the NBA must fork over the dollars to get rid of a player. That's cool. Whatever it takes to keep me from looking her in her ugly face ever again."

Heart pumping with exhilaration, she printed the document on letterhead, then carried it to Kiara, who reviewed and signed it. Alexis personally delivered the letter to the VP so he could sign it, too. When she returned to her office, Alexis happily sent Nicole an Outlook invite to the meeting, which was set for nine o'clock the next day.

She couldn't wait.

That evening Alexis prepared a simple dinner. Salmon, grilled corn on the cob, wild rice, and a garden salad with ranch dressing. She filled four plates with food, took one to her mother, and set the tray on Mona's bed before closing the door behind her.

She returned to the kitchen, picked up two plates, balanced one in each hand, and carried them to the dining room.

"Here you go. Hope you like it."

Varnell examined the meal she had prepared. "It smells good. I'm sure it tastes just as good."

"Mama, eat!"

Alexis grinned broadly. This was the first time Hayley called her "mama" and meant it. She laughed and said, "All righty, Ms. Greedy. You know I wouldn't forget about you."

After she set down Hayley's dinner, she got her food and a mimosa, then joined the others.

Alexis felt a twinge of nervousness. So far, she and Varnell had been on four real dates: the off-Broadway play, bowling, the Wings Over Houston air show, and fishing. Nice simple outings. And she'd had a good time. But still, she questioned if it was too early to let him meet her daughter.

"I appreciate you understanding about—"

"No need to apologize. I'm glad you told me. Children are gifts from the Lord. They are a blessing."

"I'm surprised you don't have any."

"Not yet. I'm only thirty-one. There's still time."

She shyly grinned at Varnell and appreciated the comfort his presence always seemed to give her.

"Well, let's eat." She started to stab her daughter's fish with a knife but Varnell interrupted.

"In my house, we give the blessing before we break bread. It's just a little habit."

"A great habit. I apologize. Can you say it for us?"

Varnell grabbed Alexis's slender hand and then reached for Hayley's tiny fingers.

She yelped. "Eat. Now."

Varnell chuckled and said, "Patience, my child."

Alexis felt warm and fuzzy on the inside. She held Hayley's other hand and bowed her head but she didn't close her eyes. She kept taking quick peeks at this man who was quietly yet authoritatively sitting in her home. The more she looked at Varnell, the more she liked what she saw.

After the blessing, they all sat together and chowed down.

"Is it okay?" she asked.

"It's great. Perfect."

"Are you sure you're not lying to me?"

"You really ought to know me better than that."

Alexis agreed with him. "That's my New Year's resolution." She grinned and winked.

She had both her BlackBerry and iPhone sitting on the kitchen counter. She kept the work phone powered on just in case her boss called. But when the iPhone rang, she pretended she was hard of hearing.

"So how was your day today, Mr. Brown?"

"It started out fine and it's ending up even better." Varnell's eyes twinkled when he smiled at her. She couldn't believe how his smile could make her blush. Alexis's heart began to melt like a chocolaty hot fudge sundae with cherries on top. The phone went silent but immediately rang again, and she knew it was Rashad. She silenced the phone. Varnell didn't flinch. He didn't question.

She was feeling this guy more and more.

Varnell helped Alexis put the dishes in the dishwasher and wiped down the counters without her even having to ask.

"Um, why aren't you married?"

"Why aren't you married?" Hayley said, imitating her mother.

"I'm happy. That's what is most important."

Just then, she heard a persistent tapping on her front door. Alexis knew that it wasn't a Jehovah's Witness or the UPS guy.

"Varnell, I need to handle this. If you don't mind, go on upstairs and make yourself at home. You know where everything is."

She was referring to her den. He'd never been in her bedroom.

"No problem."

Alexis went to grab her daughter and balanced her on her hip while Varnell started up the stairs. Before he reached the top, he called down to her, "Don't hesitate to call me if you need me."

"It'll be all right. Thank you so much."

She hesitated, then answered the front door. Rashad may have turned out to be a disappointment, but he was still her child's father. She knew that if anything went down, Varnell would protect her. Alexis stepped outside into the noisy breeze of the darkened evening. Dogs could be heard barking. The sounds of children yelling filled her ears.

"Skillet! Why didn't you pick up?" Rashad openly stared at the unfamiliar black pickup parked in her driveway.

"Please don't call me that anymore."

"Okay, Alexis. What you been up to that you don't answer the phone?"

"Busy. That's all."

"You too busy for me?"

"Obviously I was at that particular second, Rashad. What's up?"

"You don't 'what up' me."

"If this ain't some foul mess."

"Let me hold her." Rashad scooped his daughter into his arms and played with her for a minute. "So why are we outside? It's cold. And she isn't properly dressed."

"It's not that cold, Rashad. Don't even try it. How was your little honeymoon?"

"That wasn't a honeymoon." He paused. "I want to know if you heard about what happened. While we were on the cruise, Nicole texted me that she's pregnant. All hell broke loose. Did my wife mention anything about it?"

"She mentioned Nicole, but definitely not that. Hmm. Your little female Shrek is pregnant, huh?"

"Shrek, Shrek, Shrek," Hayley cheered.

"She's not ugly. But check this out . . . Kiara is pregnant, too."

"Pregnant, pregnant, pregnant."

Now it was Alexis's turn to be shocked. "No shit? Whoa! Your life has really grown into a hot-ass mess. But it's not like I care or anything. I'm glad I got out while I could."

His jaw rigid, Rashad felt frustrated at her behavior. "You've always been a pro at trying to hide your feelings. But I know even though you putting on this big act like you're unbothered, I know you still love me, even though you got some man up there probably laying in the bed waiting on you—"

"What? Why would you think I love you?"

"Because you're trying to get back at me through this new dude that has this lame-looking truck. What's his name?"

"Ha, that's none of your business. As many women as you're sticking it to, you have the nerve to be jealous."

"I'm used to you being accessible, being all mines." He sounded sadly sober. "I thought you were different. A true ride or die."

"Are you honestly trying to go there, Mr. Married Man?"

"Don't throw shade. We better than this. We been together, what, almost two years?"

"First of all, we are not together. Not anymore. And secondly, your daughter is way past two, so your calculations are way off."

Clearly agitated, Alexis folded her arms across her chest and debated whether or not to tell him what was about to go down with his new side chick. Once Nicole got fired, she would bet a million dollars that Rashad would have no interest in that woman. She knew he didn't like bum bitches and that's what Nicole would be in less than twenty-four hours.

"All I can say is you have changed—"

"I've changed? Look, give me my daughter. I've got important things to do."

"Nothing is more important than me. Nothing! You go and have your little fun, your little pity party with that man that's over there. I can see the ninja looking out the window right now."

"That's a lie because my room is in the back of the house." She laughed. "You got the nerve to be jealous. That's my mama in the window making sure nothing is going down out here."

"Tell her she don't have to worry. Nothing is happening. Literally nothing is going on."

"You got that right. We have no business but our daughter. The past is over, Rashad. You may as well get used to it. I do not belong to you anymore."

"But what if I need a place to stay if she kicks me out?"

"Ask your female Shrek!"

Rashad left in a huff. And she turned around and went back inside the house.

It was the next morning. The meeting was about to start. Alexis sat in a guest chair in Kiara's office. She wore a black suit with a white blouse. Her hair cascaded down her back. Alexis was poised and felt calm. So when Nicole entered the office and loudly gasped when she spotted Alexis, she felt energized and satisfied like someone was looking over her shoulder.

"Have a seat," Kiara told Nicole.

"What's this about?"

"Please sit down."

"I don't want to sit down."

"You may not have a choice. Sit down please."

"OK, but I feel like you're double-teaming me."

"I have no idea what you're talking about, but if you'd just calm down and be seated, we can get this meeting started."

Nicole nervously sat on the edge of her chair and clutched a university-owned tablet to her chest. For a minute, she resembled the quiet and insecure young woman Kiara first hired.

"Nicole, as you know, you were hired last May as the media coordinator for the communications department. And you understood from the beginning that during the first six months of employment, your job performance, skills, and adaptability to the workplace would be closely evaluated."

"Yeah, what about it?"

"I'm here to inform you that you didn't make probation and today is your last day. It just didn't work out. Alexis?"

Alexis took her cue and presented Nicole with the letter.

Nicole snatched the letter from Alexis and quickly reviewed it. Her hands were shaking.

"This is crazy. I-I did an excellent job. I covered all the events that you told me to do, and I wrote a ton of feature stories and co-produced videos that got good coverage. I'm more than qualified."

"If you can recall, when you first came to this job you received an offer letter that stated you could be terminated for any reason. You signed it. Do you need me to pull it from the file?"

"I bet I know the real reason for this so-called termination." Nicole rose to her feet and began pacing. Her spike heels clicked against the floor. "I don't agree with this action. I can see it if I was someone who didn't come to work half the time. Or one who didn't do her work."

"Half the time you didn't work," Alexis murmured.

"And why is she here? She doesn't even like me, and never has."

"Nicole, this has nothing to do with anyone liking you or not liking you. It's business, not personal. Now sign and date the letter at the bottom. I will need you to clear out your desk and hand in your keys, badge, and any other university-owned equipment. Give everything to Alexis."

"Including that tablet," Alexis said.

Nicole laid angry eyes on Kiara. She wanted to smack her but she knew that doing so would result in more serious trouble. She eyed her boss's slightly protruding belly. She walked up to her and reached out and tried to touch her stomach, but Kiara screamed then leaped from her chair.

"What are you doing?"

"Whose child is this?"

"W-what?"

"Whose baby is it, Kiara? Tell me."

"That's none of your business."

"That's because the baby you're carrying doesn't belong to your husband. I heard you and Mr. Osborne talking in the stairway that day. I know his voice. I heard him ask you if your baby was his. I wonder how Rashad would feel if he knew that?"

Alexis's eyes enlarged. She couldn't believe how devious and spiteful Nicole was.

"Look, Kiara. I need this job and you know I need it. Now's not the time for me to be going through this. But I will bargain with you. I know you're mad because I am having Rashad's child. But we are a team. I like my job and I need the income. It's not fair to put it all on him."

"You're sick—"

"More importantly, with your reputation, I know you wouldn't want the university to know you could possibly be pregnant by another man. So if you let me keep my secret, keep my job, and let me stay, I will keep your secret. I won't tell a soul. Is that a deal?"

"That's blackmail," Alexis said.

"And you," Nicole said, walking up to Alexis. "You have no room to talk, either. I'm not the only woman around this place who can get fired."

Alexis shot Nicole a warning look. Nicole backed down. She wouldn't want to break her promise to Rashad not to tell that he was Hayley's father.

Nicole turned to Kiara. "Bottom line is I think you didn't clearly think this through. I know you're scared of people knowing your business. I have a way to solve this."

She took her termination letter, spit on it, tore it up in dozens of pieces, then merrily tossed them up in the air.

"Effective immediately, I accept your offer of full-time employment as the media coordinator for this department. Alexis, be a sweetie and type up an official letter. I'd like a four percent raise, too. After the letter is ready, I will be more than happy to sign that one."

Nicole walked toward Kiara's door and started to open it.

"Don't forget. Keep my secret and I will keep yours. And that's a promise."

Nicole whipped out her smartphone, clicked the camera app, pouted for a pose, pretended like she dropped a microphone, then twirled like she was gone with the wind fabulous, and walked out.

Chapter 21

"Alexis, I need you to log into the HR system and cancel her termination."

"But—"

"This chick is playing hardball like she's LeBron. I must do what I need to do until I can figure something out."

Alexis could only stare at the shredded-up letter that was messily spread on Kiara's floor like some losing lottery ticket.

"I don't see how you can let her get away with this. You're the boss. You tell her what to do."

"You don't understand."

"Oh, trust me, I understand. When people have secrets they're trying to hide, they lose their common sense. I'm not talking about just you. It can happen to anybody. But if you let that nut bag do this to you now, you're letting her win. People like her can't win."

"Okay, let's think about this. If I insist on the firing, because technically I can still get rid of her even if she refuses to sign that letter, there's no stopping her from spreading all my business throughout this campus."

"Is it true, Kiara? You're having another man's child?"

"I won't know till it's born. That's all I can say."

"Regardless, I'm really sorry about all this." Alexis

continued with her indirect apology. "I want Nicole to be out of here so bad you have no idea. She shouldn't win."

"And she won't. It's just that I know in my heart I don't have to do anything bad against Nicole. She will get hers eventually."

Kiara thought about her past actions and the price of revenge.

"It's all a big mess. The Crips hate the Bloods. One gang member kills another gang member. They retaliate. And the cycle continues. Which one of us can win if we keep up the cycle?"

Alexis couldn't take it anymore. She excused herself. She immediately logged into the system that would allow her to cancel the termination. Her hands shook with every stroke across her keyboard.

Later, when Alexis was sitting at her desk eating her lunch, Shyla Perry quietly walked up to her. Alexis reached for her iPhone, but Shyla acted like she didn't care.

"Hey, Alexis. I heard what happened earlier. What you eating? Looks like humble pie. Bwahahahaha."

"Shyla, please go away. Just disappear."

"I know you wish we'd disappear. But we're here to stay. We are bosses."

Alexis played with her cell phone.

"Oh, I forgot to tell you. You know I'm getting married next month. But somehow I accidentally lost your invite to the bridal shower. Well, I've decided to take the high road and I've had a change of heart. You're welcome to attend as my special guest. Unless you'll be too busy taking care of that bastard child you got—"

Alexis pulled back her knuckle and quickly popped Shyla. Her head snapped back. Shyla didn't know what hit her. She moaned and caressed her jaw.

"Oh, my God! I can't believe you did that."

"And I can't believe what you said. What a minute. Yes, I can believe it. Stupid bitches say stupid things."

"You. Are about to be. In big trouble." Shyla rested her hand on her jaw and limped toward Kiara's office, even though Alexis never kicked her.

"Hold up a minute." Alexis approached Shyla. She was holding her cell phone.

"Look! Violence is wack. There's no justification for it. But so is going in on someone's child." Alexis placed the play button on her phone and turned up the volume. Shyla's loud and catty voice could be heard instigating an argument with Alexis.

"Oh, I forgot to tell you. You know I'm getting married next month. But somehow I accidentally lost your invite to the bridal shower? Well, I've decided to take the high road and I've had a change of heart."

Alexis stopped the recording right before it revealed the sound of her hitting the woman and Shyla screaming.

"You conniving little violent-ass—"

"I was out of order and I am sorry for my behavior. Do you accept my apology, Shyla?"

"I accept it, but you're still a conniving, violent-ass bitch."

Shyla pouted, nursed her jaw, and slunk away from Alexis.

Kiara decided to take the rest of the afternoon off. First she checked with Alexis. The termination paperwork has been a pain in the neck to cancel, but it would be done. She knew she'd have to work on trying to give Nicole a raise, but nothing inside of her wanted to do it.

She continued in her vehicle and drove to the store where she'd tried to buy the hair accessories months ago but the cashier accidentally forgot to charge her.

Kiara's heart felt a lot lighter after she took care of

that business. And when she went home, she picked up the duplicate order that Nordstrom sent her, and returned it to the brick-and-mortar store unused and in its original packaging.

"If I keep this up," she said to the cashier, who barely listened to her, "if I make the wrong things right, there's nothing I can't handle."

Chapter 22

On Thursday of that week, when Alexis was at work, she lowered her head and peered in the darkness underneath her desk. She placed one finger against her lips, signaling to Hayley that in order to win this little game they were playing she must be perfectly quiet. She handed her daughter a miniature flashlight to play with so it wouldn't be so shadowy when she hid in the corner. The space under the elegant U-shaped hardwood desk offered ultimate privacy. Hayley would be safe from view.

All that morning Alexis tried to act like everything was normal. She had to do her job plus make sure Hayley wasn't seen or heard.

When Shyla and Nicole scurried past mid-morning, Alexis felt Hayley playfully tapping her leg. Alexis ignored her. Hayley began to hum and persistently yanked on her mother's skirt.

"What's that noise?" Shyla asked, stopping to listen. "Did you hear that?"

"What noise? I didn't hear anything."

"Lessie."

Alexis wanted to correct Hayley but couldn't.

"Hey, ladies," Alexis said in a loud voice. "Some nice

person brought kolaches and doughnuts to work this morning. A dozen of them are still left in the kitchen."

"I can't eat that shit. Remember I'm watching what I eat these days."

"Oh, chile, you so wrong for that." Shyla laughed at Nicole's catty remark.

"Well, why don't you get on about your business and do some work, since you're making all this money these days."

Nicole plopped her new leather purse on top of Alexis's desk.

Hayley poked her little head from the side of the desk. Part of her head was hidden but Nicole still could look directly into the little girl's eyes.

"Oh, my God."

"What?"

"She's what I heard."

Hayley completely emerged from her hiding place. Aware that she had an audience, she rocked back and forth in her tan suede boots. She wore a dark brown knit dress and some textured tights. A little purse was hanging off her arm.

"What's she doing here?" Nicole asked. Nicole lifted up the little girl and held her. "I can't believe this. She's grown since the last time I saw her." Nicole wanted to be nice to Hayley. This was her lover's child, sort of her stepchild. Plus, she really did love children.

Alexis felt protective of Hayley. She wanted to tell everyone that this was her kid, but the workplace environment had treated her so unfairly.

At that moment, when Alexis saw her big, looming desk, she saw her sister. The desk was a custody agreement, a keeper of secrets, the hider of a Freakum Bag, and a clever way to conceal her truths. She was sick of burying truth inside of lies.

Hayley's eyes lit up. She gurgled and seemed so happy, so accepting, no matter what was going on around her.

"This beautiful child is my daughter, Hayley. I'm in the process of obtaining full custody of my baby. And the day care center has admitted her, but they won't have an opening until tomorrow. I chose to bring her here where I could watch her. And I—"

Why am I explaining my situation to them?

"Hayley will be here as long as I want her to be. You got a problem with that?"

"I know all about it. You're just doing what you have to do."

Nicole ruffled the little girl's hair and set her in Alexis's arms.

Shyla stared at Hayley and smiled. "She really is a cutie pie. Just like her mommy."

The two women walked away, leaving Alexis alone with her daughter.

Alexis allowed Hayley to sit next to her on a guest chair that she positioned on the side of her desk. She did her work for the remainder of the morning and was surprised that none of her coworkers gave her odd looks. But when lunchtime arrived, she quickly scooped the girl up and whisked her out the door. She drove Hayley to her cousin Fendi's apartment. Mona Hooker, who normally watched her, was tied up all day at several doctor's appointments and couldn't keep her. So Alexis had to make other plans.

"I have a meeting that I need to attend . . . Thank you so much," Alexis told her cousin and handed her some cash.

"I got a hair appointment later—"

"Don't worry. I will pick her up. Just let me know when. Text me."

"All right, cuzzo."

Alexis drove back to work feeling more at ease. She was someone's mother. She knew it was time to start acting like it. She wanted to phone Rashad but resisted the urge. She needed to learn how to face tough situations on her own.

Approximately an hour before she was scheduled to get off work, she heard a commotion down the hall near the entrance of the building. She tried to concentrate on her typing, but couldn't.

The sound of multiple voices disturbed her.

"Whose little girl is this? She's so cute! Look at those little Timbs."

"Aww, she's got some pretty ole eyes. This baby is too precious."

"I got next when you're done holding her. I love babies."

Alexis was mildly curious. She loved babies, too. She was about to rise up from her seat when she saw a silhouette of someone creeping down the hall. Two shapely figures. She heard the soft pitter-patter of tiny feet. Then the sound abruptly stopped.

"Mama."

Hayley's unmistakable voice. Alexis saw Fendi rushing behind Kiara. Kiara whisked the little girl in her arms. She held her and talked sweetly to her.

Alexis froze on sight, unable to talk or think.

Kiara set the child down. Hayley burst into a wild sprint and zigzagged through the corridor. Kiara laughed and began to chase her.

Hayley stopped in front of Kiara's office, then dashed inside.

Alexis reclined in her seat and shut her eyes tight.

Soon she heard, "Dada. Hi, Dada." Alexis presumed her daughter saw the family photo with Rashad in her boss's office.

After that, the sound of cruel silence.

Until Fendi interrupted. "Cuzzo, you all right?"

"Why are you *here*?"

"I had to pee and now I'm 'bout to go. I told you I had to get my hair did. I'm already late to my 'point-ment . . . holla."

"I. Was supposed. To pick. Her up," Alexis spoke to the shadow of her flaky cousin, who quickly left the building and disappeared out of sight.

"I paid you. I . . . ugh."

Not long afterward, Kiara slowly traipsed down the hallway. This time she was holding Hayley in her arms. The little girl patted Kiara's cheeks with her fingers as she softly sang. Kiara silently marched until her long trail ended at Alexis.

"So *this* is my husband's daughter."

This time the boss didn't want to meet with Alexis in her office. This time she demanded the woman follow her down the hall, through the exit doors, down the steps, and away from the four walls of their building and onto the college campus.

Kiara, still holding Hayley in her arms, trooped ahead like she was Sofia in *The Color Purple* wearing her flowered hat. Her loud footsteps banged the pave-ment, her neck straight, as she headed to a place un-known. She finally stopped at an empty wooden bench that was seemingly planted in the middle of nowhere. Trees with swirling leaves towered over them. Students rushed past, headed to classes. The air was cold and brisk, and the wind howled like it was scared.

Hayley coughed and shivered.

"This won't take long."

"Kiara, I'm so, so sorry."

"Are you?"

"Yes. This." Alexis mournfully sighed like it finally hit her. "This. This."

"I don't know. I don't know what to say. What can you tell me to make this situation good? Acceptable?"

"I understand if you hate me, Kiara. I'd hate me too if I were in your shoes. I wanted to tell you, I was dying to tell you but he—"

"I just wonder why it's taken me so long . . ."

Alexis nervously rubbed her hands together. Her face was pinched, her normal portrait of a confident, beautiful, sexy, desired woman gone.

"But I always knew."

"You knew?"

"When a woman really wants to know, she knows. He can lie as much as he wants. *I* can lie as much as I want. I didn't know everything, but I knew something. The hints were there. My God, she favors him."

"Again, I wish things had been diffcrent. Everyone has faults and does things they regret. I'm no different and I—"

"I don't need the speeches. I hate speeches. Worthless, meaningless, this shit ain't gonna change nothing speeches. My heart feels like a big pile of dust right now." She looked Alexis squarely in the eye. "Do you know what that feels like? To realize that everything you've ever believed in, everything that ever made you feel warm inside, and safe, and loved, and significant, is all questionable? No, you don't know. I don't care what you say. You have no idea."

Hayley squirmed in the tight clutch of Kiara's arms. Alexis's impulse told her to grab her daughter. Get her. Save her. She reached for the child, but Kiara coldly turned her back to the woman.

"I guess this is what I get," Kiara said. "What I deserve."

"No, don't say that—"

"No, wait. I'm not done yet." She faced Alexis again and spoke. "When my husband and I first met, I was single. But he was already in a relationship. Not married, nothing serious, but he was casually dating someone. And I saw him. We talked. We clicked. I went after him. I spoke us into existence. That's what I do. And I worked hard at it. We were married. I probably loved him more than he loved me at first, but he grew to love me. He grew to understand the things I wanted and needed from him. And he gave them to me. He did an excellent job making me, us, look good. But after we had the baby, things shifted. I started feeling like a single mom. His contracting business felt like the new 'outside' baby, a kid by another woman that I had to learn how to deal with because he was spending so much time with the 'kid.' He was loving that kid, and I felt like he loved that other child way more than he loved me. I got scared. I hold on to the ledges when I'm scared. And maybe, just maybe, the tight grip I had made him feel trapped, and it scared him away."

"Look, I already feel like crap and listening to you pour out your heart, Kiara. All I can say is, thank you for sharing that with me. We seem like two different women, but I think we have more in common than you think."

"Oh, thank you very much for that. That really makes me feel so special."

"No, I need you to please believe that I'm as much a victim as you are. But I'm not like Nicole. I won't cause you any trouble. I-I—"

"I-I, shut up!"

Kiara handed Hayley to her mother and gave the child a stony, miserable look. Even she couldn't deny the resemblance. Rashad's lips, eyes, and ears, the dimples in her tiny fingers.

"Ghetto twins." She laughed and discreetly caressed her belly. "My husband, the overachiever. Who else can go from one child to four in a few months? I gotta get out of here."

Alexis was still full of questions. Did she still have a job? Would she be forced to type up her own termination letter? But a blank expression rolled down Kiara's face like a theater curtain going down after the final act, except Alexis couldn't hear any applause.

Chapter 23

Kiara left work two hours early the day she saw Hayley. She could not bear to be in the office any longer. She had so much energy she felt like going home and cooking a big meal, for herself, Myles, and the unborn child. She was in the kitchen trying to remove the tray of cornbread, but pain shot through her knees whenever she tried to squat.

"Myles!"

"Yes, Mommy."

"Be my little man and grab that oven mitt, open the door, pull it as hard as you can, and take the mitt and get the cornbread out before it burns."

"Okay."

Little Myles stuck his tongue out the corner of his mouth and pulled open the heavy metal door with all his might. He skillfully removed the metal pan and stood on his heels as he set the baked bread on the counter just like Kiara instructed him.

"You're my little buddy. Thank you, my love."

A few minutes later Rashad came and rang the doorbell. She had taken his key but let him come in if she was there and he needed access to his clothes or other belongings. He still lived with her, but she told him he'd have to get out soon. So much of her situation reminded her of Mama Flora that she wanted to laugh.

Kiara opened the door and let Rashad in.

"I gotta hit the shower and head back out. I know you want me to get out but this is about to be a real busy week. And no, I'm not lying. I will show you the quotes that I issued recently."

"I believe you. Do your thing, king."

He ignored her sarcasm and ran to the master bedroom. After a few minutes she heard the sound of the shower running. Rashad took long showers.

Kiara went to her closet and retrieved an iPhone she'd secretly purchased just for one specific reason. She powered up the phone and went outside to Rashad's work van. Just like she suspected, he forgot to secure the locks. She opened the front door and slid her iPhone underneath his driver's seat. She quietly closed the van door and returned to the kitchen.

Rashad was still in the shower. She could hear him loudly singing the lyrics of "Make the Money" by Macklemore & Ryan Lewis.

When he emerged dressed and smelling good, she called out to him right before he escaped through the front door.

"You need to take time to find another place to live. Even check into a hotel. I can actually help you find one."

He sighed. "Kiara, okay, okay. You know I'd rather us work things out."

"That's not going to work. I'm giving you two more days. Then you must leave."

"All right." He pouted. "I'm running late. Bye."

Kiara waited a half hour before she logged onto her tablet. She signed into iCloud. She clicked the Find My iPhone icon.

She closed her eyes and held her breath as the page loaded. A map appeared. A blue flashing dot displayed on the screen.

She called out to Myles and told him to put on his jacket. For a mid-October date, it was surprisingly chilly outside and raining. But she was going anyway.

She printed a copy of the map location, took out her main cell phone and turned on her GPS. Soon she was on her way.

Kiara drove calmly and steadily down the wet and slippery highway.

When she arrived at the location on the map, she quickly saw Rashad's white van. It was parked in the driveway of a little house. Her heart beat out of its chest as she stepped out of the car. She saw Nicole's Mustang and her heart dropped.

"So this is where she really lives." She jotted down the address.

Kiara walked up to the door, stood on the welcome mat, and stared through the front window. The curtains weren't drawn and she could easily peer through the miniblinds. She saw Rashad first. He was shirtless. His bare chest was exposed as if everything he had could be claimed by whoever would have it. She gasped. Nicole Greene was holding a spoon in her hand. She lifted it to Rashad's mouth. He licked the food off the spoon, chewed it, said something to her, and leaned in for a kiss.

Kiara watched her husband's lips press against another woman's. His comfortable appearance made it seem like he'd kissed Nicole a thousand times. Bile rose in Kiara's throat. She wanted to leave, but she kept watching.

She saw Nicole wrap her arms around Rashad's neck. She saw the joyous grin the woman offered to him.

She's in love with my husband.

"Is that Daddy in there?"

Kiara quickly said no and covered her son's eyes. But she kept watching.

She observed their body language. They stood close to each other, like familiar territory. She saw Rashad's mouth move like he was telling Nicole something. She saw Nicole laugh and reach up to caress his head; she stroked his hair and touched his body as if she owned him.

Then Nicole took Rashad's hand and placed it against her belly. He bent over and kissed it.

Kiara snatched Myles's hand. She dragged him into the car. The rain fell on their heads. She didn't tell him to put on his seat belt. And she forgot to put on hers. She started the ignition and began to slowly drive away from Nicole's house. She pulled out her cell phone and dialed Rashad's number.

"Pick up."

He didn't pick up.

She hung up and called him back.

It rang and rang.

She hung up and called him again.

She dialed Rashad's number eleven times before he answered.

"Hey." His voice sounded muffled.

"Where are you?"

"Working."

"Working where?"

"Same old same ole."

"Are you alone?"

"No."

"Who else is there?"

"Me and some of my men. Why? What's with all the questions?"

"Are you at her house?"

"Her who?"

Kiara hung up.

A few hours later, Rashad drove his white van into the driveway of their meticulous home. The lawn was perfectly mowed. Beautiful gold and purple flowers lined the sidewalk leading up to their house. He turned off his cell phone right after he'd picked up a call from Nicole. She'd been crying and saying she missed him and that she wanted him to spend the night with her and their unborn baby. He told her he would and got off the phone. Then he mentally switched gears. In his mind, Fresno was headquarters. No matter where else he spent time, Fresno had always been home.

He walked into the house and checked the mail in the front hallway. Nothing.

The song "Tyrone" by Erykah Badu was loudly playing on repeat.

Rashad sniffed and detected the aroma of his favorite dinner. His nose led him into the kitchen. Just when he was about to open the refrigerator to grab a beer, Kiara appeared from nowhere.

"Stop it."

"What are you talking about 'stop it'?"

"There's nothing in there, in here, for you, Rashad. You best be on your way."

"Here you go again. How many times do I gotta—?"

"I finally realized, Rashad. You don't get me."

"Kiara, I heard you."

"You hear me but you don't hear. You don't get me . . . and Nicole Greene, too. That's not dope."

"What—"

"You think it's okay to stick your tool in a woman's hole whenever you get the urge. Call yourself taking a break." She paused. "I know about your 'break' baby."

"What break, baby?"

"Rashad, stop the lying. I know about your daughter. Hayley. I met her. Alexis confessed. The child looks just like y'all. How could you do this to me? How can you put on this façade all these years?"

"Babe, it's not what you think—"

"I don't want to hear it. You don't have break babies on me, you hear me. We have never been on a break."

He stood there looking as stupid as he had ever looked. At that moment, Kiara hated her husband. It was a feeling she never thought she could have for someone whom she'd loved with all her soul.

Rashad attempted to hug her. Kiara balled up her fist and beat his chest with her hands. "I hate you for what you've done to us. Don't you touch me ever again. You hear me?"

"Don't hate me. Please. I know I fucked up. Sorry."

Something in her broke. She realized his weak apology was the only confession she'd ever get out of this man.

"I'm not taking the foolery and the mayhem anymore. You've got to get out. I don't care where you go, but I will not live with your disrespect one minute longer."

"This is my house, my family. I ain't going anywhere."

"I can use a butcher knife, a hammer, or some hot grits. Take your pick."

Rashad saw the lifeless look in Kiara's eyes. He stormed away and quickly packed his belongings, stuffing clothes in garbage bags; the makeshift luggage for a man kicked to the curb. Erykah Badu's authoritative voice could be heard singing "Tyrone" in the background, telling her man to come get his shit.

Before Rashad left, he twisted the knob on the front door and looked back to stare. Kiara never met the gaze of his eyes. She just pointed.

"You know the way out."

He slammed the door behind him and left a hollow echo. Paint chips fell from the ceiling and crashed to the floor. The impact felt instant and irreversible. The house was eerily quiet, his dresser drawers empty. Even his scent was fading away.

"I love you, but you're an ass."

Hot tears streamed from her eyes, spread across her cheeks and dripped from her chin. Salty liquid filled her mouth.

Kiara's husband was gone. Life as she knew it was ending. But she wasn't afraid. Fear couldn't win anymore.

She wiped away her tears until she could think clearly. She picked up her iPhone and dialed a number.

"Hello?"

"You wanted him. You got him."

Chapter 24

Rashad was at a crossroads. Even though he promised he'd never get rid of any of the women in his life, he knew it was impossible to live that way. Something had to give. He knew he'd blown it with Kiara and he felt regretful. She really was a good woman. And he wanted to try to be a better husband, but pussy was his weakness. Selfishness was his vice. He decided he needed to do something different. He would intentionally hurt someone in order to save himself. It scared him to become a man who was different than his dad, but he would give it a try.

So he stayed at a motel the night that Kiara kicked him out of the house. He lay around all night long tossing turning and thinking. The next afternoon after he checked out, he drove around for hours. His cell phone was off all that night and day. But suddenly, his mind was more clear. He powered up his phone. Only Nicole had tried to contact him. He neglected to read her messages. Instead, he typed up a text and then pressed send. It read:

Hey. We need to talk. Can u pls meet me today at 4 at the spot.

Nicole texted him back.

K. What you want me to wear?

Right before he could respond, his cell phone rang.

It was Alexis, "Hey. I got your text. I'm assuming this is about Hayley. I can meet you but I will be running twenty minutes late."

For the first time in his life, Rashad wanted to die. He didn't mean to send a group text. And he couldn't be in two places at one time. Or could he?

Which woman should I go meet? Which one will I eliminate? I feel like a judge on Chopped.

He decided to meet Alexis. Since Nicole was the more emotional one, he'd deal with her later.

He got to the restaurant before she did. Hayley was with her. He smiled and turned off his phone.

"Hey, Rashad, what's up. You texted the wrong woman." She smiled. "I saw it was a group text, but the facetious side of me decided to meet you anyway."

"Oh, yeah." He blushed with embarrassment. Alexis acted hard but Rashad felt she was so chill in spite of her spunky attitude. "You know you ain't right, but I'm glad you met me anyway. I'm here just to try and gain some understanding. Try and be a better man."

"Oh, really? How will you accomplish that?"

"I came to give you my blessing."

Alexis yelped and laughed. "Thank you for that, Jesus."

"Seriously. I don't have a right to keep you from your happiness. If dude makes you happy, go for it."

"Wow! I'm touched. I am skeptical, but touched."

He laughed too, knowing he probably sounded foolish. "I know you think I'm bugging. This new me will take time. You ain't used to this type of Rashad Eason."

"No, I'm not."

Rashad felt like a burden had been lifted. Maybe he needed to be more truthful so everyone could be happier . . . including himself.

"But you're used to this Rashad. Order whatever y'all want from the menu. Last night, Kiara pushed me out the nest. And can you believe she cooked and did not even let me eat one green bean? I fasted all day like a Roman Catholic. So I'm starving, too."

"Let's eat," Hayley yelled.

"Let's." Alexis smiled. For a minute she felt sorry for Rashad. He looked like hell. But it was his own entire fault. She told him that she appreciated his honesty, and confessed she was ready for something different, too. And that it did include her new man, Varnell Chester Augustus Brown.

It felt good for both of them to just talk to each other like adults with no arguing. They ate and enjoyed a nice, pleasant conversation.

An hour later he powered on his phone.

Frantic texts started loading. All from one woman.

Where R U?

I came to the spot. U weren't here. What's up?

R U Ok. Call me!!!

Kiara had been super busy that evening because Myles started throwing up as if he had a stomach bug. She stayed home and cared for him. But she realized she needed to run out to the store real quick to stock up on some medicine, soup, and orange juice.

By four-thirty, she managed to get Myles settled in the front seat of her car. She put the car in reverse and pressed the button to raise the garage door. She glanced at the rearview mirror. A lone figure stood directly behind her car. And it wouldn't move.

Kiara peered closely. It was Nicole. She blew her horn.

Nicole continued standing directly in front of the trunk, blocking Kiara from being able to leave. Kiara pressed on the horn again.

Finally Nicole walked up to the driver's side window. Tears streamed down her face,

"*P-lease*," she wailed, "I want Rashad. Give him up."

Kiara gasped. She got out of the car and faced the distraught woman. Nicole didn't back away. She grabbed her boss by the arms and shook her. "You need to face reality. Y'all had your time together. But it's not working out anymore. If Rashad really loved you, if he was happy with his life, he wouldn't be kicking it with me."

"Nicole, please don't say these things—"

"But as long as he thinks he's supposed to be with you and trying to work it out, he will continue holding back from me. Let him go. I don't want him to sneak around anymore. I know what I want. You're still young and pretty, Kiara. You can get a second husband. I've never had even one."

"You're crazy. Nicole, I'm serious, get away from me with that mess or I will call the police on you so fast—"

"Are you sure you want to do that? You actually want to involve the police in this? Because if I told Rashad that you're fucking around with Eddison Osborne, I will spill some tea that even Molly Maid can't clean up."

At first Kiara felt that fear rise up in her, but something made her want to face it. She could either face it or run from it.

"You can't handle all this, Kiara. You're greedy as hell seeing that you're fucking two men. Two! All I'm asking is for one of them."

Kiara realized Nicole had no idea what she was talking about. She felt sorry for the chick.

"My son is in the car. Hush your mouth."

"I'm going to open up my mouth like I should have done all along and tell Rashad what's really going on with you."

Kiara felt so much hatred for Nicole right then.

"You know what? Go ahead. Call Rashad. Tell him I had sex with another man. I don't give a damn anymore."

Nicole looked shocked. "You don't?"

"I don't. So call him. See what he says. I'll be waiting right here for him. Because I know he's going to be running back to me."

"You wish he would, psycho bitch."

"Hold on, Nicole, I get sick of the way you talk to me as if you don't work for me."

"When I'm off the clock, I can say what I wanna say." Nicole looked angry. "In fact, I dare you to fire me. I will put you on blast everywhere I can. Twitter. Facebook. Instagram."

It took everything inside Kiara not to put her fingers around Nicole's neck and choke the life out of her.

"You know what?" she said. "We aren't at work right now. Get the fuck off my property, bitch."

Chapter 25

Kiara was at her wit's end. She knew it was time to execute her plan. After she rushed to the store to pick up the items for Myles, she came back home and placed a call to Eddison.

"Eddy, it's me. First, I want to apologize for how things went down the last time we talked."

"Yeah, you made me feel real shitty."

"And I'm sorry. I am. I wasn't thinking clearly. You've been so very good to me. I know this. So I've had time to think. And my plans for making it work with Rashad simply haven't succeeded. I thought giving it a try was the least thing I could do. But now I have come up with a new plan. Eddy, if you'd have me, I-I want to see what it's like to be with you. I feel so safe with you. I care about you too."

"Are you sure, Kiara?" He sounded doubtful.

"Come on, Eddy. I've been through hell. Give me a pass. Please!" She was almost in tears. "These last few months have been trying. You know this. You've been there all along."

He was silent for a few minutes.

"And I still plan to be there," he finally responded.

His voice was forgiving and his heart felt less stony. After all, he did care deeply about Kiara and believed if it was meant to be, he'd hear from her again. He was glad she called.

Kiara felt relieved. "That's why I called you. I just wanted to apologize . . . and tell you I've missed you a lot. And, if it's not a problem, can we come by tonight? Myles and I want to stay the night. He's been yakking about those trains that you have."

"Are you sure? You think it's okay to do that? Are you positive you're up for it?"

"Honestly, I feel just a little emotional, that's all; things aren't always easy to face when your life drastically changes, especially when you never planned on them."

Eddison could relate. Losing his soul mate had deeply affected him. He never thought the sorrow from her death would end. But now he was on the mend. He wanted a better life and he wanted Kiara to be part of it; both her and her son.

"Things won't always be easy. But I am here to help you along the way. Tell you what. I will leave the front door unlocked. I can prepare the upstairs master suite for Myles. It's that room in the front of the house. I need to open the window and air it out. It hasn't been used since . . ."

"Since Nina used to live there?"

"You got it."

"Okay, Eddison. Thanks."

Kiara hung up the phone. She caressed her stomach and whispered, "I'm so sorry."

She went to the front hallway and stared at all Rashad's things that she'd thrown in his luggage a while ago. It got filled up with his belongings, but he never took it with him when he left.

She went to her walk-in closet. She hauled dresses

and shirts, shoes, and maternity clothes. She dumped all of her belongings inside some of her own luggage. She got a makeup bag and placed toiletry items in there. She toted her bags downstairs and set them next to Rashad's luggage.

She went into the refrigerator and poured a tall glass of lemonade and filled it with ice cubes. She removed a plate of leftovers that Rashad was supposed to eat the other night. She set it on the table.

Then she walked up the spiral staircase and went looking for Myles.

He was in his bedroom. Toys were scattered everywhere. There was barely any room to walk.

"Your daddy's going to kill us," she said. "Why is your room such a mess?"

"Daddy is going to kill you?" he said.

She gasped at his question then nodded. Her cell phone was in the pocket of her sweater. She discreetly placed her hand on the camera recording app but didn't press it.

"What did you just say, Myles? Say it again. Louder." She pressed record.

"Daddy is going to kill you," he yelled.

She screamed. "I can't believe what you just did." Then she stopped recording. Her hands were shaking. She stared into space.

"I'm sorry, Mommy. I will clean up."

"Don't bother. It won't make any difference."

She instructed Myles to pack a few things in his backpack. Then she calmly dialed Rashad.

"Hello?"

"Rashad. You forgot your suitcase. I thought you'd want to come and get it."

"I was on my way. Nicole told me something about you and another man. What the fuck is going on?"

"Just come and get the rest of your stuff. Myles and I are about to leave any minute."

"Where are you going? Don't go. Please. We can talk about this."

"It's too late now. Nothing can change this situation."

"I'll be there in three minutes."

She hung up. She called out to Myles and told him to go to the garage.

"Go sit in the car. Get in the backseat. Wait for me. Do not leave the car for any reason. You hear me?"

"Okay, Mommy."

Before he turned around to go, she wondered if it would be the last time she ever saw him again. She kissed his little cheek.

"I love you, Myles. I tried to be the best mommy. If I failed you, I'm sorry. But I tried."

He gave her a confused look. "All right."

She asked him to go to the car and wait.

Then she went back in the house and walked up the long spiral staircase.

She knew Rashad would go through the front door. Minutes later when he pushed the door open and saw her things in the suitcase lying in the hallway, the look on his face said it all. He never looked scared . . . until then. He stepped inside the doorway and left the door wide open.

Kiara gazed down at Rashad.

"What are you doing?" he called up to her.

"Hi. I've been waiting on you."

"I'm here. What's this I heard about you and some dude? Who is he?"

"I can't tell you, Rashad."

"So it is true?" He sounded despondent.

"It's true."

"And your bags . . . why are they packed? Where are you going?"

"I need time to think. So I'm leaving for a couple days."

"Where? To be with that man?"

"Rashad, you'll never be satisfied, especially after knowing the truth."

"You fucked another dude? What he got that I don't have?"

"It doesn't matter now. Good-bye. Oh, I made you a plate of food and there's a glass of lemonade, too."

"Huh? Are you trying to choke me? You hate me that much that you want me dead?"

She just shrugged and said nothing.

"Kiara, please, come downstairs so we can work this out. You're not the type to have an affair. You are my Super Woman."

In the past, him calling her that would have made her swell with pride. But now?

She reached in her other pocket and tossed a handful of her secret bank account receipts.

"What's that?"

"Something the police will want to know when this is all over."

"You don't look right and you don't sound like yourself. Did I do that to you?"

She stood at the top of the stairs and looked down.

"You had it all, but you threw it away to live a secret deceitful double life. You made a fool out of me, Rashad. Now you have a disgruntled woman who had an affair, a pregnant woman trying to get away from her husband . . ."

She closed her eyes and began to lean over the railing.

"No," he screamed.

Right then, the screeching of tires sounded outside.

Someone shouted "Myles."

Kiara opened her eyes. She recognized a neighbor's voice. She ran down the stairs. Rashad followed her out the door.

A tiny crowd gathered in the street in front of their house. Little Myles was sitting on the curb in a daze.

A car a couple yards ahead was idling with the driver side door opened. A man was crouched next to Myles asking him how he felt.

"He ran out of nowhere and dashed in front of my car. I could barely brake. I think I hit his foot but it appears he sustained no injuries," the driver explained. "He's just a little shaken up."

"My baby," Kiara said. She ran over to Myles, examined his foot, and hugged him. Then she fussed. "You could have gotten killed. Then what would I have done? I told you to stay in the car but I can tell you're hard-headed."

"Kiara, please," Rashad told her. "Our son is alive. He's OK. That's all that matters. His wellbeing is all that really matters."

As Kiara stood next to Myles it became crystal clear how crazy things had gotten. She would never want her child to die, and she thought about herself, she knew she wasn't ready to die either. Life was a gift. And she wanted to stop the madness, stop flirting with danger, and start being a responsible mother.

As the crowd dispersed, and the man who had almost injured his son drove off, Rashad felt sad in his heart.

"What are your plans?" he asked.

"I plan to take it easy. I'm thankful God intervened and nothing worse occurred."

"Me too. So, if it's okay with you, may we please go back in the house and really sit down and have a heart-to-heart?"

"So much has happened." Her voice sounded hoarse. "I just need a little getaway for now. Maybe we can have that talk one day, but I can't promise you anything right now. Take care, Rashad."

She made sure that Rashad was far gone in his car and had completely left before she was able to lock it up and drive away . . . drive away from the house and everything she'd built up. The hopes and dreams that she knew she'd have to eventually release before she could really live again.

Chapter 26

A few days later

"Hey, move that chest of drawers over there. And push that couch against that wall. Thank you, babe."

Nicole observed the new bedroom with supreme satisfaction. The renovation work on the house felt good and looked picturesque. Since Rashad accepted her invitation to move in, he had stepped up to the plate. He ordered furniture for the room that they turned into a nursery. He came home every night at a decent hour. He allowed his work crew to do the late evening and weekend projects.

According to Nicole Greene, things were looking up and couldn't be better.

"I am about to put a load of clothes in the wash, so if you need something cleaned you should add your stuff to it. I'm starting with colors."

"All right," he said.

Being at Nicole's house in this capacity felt a bit odd. Her ceilings were much lower and looked nothing like the ones at Rashad's former house in Fresno. And she didn't have an oversize garden bathtub; at the other house, he'd had two of them. But for now, this was home.

She came and gave her man a tight hug from behind. After all this time, and well over two months of pregnancy, she still knew how to get him going. She pressed her lips against his neck and kissed him like he was the best she ever had.

"Now that's dope. Keep going."

Pretty soon they were making love from the bedroom to the bathroom. Rashad knew Nicole would give him everything he needed during those life-changing days. She was his little ride or die and she was exactly what he needed to face what life had presented to him.

Alexis beamed with happiness. The tour boat cruised at a relaxing pace. She couldn't believe she and Varnell and Hayley were sitting together on a bench as they drifted along the Riverwalk in San Antonio. Her arms hung over the railing as she took in the sights of the outdoor restaurants and listened to the tour guide provide the rich history of this beautiful place.

Her child was smiling, her man was grinning, and she was elated to finally get her simple wish. Alexis finally felt like the woman she knew she was: a main chick. And she loved it.

Rashad and Nicole were adjusting to their relationship. She treated him like a king. He liked the attentiveness she gave him, but he still wondered about Kiara. What was she doing? Did she miss him like he missed her? He couldn't believe that she stuck to her rule of not letting him back into their house. Her shutting him down felt unreal, unfair, and it made him quite angry. Kiara Eason was his first love and he couldn't imagine any other man ever replacing him. Somehow, he'd have to get rid of her new corny dude and convince her that he alone was Kiara's true king. Somehow, he would try to get things back to the way they used to be.

It was a late October evening. Kiara, Myles, and Eddison were on foot, traveling in the dark from house to house on Eddison's quiet street. The wind was swirling and screaming but otherwise it was a pleasant night. Wearing a Spider-Man costume, Myles bounded up the walkway to the decorated doorway of a family that was handing out candy and treats.

"Thank you. Happy Halloween," he said.

Kiara, clothed in a Super Woman outfit, smiled and snapped a photo of her son. All she cared about was him being happy and stable. At this point, stability and happiness were what she wanted, too.

"Thank God, the weather cooperated," she told Eddison, who wore a red Superman cape.

He squeezed her hand. They walked together deep in their thoughts.

"So what about the next holiday?" Myles asked. "What are we doing for Thanksgiving?"

"I ask myself the same thing," Eddison said. "It's been a heck of a year."

"We're going to be thankful. And then we're going to get ready for the next holiday, and the one after that," Kiara said firmly.

She sounded confident but she had no idea what life had in store for her. So she looked cheerful but she felt nervous. Maybe it was because Kiara didn't know that in the shadows of the darkness, her husband, Rashad, had his eyes on her and Eddison. He slowly followed them in his rented car, circling the block, like a shark waiting to draw blood.

Don't miss the next book in the
Love & Revenge series,

My Married Boyfriend

On sale wherever books and ebooks are sold in
September 2016!

1
The Sky is Crying

Rashad Eason reached across the desk and handed the woman a fifteen-hundred-dollar cashier's check. She had pasty, pimpled white skin, a buzz haircut, and a thick mustache. She was very unattractive. To Rashad, she resembled a proud lesbian but that didn't matter. He had extensively researched Lily Tangaro online. He admired her track record and needed a competent person to do the job.

"You think you can get me everything I want?" he asked.

Lily examined the check, then reclined in her leather swivel chair. "You're serious about this, aren't you?" she said.

"More serious than a triple bypass."

"But it hasn't been that long since you physically separated from your wife."

"I know that. But if I don't do something fast, I may change my mind."

"I see." She paused. "We always recommend that the plaintiff think about the decision for six months."

"I can't wait that long. Thinking about this for six months would kill me."

She nodded and secured the retainer payment inside a classified file folder. "Sign these documents and we will get started on your case right away."

Rashad eagerly reviewed several papers that Lily gave to him. He took a blue pen and scribbled his name and the date. Then he stood and shook her hand.

"Thank you, Ms. Tangaro."

"Call me, Lily."

"Will do, Lily. And my son, Myles, really thanks you."

"Seriously? He's only six—"

"He's seven. Myles knows what's up. He's seen a lot, unfortunately. And this is why I gotta do this. It may be the only way I get to spend quality time with him. Plus, I don't want my son around his crazy mama any longer than he needs to be."

"Totally understandable. We'll be in touch."

"No doubt, Lily. I appreciate this."

Rashad drove away from his new attorney's office feeling more hopeful than he had in weeks.

It was a rainy Friday in Houston; the day after Thanksgiving. Rashad was lucky that Lily had agreed to meet him briefly in her office to sign his paperwork.

Light drops of water drizzled from the sky. Rainy days made Rashad feel depressed. But he had to shake it off and keep it moving. It was time to go see Myles. And spending time with his son was one of the few things he could be happy about these days.

When Rashad arrived at the designated pick-up spot, which was in front of Mama Flora's house, he let the car idle next to the curb. Technically, she could be considered his grandmother-in-law. Mama Flora was his wife's maternal grandmother, and the woman that raised Kiara. She was sensible and didn't stand for drama. Rashad and Kiara both agreed that exchanging Myles for visits at Flora's place would be the best option.

Rashad impatiently drummed his hands on the steering wheel. He listened to raindrops splatter on the ground. Minutes later, Kiara drove up and parked directly behind him. He observed her through the rearview mirror.

"Damn, I can barely see her but the woman still looks good," he admitted to himself. He hadn't laid eyes on Kiara in weeks. And after all they had been through, she still tugged at his heart.

He saw her mouth moving and assumed she was talking to their son. After a while, both Kiara and Myles emerged from the car. Wearing white gym shoes, the little boy ran behind the car then raced ahead of her. He fled into the street instead of staying on the sidewalk. Soon he tugged at his father's locked door handle and yelled.

"Hurry up, Daddy. I'm famished."

Rashad laughed and popped the locks. He got out of the car and scooped Myles off his feet and hugged him tight.

"Really Myles? You're famished? Where'd you learn that word?"

"The Food Network."

Rashad chuckled as he set him back down.

"Oh, so I don't get a 'hey, Daddy how you doing? I miss you. I love you, man'?"

"Hey, Daddy, I missed you. Can we go to Steak and Shake for dinner?"

"Myles," Kiara interrupted as she hurriedly approached them wearing a short, purple long-sleeve dress and four-inch wedge heel sandals. "I told you about running in the street. Are you crazy? Do you wanna get hit by a car? It's raining and that makes it harder for drivers to slow down in this weather."

Kiara eased up next to Myles. She thumped him on his forehead.

"Ouch, Mommy."

"Don't do that," Rashad scolded. "My little man misses me, that's all. It's been a minute."

"Whatever Rashad," she spat at him. "None of that matters. He knows better than to do something reckless like running in the street. He doesn't listen."

"I do listen, Mommy." Myles mostly ignored his mother as he happily gave his father a few daps. The little boy always seemed calm and sure of himself when he was in Rashad's presence.

"You're a chip off the old block, son," his father said. He knew the danger of Myles not looking where he was going but Rashad didn't notice any cars coming down the street. He could tell how much his boy deeply missed him and that made him feel good.

"Damn, I've been dying to hang out with my little man. Has he gotten taller? What the hell you been feeding him?"

"That's a stupid question and you know how I feel about those."

"I was just joking, Kiara. Lighten up."

"Ain't got time for jokes."

Suddenly the air grew tense. Rashad felt himself getting agitated.

"Look, this is the holiday season. People are supposed to be merry. But you act like you on something. You been drinking? Can't you ever be happy and just chill?"

"Lord Jesus. More stupid ass questions. Don't start."

Kiara gave Rashad a sober look as she handed him Myles's backpack.

"Lucky for you, Mama Flora is away from her house right now. At the last second, she had something to take care of and she had to leave. So we both have to be mature enough to handle this without her."

"That's cool. I got no problem with that."

"Anyway, all his things are in there: two pair of pants, some shirts, underwear, pajamas, favorite electric toothbrush, all that."

"Hmm, seeing this makes me realize I gotta stock up on some stuff for him to keep at . . ."

He wanted to say he had to buy clothes for Myles to keep at his other place, a home he started sharing with his pregnant lover, Nicole Greene. Weeks ago, when his wife forced him to leave the house because she got sick of Rashad's lies, Nicole instantly suggested that he come stay with her. On that short of a notice, he had nowhere else to go. So he took her up on her offer. And now he was adjusting to his 'new normal.'

Rashad mentally switched gears as he gazed at Myles.

"Damn shame we couldn't eat turkey and dressing together, and watch the Lions and Cowboys game. That's what I did with my dad every Thanksgiving when he was still alive. I was *always* with my daddy on that holiday. Sitting up in that cold ass living room. Eating good food and talking smack. I wish we could have done that, Myles."

Rashad stared at his son but he was talking to Kiara.

"Um," she responded. "We had the whole day already planned so he wouldn't have had a chance to come by anyway. We went to the parade downtown. We ate a wonderful dinner. And then we drove down to see the Festival of Lights at Moody Gardens. Myles ended up having a *real* good time with us, didn't you?"

"Uh huh," he said.

"Cool," was Rashad's clipped response. "I'm glad for you."

He acted like he was unbothered. But Rashad hated that Kiara stopped him from spending time with his child two holidays in a row. *She* got to pick his costume and take Myles trick or treating. And *she* got to eat turkey with him too. What gave her the right? Just because she made him leave the house, does that mean she could enforce all her own rules as well?

Rashad fought to hide his anger as he leered at Kiara on the sly. She was holding one of those huge pink and black golf umbrellas in her hand. Even on a dreary looking afternoon, somehow this woman managed to appear elegant and beautiful. Her eyes were full of spunk and passion. It seemed she didn't have a care in the world.

And he hated it.

But at the same time, Rashad was strangely tempted to grab his wife in his arms, slap her one good time, kiss her, and tell her that they were both acting silly. He wished they could get their emotions in check, work things out, save the marriage. He really didn't want to file on her, but she was acting unreasonable. He wished she could get some sense into her stubborn head. Maybe she'd listen and let him come back home where he felt he belonged. But that scenario was a hopeless fairy tale. He knew Kiara was still pissed and he didn't want to risk getting swung at in public.

"All righty then," Rashad spoke up, anxious to leave. "Since I have less time than I originally thought, we need to make that move right now. I will have little man back here on Sunday night around eight."

"Eight?"

"Okay, then. Seven."

"Sunday *afternoon*, Rashad. I need him here by two so I can make sure he has time to take his bath, complete his homework, and eat dinner. Plus, if we decide to go check out that new Madagascar movie he's begged us to see, we will probably want him around noon."

We.

Rashad knew his wife was referring to her new man when she said "We."

"Back by *noon*? That means I won't even get to spend, hell, even a full twenty-four hours with him—"

"Sorry, but that's just how it is."

"You're not sorry, Kiara. You're selfish. I haven't seen my son in God knows how long. I have a right to be with the boy just like you do. And I will bring Myles back when I'm done with him."

"Wait one second here. I find it so strange that all of a sudden you are so desperate to spend time with him. You should have thought about how important he was back when you were sacrificing time with your son to go lie up and bump your nuts on that whore."

"W-what did you say?"

"You heard exactly what I said. If you hadn't done what you did, we wouldn't be out here on these streets doing this; exchanging a child like he's a drug or a piece of currency. Do you know how mad this makes me? I did everything and I mean *ev-e-ry*-thing I could to make you happy, but no, no, no. Nothing I did was good enough. You had to go get yourself a damned side piece. Her pussy must taste like Skittles."

"Kiara, you best better shut your mouth."

"So it's true? Her coochie taste like Gucci?"

"I'm warning you."

She was ready to attack him with more angry words, but she grew alarmed when she noticed a frozen smile gripping her son's face. He resembled a mannequin; he looked like he was scared something bad would happen if he moved an inch.

Kiara realized she'd gone too far. But she usually did when it came to Rashad. She hated that his whorish ways had destroyed their perfect family life. She hated that not only had he knocked up that heifer Nicole Greene, but he'd also been hiding a two-year-old daughter that he had with another woman who worked for her: Alexis McNeil, her own administrative assistant. Her hubby hiding baby mamas and side chicks that worked in her office was too much. Rashad made her look like a fool. The more Kiara thought about it, the crazier she felt in the head.

She reached and grabbed Myles's hand as if to snatch him back toward her car.

"What are you doing?" Rashad asked.

"Let me be clear. I don't know if we're ready for this informal custody sharing thing. I know it's the decent thing to do, but hell, I'm not feeling 'decent' right now. I think we need to take baby steps. So if you can't bring him back by noon, then he's going home with me right now. I'll let you have him in two weeks. For a full weekend. Promise."

"See, this is bullshit. I was supposed to get him last weekend, remember? You broke that so-called promise. Why you always got to be in control?"

They were still standing in the street next to Rashad's idling sedan.

"Why you always try to run shit like I'm your child? Or your employee. Huh? I'm a grown ass man." He stepped closer to her. "Who the hell put you in charge of me?"

Kiara snatched Myles's bony little arm and pulled so violently that he screamed, "Ouch! That hurts."

"Your crazy ass better let go of my son." Rashad grabbed Myles's other arm.

"Shut up! I don't like how you're talking to me."

"I don't like the fact that you fucked another nigga; now you pregnant. I guess we should go on the Maury show to find out who the real father is."

"What the hell? That's it. Forget this. Come on, Myles." She yanked him again.

"Mama, I want to stay with my daddy. I want my daddy." Myles inched closer to Rashad.

"I don't care what you want. He doesn't deserve you. We're leaving. Come on."

Raindrops poured from above as if the sky was crying. Kiara tried to hold her umbrella in one hand and drag away Myles with the other.

But the boy wrestled with her, pulling back from her, and tried to free himself.

"My arm. It hurts. It *hurts*. I don't like this. Let me gooo."

Kiara wouldn't release Myles, but Rashad did.

He'd been taught that real men don't cry. But right then, he was filled with uncontrollable rage and a lingering frustration that made his throat swell with pain. It wasn't fair that since Kiara banned him from their house he hadn't played with his son, hadn't looked him in his eyes, or helped him with his homework. He missed fixing Myles's breakfast and shooting hoops with him in their backyard. Little things meant a lot. And Rashad resented the legal system which granted numerous women so much power when it came to a man, his money, and his children.

He stared at his wife, almost in disbelief that feelings

of pure hatred were boiling up in him and making him flush with so much anger that he started sweating.

"Mommy, I want to be with my daddy. Let me go."

"Stop all that yelling, Myles. I want you to come back home with me."

Several cars slowly drove past them, which infuriated Rashad. "Look at this shit. You got people staring at you like you're crazy."

"The hell with them. I'm not crazy. I'm just doing what I have to do to protect my son."

"He's my son, too, Kiara. I don't know why you seem to have forgotten that." If his wife wasn't pregnant there was no telling what Rashad would have done to her. He didn't want to fight, but her unpredictable reactions drove him to respond in ways that he hated.

"All I know is, it's damn near Christmas," he continued in a choked voice. "I wanted to take Myles shopping this weekend. I-I-I have all *kinds* of plans for him, don't you understand that?"

"I don't give a damn about your stupid plans," she retorted. "You better learn how to speak to me like you have some sense. You can't just say anything in front of a child."

Rashad felt like his wife was a hypocrite. She clearly saw his sins but was blind to her own. But he counted to ten and calmly told her, "Kiara, I apologize if it seems like I was disrespecting you. But can we let go of this argument? Please. And let me give Myles the chance he deserves to hang out with his father . . . his *real* father."

"Oh hell no. I know you're not trying to throw shade at Eddison who's been nothing but remarkable to us. Plus, that boy's not stupid. He knows who his daddy is."

"Mommy, you're hurting me. Please let me gooo."

Kiara then realized she had Myles in a death grip. She felt his fragile bones between her fingers. She heard the hurt in his voice. She released him.

"Oh God. I'm sorry baby. I-I . . . please forgive me."

With tears in his eyes, he nodded and leaned on his father's stomach.

"Kiara," Rashad said in a gentle tone. "So you're going to let him be with me till Sunday night?"

She hesitated and reached in her purse. "Fine. I'll let him go with you since we went through all this trouble in the first place. We can negotiate a fair time for his drop off. But I want you to know that I bought him his own cell phone today. Whenever he's away from me, he must keep it on him at all times. And we taught him how to use it. In case of an emergency."

"You really don't trust me, do you?"

"No, I do not. But that's beside the point. I just want Myles to be okay. I just want him to be happy." Kiara's voice caught in her throat as she wiped tears from her eyes.

She kissed Myles's little cheeks and allowed a brave smile to brighten her face. "Bye baby. I love you."

"Love you, too, Mommy. Come on, Daddy. My stomach is growling. Can't you hear it?"

"That's a damned shame. We'll go eat right now, son."

Kiara swiftly turned around to leave. The street was slippery and wet. In her rush to get away, her feet got tangled together. The wedge heels were narrow and clumsy. Her right ankle twisted and gave in underneath her. Her umbrella plunked to the ground. She slipped on a pothole, and fell forward, but landed on her thigh. Her hand scraped the rugged, scraggly surface as she braced herself from injury.

"Ugh, ouch. Dammit."

She lay on her side feeling totally embarrassed and wincing. Rashad wanted to ask if she was all right, but he simply stared at her.

Rain water sprayed her hair and cheeks. Her hair became a matted mess.

"I can't believe this. Rashad! Can you help me up or are you just gonna stand there?"

He gaped at Kiara and wondered if she just got what she deserved.

She'd made life so difficult for him recently. Rashad knew she was now seeing that man from her job, Eddison Osborne, and Nicole told him that they'd had an affair.

Rashad could clearly see Kiara's tiny baby bump. He wondered if the baby was his, even though she'd told him that it was.

"Rashad, did you hear me? I need your help."

"Why should I?"

"Huh? I can't believe you said that!"

He had the eyes of a reptile; cold, curious, and calculating.

"I don't know whose baby you got inside of you."

"Rashad, oh my God. How can you go there?"

"Because *you* went there—with that other nigga!"

"Now is not the time. Help me up, please."

He stared down at her belly. And so did Myles.

Kiara felt completely humiliated. She never wanted their son to see her like this.

"Rashad, show your son how to treat a woman. *Show* your *son* how to *treat* a *woman*!"

Rashad looked skeptical and unmoving.

"Myles baby, please."

Myles raced to his mother and immediately grabbed her outstretched hand. His tongue stuck out of his mouth as he struggled to help Kiara. Rashad suddenly rushed to the other side of her and held out his hand too.

Wincing in pain, she got on her knees, and leaned on Rashad as he hoisted her to her feet.

"Thank you, baby." She ignored Rashad. "You are my precious son. You must always remember to be a gentleman, and help your mother. And always be good to a lady. Promise me."

"I promise, Mommy."

"Ha!" Rashad muttered.

"All right, okay. I can do this," she said to herself. "I can make it to the car."

"Bye-bye, Mommy. Don't forget to pick me up on Sunday."

"I can never forget anything that has to do with you."

She watched Myles excitedly race around to the other side of Rashad's sedan. He went and opened the passenger door for his son. Kiara waited until Myles was safely inside the car. She rubbed her hip and hobbled over to Rashad.

"You didn't act concerned about our unborn baby for one second."

"I don't know whose baby that is." He paused. "How many times did you fuck that dude?"

"How many times did you fuck both your baby mamas?"

"Oh, so you hooked up with him just to get revenge? Was his dick bigger than mine? I don't care how big it was, no man could ever love you like me!"

"Oh my God! Just be quiet with all that. I can't believe I used to love your pathetic ass. And you best believe that part of my life is gone. I'm moving on. And you're acting like a dick and trying to shame me in front of Myles is unforgivable. You'll never get this pussy again."

She turned away again, this time moving more slowly than the first time. Then she quietly limped away. Hair soaking wet, but head held high.

After Kiara slid into the vehicle, she slammed her door, revved the engine, and waved her middle finger at Rashad as she drove past him.

Eason v. Eason had officially started.